Too Near the Edge

Also by Lynn Osterkamp

Stress? Find Your Balance (nonfiction)

How To Deal With Your Parents When They
Still Treat You Like A Child (nonfiction)

Too Near the Edge

a novel

by

Lynn Osterkamp

PMI Books

Boulder, Colorado

ISBN-13: 978-1933826-22-6
ISBN-10: 1-933826-22-3

Front cover photo © Vlag Turchenko
Image from BigStockPhoto.com

Published by
PMI Books
an imprint of
Preventive Measures, Inc.
254 Spruce St.
Boulder, CO 80302

Printed in the United States of America

For information regarding special discounts
for bulk purchases, visit our website at:

pmibooks.com

"The bottom line in this case is the difference between accidental death and a homicide is the push of a hand."

Deputy Brett Rye

Prologue

Going over the edge at the Grand Canyon doesn't allow for do-overs. Rocks are hard and nature has no airbags. In the early morning of April 15, Adam Meyer became the first canyon fatality of the year. Later in the day, his blood-spattered and torn bright yellow Marmot precip jacket led rangers to his crumpled body almost 300 feet below the rim, where one ranger vomited at the sight of Adam's crushed skull and broken neck. A rescue team sent to document the scene and remove the corpse by helicopter, noted that despite the victim's fatal injuries, his cell phone, clutched in his right hand, remained intact.

Adam had started the day with high hopes the transcendent power of nature would open his heart and calm his fears. After a fitful night's sleep, his alarm clock woke him at 5:30 am in time for sunrise over the canyon. He pulled on jeans, turtleneck, a fleece pullover, boots and his Marmot jacket. He put on his backpack—packed with food, water, and a map— grabbed his wind-proof gloves and hat, opened the cabin door and stepped out into the icy morning.

He'd arrived at the Bright Angel Lodge cabins in darkness the night before, so this would be his first view of the six-million-year-old canyon. His head overflowed with information about it—close to a mile deep, ten miles wide and 277 river-miles long. Anticipation made his gut queasy and he almost fell stepping across the slippery parking lot behind the cabins toward the rim trail. As he stood on the edge looking down at the gigantic gorge, Adam became momentarily disoriented—like he was being sucked into the opening.

He turned his focus to the individual spires and buttes in the shadows before him and regained his equilibrium. He had, indeed, come to the right place. The awe-inspiring view more than met his expectations. As a burst of excitement and joy washed through him, he wished Sharon and Nathan could be with him to share the breathtaking sight. He loved them so much. They were the lights of his life, and he missed them. But this was not a vacation for Adam.

He'd come to the canyon to resolve an unrelenting worry. First, he looked for help at home in Boulder, Colorado—a town with more therapists and healers per square inch than ants on a discarded candy bar. But each time he got close to discussing his concerns, fear stopped him from disclosing any details. Thinking about it wore him out. Every way he explored the problem it got more complicated. Deep down, he believed he had stumbled into pure evil. Terror was eating away at his spirit.

Even worse, his anxiety was contagious. His preoccupations created distance between himself and his wife, Sharon. She'd pleaded with him to tell her what was bothering him. But he couldn't talk to her about this, despite the intimacy they shared. Now fear of losing her tormented him. He worried he'd pushed her away, and neglected Nathan, who was only eight and missed his attention. Adam needed direction in a way he never had before. He hoped to find it here.

Friends in Boulder told him about a homeopathic principle that works on desperation of the soul or spirit. The principle says you can treat an undesirable condition by choosing weather and landscape to match your mood, and immersing yourself in it for a few hours. For example, meeting bleakness with bleakness has a powerful cleansing effect.

He took the advice and decided to visit the Grand Canyon. He believed nothing but the vast space of the canyon could be a match for his huge problems and his emptiness. Perhaps the 18-mile rim walk and the view of its spires and spaces, would help him find his bearings.

Now he hiked slowly along the paved trail between Bright Angel and Maricopa Point. The rising sun began to brighten tips of pinnacles below. Gradually craggy hollows came to life. Spellbound, he gazed at the changing patterns of light and shadow, and absorbed the natural quiet of the canyon. Its magnetic energy connected him to the earth. His problems shrank in the face of the permanence and enormous size of rock formations below.

Farther along, the trail changed to an unpaved path, some sections narrow and close to the edge with no wall between the hiker and the chasm. Adam stopped to peer over a 3,000-foot precipice called The Abyss, where sheer rock walls dropped steeply to the shadowy cavern bottom. Scraggly evergreen trees clung tenaciously to hillsides, wherever they found enough sand for their roots. Countless slag heaps of fallen rocks attested to the restlessness of nature.

Standing at the rim in the early-morning hush, he began to relax. It was as if the world stopped to let him meditate.

After a few minutes scratchy noises from a ground squirrel scampering by distracted him. Then he heard soft sounds of footsteps on the path behind him. He turned to greet a fellow hiker, but saw only an empty tree-lined trail. His eyes stopped at a red and black sign immediately on his left. "Danger!" the sign proclaimed in large block letters. "Use caution near the edge," the warning continued. "People die here falling from the edge." He peeked over the edge again and shuddered. His stomach heaved as he imagined the long fall to the hard canyon bottom.

Suddenly, a hand struck the center of his back, pushing him towards the yawning canyon. "Hey!" Adam yelled. He slid across the icy path to the rim of the chasm. "Stop! Help me!" In a futile attempt to stop the fatal fall, he grabbed at a stunted bush to halt his skid toward the brink. For a brief moment, he dangled over the edge, but the branches ripped out of his hands like a kite string in the wind. "Help!" he cried, reaching into his pocket for his cell phone in a useless attempt to make one last contact.

Adam's bloodcurdling screams echoed through the canyon as he sky-dived head first toward the mighty Colorado River 5,000 feet below. He rotated in the air five or six times, slammed head-first into a rocky cliff, bounced off onto a ledge and rolled to a halt on his back.

1

When the phone rang on that scorching hot Saturday morning in July, I was sitting cross-legged on my covered front porch, gazing intently at a potted red geranium flower. I tried to let go, to let my mind drift into frictionless flow like Masuka had us doing in class yesterday. My eyes kind of crossed, and the geranium took on an impressionist tone. But I couldn't empty my mind the way I knew I should.

Pablo kept popping up in my mind's eye. I could see his thick black curly hair that I love to run my hands through, his chocolate-brown eyes, and his solid muscular shoulders. So nice. But then, I saw his scowling face from last night's argument. Why didn't he give me more respect? I wanted him to accept my work as every bit as important and significant as his own, but instead he focused on the parts he thought were flaky. Had I made a huge mistake telling him about Tyler?

I wanted to refocus, get clear. Why did I continue to let Pablo dominate my thoughts? Over the past few years, I'd spent countless hours agonizing over our relationship. Do I love him? Does he love me? Do we have a future together, or should we go our separate ways as we did once before? Oops…now I was beyond distracted.

Would I ever learn to be centered the way Masuka is? Like many meditation teachers and devotees in Boulder, Colorado, Masuka floats through life like a wispy cloud on a summer day. Nothing ruffles her. In meditation class the week before, when Bill accused her of pretending and putting on airs, Masuka smiled gently at him and said "However you see me is what works for you now." Bill decided he didn't want to see her at all. He got up and stomped out. Masuka simply directed our attention back to the bamboo that was our focus, and reminded us to tenderly clear our minds of upsetting thoughts.

I wished I could be that blasé about Pablo, but I was nowhere near that. Actually the more I thought about last night, the more his reaction struck me as intolerant arrogance. My anger grew until I could almost feel steam blowing out my ears. Arghh! No way could I sit in front of this geranium anymore. Instead of peaceful calm, energy coursed through my body like an electric current. So when my cell phone rang, I jumped about a foot and dropped the phone when I tried to grab it out of my pocket.

"Cleo Sims Grief Counseling," I answered, hoping the phone had survived.

"Hey, Cleo. I have a new client for you. You absolutely have to help my friend Sharon, whether she wants it or not." I recognized the gravelly voice of my close friend Elisa, who had a way of being sure of what would help someone else, without giving much thought to that person's own ideas.

"Hey, Elisa, slow down. I have enough difficult clients without taking on people who don't want my help."

"She does want it; she just doesn't know it yet. Anyway, she'll be at our party tonight so I can introduce her to you. I just wanted to make sure you're coming."

"Wait a minute, Elisa. Who's Sharon? I can't remember you mentioning her before." Elisa can be outrageous, but that's one of the things I love about her. She keeps me laughing. And she's a good-hearted, caring person who has helped me over and over again when I needed someone. So I wanted to hear more about what she wanted me to do for her friend who might not want my help.

"Sharon Meyer. Her husband passed away at the Grand Canyon last April and she …."

"He passed away at the Grand Canyon? What, was he fatally ill when he went there?" I interrupted, enjoying my chance to match Elisa's outrageousness. It's a game we play. "Did he have his hospice nurse along with him?'

"Of course not. He was hiking at the Grand Canyon and slipped off the trail where it was icy," Elisa replied.

I sighed. "Elisa, you know how I feel about the euphemism 'passed away,' especially when we're talking about a violent death. Passing away after a long battle with cancer is one thing, but when a person dies in an accident, let's just say 'died' or 'was killed' and be done with it." I paced wide circles in my yard as I ranted.

"OK, died, whatever," Elisa said. "Just be there tonight, OK? Sharon needs some help, and I want you to help her. I'm not suggesting her for grief counseling, although she could use some. It's the Contact Project I want for her."

"I'll be there, and if you want to introduce us, that's fine. But she would need grief counseling if she's going to be in the Contact Project. I'm not a medium conducting séances here. This project is a part of grief counseling."

I knew Elisa was quite aware of this caveat, but chose to overlook it for her own reasons. Since I'd known her for almost fifteen years, I was totally on to her tricks.

"It may take some convincing to get her to do it, though." Elisa ignored my jibes and plowed right on. "Sharon's father is Donald Waycroft. I know you've heard of him. He's a big-deal behavioral psychologist at the university. Anyway, he rejects most areas of psychology other than behaviorism as unproven, and hates parapsychology with a passion."

"I read some of his articles in graduate school. He's definitely a stimulus-response sort of guy. I can only imagine how he'd view my work."

"Well that's his problem, isn't it? We can't let his rigid beliefs get in the way of you helping Sharon."

I knew it wouldn't do my professional reputation any good to look like an ambulance chaser, or to get on the wrong side of a psychology faculty member, so I was a little wary of this client referral. "Elisa, I'm not going to talk her into signing up! You know you're not doing me any favors with a referral like this," I said. "It's not like I'm desperate for business."

"Whew, honey! You're in a mood." Elisa barked.

"You're right. I'm not in the best mood," I said, thinking that I wouldn't have gone off on Elisa that way if I hadn't been so rattled when I picked up the phone. Even if her friend sounded like trouble for me, I should at least listen to what Elisa had to say. And Sharon very likely could benefit from grief counseling. So I took a deep Masuka-like breath and said, "Tell me a little about Sharon and her husband."

"Adam Meyer was a web site designer," Elisa said. "Kind of cute. Medium height, very fit, blue eyes, reddish-brown hair, big smile. You might have met him at one of my parties."

"Elisa, that description fits half the men in Boulder," I laughed. "I don't remember meeting him, but you always have so many people at your parties. What was he doing at the Grand Canyon in April? Not the best weather there at that time of year."

"It was some kind of midlife crisis thing. I don't know all the details. He fell into the canyon and broke his neck, so he was dead when they found him. I feel terrible for Sharon. They're just about your age—she's 35 and he was 37—and they had only been married two years."

"Horrible," I said, trying not to picture the man's battered body impaled on some rocky spire.

"The strange thing about it is that Adam was a big-time hiker. He climbed a bunch of fourteeners, belonged to the Colorado Mountain Club, and absolutely knew his way around in the mountains," Elisa said. "Sharon said he was stressed-out and anxious about something, but it's not like him to be careless."

"What was bothering him? Does she know?"

"No. He wasn't the kind of guy who shared his feelings easily. He was a good match for her—funny, sweet and very loving with Sharon and her son, Nathan. They're outdoorsy and active, and so was he. Adam even coached Nathan's soccer team. But he was more of a doer than a talker, so Sharon never found out what he was so upset about."

"So why are you so keen on getting her into the Contact Project?"

"It's been almost three months since Adam died. It was April 15. I remember because we were rushing our taxes to the post office when I heard. But even after all this time, Sharon isn't accepting it at all. She's convinced herself his fall wasn't an accident, even though the park rangers have investigated and told her it was. She tried to get the police to investigate, but they won't because the fall has been ruled an accident. Sharon just can't let go of it, and I'm thinking if she could contact Adam, maybe she could find some peace."

"OK, I'll plan on meeting her tonight and see if she wants to make an appointment to come in to the office and talk more. Hey, Elisa, I need to go. This drought and the watering restrictions are doing major damage to Grampa's garden. I need to go do some watering or Grampa's ghost will be tracking me down. I'll see you later."

While I watered the garden, I thought about what I would wear to the party. Sometimes, when I'm around Elisa, I end up feeling like an awkward teenager. Elisa's self-assurance is much different than Masuka's, but just as effective. She's a beautiful woman, tall and thin with thick blonde hair, layered in a casual style that always falls attractively no matter what she's been doing. She has a look of entitlement about her. Her clothes are expensive, always natural fabrics—fine wools, brilliant silks and soft cottons or linens. Her jewelry is simple but stunning—a jade or turquoise necklace or intricate sterling silver.

Don't get me wrong. I'm quite satisfied with being 5'4" tall, with medium length curly brown hair and green eyes. I really have no desire to stand out in a crowd or be a fashion plate. But Elisa sets a high standard. She's the woman other women take in and instantly envy—even though she recently turned 40. One glance at Elisa leaves most women feeling mismatched or pinned together. They check their clothes in the nearest mirror or store window, pulling and adjusting to restore their feelings of attractiveness. Elisa is always surprised to hear she generates this reaction. In fact she refuses to believe it.

For me, that much style is usually way too time-consuming, which is why I had on old khaki shorts and a ragged Earth Day 5K tee shirt, while I pictured Elisa sitting on her deck looking gorgeous in some perfectly fitted tank top and shorts, sipping herbal iced tea and enjoying the foothills view while making her pre-party phone calls.

But I can clean up and look almost as sophisticated or sexy as she does when I want to. I felt the urge to do it for that night's party. I resolved to spend some extra time getting ready, not just to feel well-dressed next to Elisa, but also because her parties draw exciting people. Pablo would be at work, so I'd be on my own. Maybe I'd meet a cute guy who'd take my work seriously.

2

The watering took me over an hour. Time-consuming home-and-lawn-maintenance is a clear downside of my house, which was built in 1872 by an early settler whose family raised fruits, vegetables and flowers on the land that is now Settlers Park in west Boulder. It's the sort of place real estate ads today describe as a "historic stone farmhouse," which is code for sloping floors, small closets, and aging plumbing. But for me, this house is as comfortable as my favorite jeans and fits me just as perfectly. I love the cozy rooms with hardwood floors and mahogany doors. And I especially love the location, nestled against the Boulder foothills and acres of what is known in Colorado as open space.

My grandmother, Martha Donnelly, who was once a prominent Boulder artist, is the actual owner of the house. She's been gradually losing her mind to Alzheimer's disease for the past twelve years, and now at age 87 lives at Shady Terrace Nursing Home. I love her dearly. Watching her essence be eaten away by this mind-snatching disease is so excruciating that some days I'm glad Grampa isn't here to see any more of it, even though I miss him deeply.

Gramma and Grampa bought the house when they first moved to Boulder back in 1950 when it was a small college town of only 20,000 people. Grampa fell in love with the big garden area, and for Gramma, the stone carriage house in back, which became her studio, was perfect.

Starting at age nine, I spent every summer with them in this house. Boulder always felt more like home to me than Topeka, Kansas, where I lived the rest of the year. I remember those summers as quiet times where the days slid by harmoniously—so different from the sharp bickering I was used to at home.

To this day, the smell of oil paint in the studio takes me back to those summer mornings when I painted there with Gramma. And the cool feel of the flagstone patio on my bare feet recalls the afternoons Grampa and I spent there surrounded by the gardens and shade trees. We talked about everything from Egyptian pyramids to tomato plants. He taught philosophy at the University, and he was as curious by nature as I am. No matter what I came up with, he took an interest. Some days we ended up at the library, where we spent hours looking for answers to my questions, like how bees know which flowers have the best nectar, or why Colorado has mountains but Kansas doesn't.

Grampa was the one person in my life who I could talk to about anything. I loved everything about him. He's my model for what a man should be and I've yet to meet his match. I miss him terribly. In some way his plants seem like part of him, so taking good care of them is important. It's a lot of work, but spending time in his gardens brings to mind fond memories of him and our times together.

I got interested in grief therapy when I struggled with my own grieving after Grampa died. I was a doctoral student in clinical psychology then, and barely managed to stick with it in the face of my overwhelming sorrow. I knew Grampa would never want me to quit, so I learned to focus on my positive memories of him to keep me going. It worked, and inspired me to go on for extra training to become a certified grief counselor. Death fascinates me because it's both mysterious and inevitable. Helping people cope with it has become the focus of my practice. It's a universal issue, although most people don't like to think about it.

My current approach to grief therapy isn't the most traditional one, but it's not unique either. After my first few years in practice, I moved away from steering people through the stages of the grief process. I found that what causes people the most pain is a need to resolve unfinished business with their dead loved ones So I began using a process that helps them work through bottled-up feelings and complete their relationship with the person who has died.

Sounds pretty reasonable so far, right? Well here's where it gets a little unusual—some would say weird or even flaky. The Contact Project is where I help people see and actually talk with dead family members or friends using a process I discovered while trying to reach Grampa after he died. Yes, I know. Sounds kind of wavy-gravy, but that isn't me. I may not follow mainstream methods, but my project is respectable. It's not like I'm telling fortunes over the internet or running some 900 psychic hotline scam.

The contact process doesn't always work, and people rarely get what they expect, but many get some satisfying communication. Most of them can only make contact once or sometimes twice, so it's not like they have the deceased back for nightly conversation. But overall it helps.

The exception to the one-or-two-contacts rule so far is Tyler, who now visits me whenever he gets a notion to do it. He was the first dead person I ever talked to, and oddly he was someone I didn't even know. He showed up a couple of years ago while I was trying for about the hundredth time to contact Grampa, who had been dead for five years. Grampa was very interested in the whole area of life after death, which he hoped existed but deep down didn't really believe in. He was particularly fascinated by Harry Houdini. Grampa told me many times that Houdini had made a pact with a friend that, if he died first, he would contact this friend from beyond the grave.

According to my grandfather, Houdini never contacted his friend. This, of course, made Grampa even more skeptical. Nevertheless, he still had hope. He told me he would contact me if he could. After three years passed with no messages from my grandfather, I decided perhaps I had to put some effort into reaching him in order for it to happen. I started reading about methods of reaching the dearly departed. And eventually I began trying out some of the less bizarre approaches.

The method that eventually brought me face to face with a dead person involved constructing a homemade "apparition chamber." In an upstairs bedroom I mounted a four-foot square mirror on the wall about three feet above the floor. I surrounded it with a black velvet curtain hung from the ceiling, using a curved curtain rod to create a small curtained booth. Inside the booth, I put an easy chair with its legs removed and a block under the front to incline the chair slightly backward. This allowed me to sit in the chair and look into the mirror without seeing my own reflection. When I sat in the chair and gazed into the mirror all I saw was a pool of darkness.

The theory behind this is that throughout history people have reported seeing visions in reflective surfaces such as clear pools of water, polished brass cauldrons, crystals, and mirrors lit in the midst of blackness. The apparitions appear as the viewer gazes into the clear dark pool.

I had actually reached a point where I thought I might be getting close to Grampa when Tyler appeared for the first time. I felt strangely lightheaded, looked up to re-orient myself, and saw a blond, blue-eyed guy in a faded gray "Never Stop Surfing" tee shirt, black nylon shorts and gray rubber sandals. He sat there in the mirror, cross-legged, like he was ready for yoga class to begin. I nearly fell off my chair! And he looked as surprised as I was.

"Yo! What's up, dude?" he said.

"Um…who are you and what are you doing here?" I asked, taking a deep breath.

"I'm Tyler. Where's here? I'm clueless."

I had no idea where to begin. "Are you dead?"

"I guess."

I wondered how he could not know whether he was dead or not, but pursuing that seemed rude even to a highly curious person like me. So I moved on. "How did you get here?"

"Surfing the mean everlasting waves. And then I bailed."

That fit with his tee shirt, but otherwise I was more confused than ever. "Wow! I was trying to reach my grandfather, James Donnelly. He died in 1996. Do you know him?"

"It's not like that there. Knowing people is totally weird."

"Look, I know it's not your fault, but this is pretty frustrating," I said. "I was following the instructions for reaching dead people, and then you show up, and you don't even know whether you're dead or not. Let's see whether I can touch you."

As I reached out to grab his hand, I felt a sharp tingle between us and he was gone. Nothing in the room looked any different than it had before Tyler showed up. But I felt absolutely positive he had been there, that he was not a figment of my imagination. I was pretty sure that if I were going to imagine someone, it wouldn't have been Tyler.

I wanted to find out more about Tyler that day, so I stayed in my apparition chamber, gazed intently into the mirror and tried to conjure him up again. This was the first of many failed attempts to get Tyler to show up on demand. As I got to know him, I quickly learned that like many of us, Tyler does not respond well to directives. Over all the time I have known him, he has made a point of appearing when it suited him rather than when I've tried to summon him.

I've learned to take Tyler seriously, even though he has an annoying way of giving me instructions that are mostly confusing. I don't take well to being told what to do either, so I more or less ignored his suggestions in the beginning. But last year I got into a jam I would have avoided if I'd taken his advice, and to my surprise he pretty much got me out of it, so ever since then, I've paid attention.

Tyler isn't someone I knew when he was alive, nor is he someone summoned by one of my clients. In fact, I don't know anyone who knew him. I assume he did exist, but even though I've Googled him and done other types of web searches, I haven't been able to get enough information about his earthly life to look him up in records or anything like that.

Talking to a dead person is different from what you might imagine. Of course the dead person has all the power. After all, they've been where you are, but you haven't been where they are. They come and go at will—that's their will—and they give out remarkably little information. There's so much we want to know from them, but they don't seem to find that important. Tyler, for example, brushes off most of my questions.

"Can you see us here on earth going about our lives?" I asked him once.

"We could, but it's totally boring," he said.

"Well, what are you doing that's so interesting then?"

"It's awesome. Endless summer. Riding the big waves every day."

I expect we could go on and on like that—but usually his visits are short so we don't. I figure Tyler finds it too tedious to talk to a living person at any length.

Until yesterday, I hadn't told anyone about Tyler. As a licensed psychologist with a private grief-therapy practice, I'm more than a little touchy about being seen as unprofessional, eccentric, or, even worse, fraudulent. But last night, in a fit of intimacy that came on as I gazed into Pablo's adorable dark-brown eyes, I spilled the whole thing. He's a police detective, so it's his job to be skeptical. But he's also an artist, and he meditates, and he can be a tender, sensitive guy. Except when he isn't. Like last night.

"Cleo, it's easy to imagine something that you really want to have happen," he said. "Some of the stories we hear at the station are even more incredible than this. But use your common sense. Contacting dead people is not very likely. And, if by some miracle you were able to reach someone, wouldn't it be your grandfather? Why would some dead surfer dude be hanging around visiting you?"

"I don't know why Tyler visits me. But I do know I'm not making him up. And I have actually reached Grampa once, but I never told you because I was afraid you would say I imagined it. Silly me!"

"Okay, Cleo. I thought we agreed not to talk about this contact stuff. You know how I feel about it." Pablo knew about this aspect of my grief therapy practice. It's not like I keep the Contact Project a secret. But he has never approved of me helping my clients get in touch with dead people. Basically he thinks it's a situation where grief-stricken people delude themselves into visualizing the person they want to reach.

"You're right. I never should have told you about Tyler." I was mad at myself for telling him, but even more mad at him for not taking me seriously. "Come on Pablo, be a little bit open-minded. I thought you were trained to look at all the facts. Couldn't you at least consider that what I'm describing has actually happened?"

"Facts! What facts?" Pablo circled my living room like a dog in need of a walk. His eyes, no longer so adorable, bored holes in my head. "I've tried to be understanding about this 'new direction' in your grief therapy practice. But you're right, I'm trained to look at facts, and I don't see any here. And it doesn't help my standing in the department that I hang out with someone who talks to spirits."

Our debate continued in that vein for a while, tensions rising. Finally, I reached the end of my patience. "Out," I screamed, pointing at the door. "I can't imagine why I ever thought a policeman would understand."

"I understand a lot more than you think I do," Pablo said just before he slammed the door.

As if I needed reassurance Tyler was real, he appeared that Saturday evening when I wasn't even in the apparition chamber. I was in my bedroom getting ready for Elisa's party, deciding between a soft cotton brown and black batik pants outfit or an aqua and white floral print linen sundress. The pants outfit won. It's one of my favorites, because I think it makes me look taller. The light was dim, and I was doing a final check on my appearance in the oversized Mexican mirror that hangs over my dresser, when I felt the lightheadedness. I turned to sit on the bed, but before I could move toward it, I saw Tyler lounging on it. I wanted to be careful not to scare him off, so I slowly and quietly sat down on the floor.

"You're back," I said.

"Duh!" Tyler replied.

"I've been trying to reach you all week, but I couldn't do it."

"Hey, chill. I'm right here."

"So, what made you decide to show up now?"

"I have a 411 for Sharon."

"What! You know about her?"

He didn't answer.

"I thought you told me you don't do messages," I said.

"Yo. Check it out. I have a message."

"OK, let's hear it."

"Sharon needs to watch her back, watch for sharks."

"Could you be a little more specific?"

"No – that's it. I gave you the word. Now it's all you. She needs some serious help."

And with that, Tyler vanished. I dashed to my apparition chamber, hoping to catch him so I could drill him for more information about Sharon. But the chamber was empty. It felt more like a slightly shabby dressing room than any mystical place. I couldn't get a sense of any energy having been there recently.

This whole thing with Elisa's friend Sharon was beginning to look a lot more interesting than I had expected. My curiosity was seriously piqued. I found myself looking forward to Elisa's party with a mixture of excitement and apprehension.

3

Elisa and Jack Bonner's house is perched on the side of a mountain in Pine Brook Hills, a fifteen-minute drive from Boulder, with views of the foothills and the Boulder city lights that add thousands to its value. They built the house in 1991 when Jack started making big money in commercial real estate, and like everything involving Elisa, it was done on a grand scale. Vaulted ceilings, soaring windows, hardwood floors, custom lighting, natural stone fireplace—the works. No question they spend money where it shows. I'm not always comfortable with that. Sometimes it strikes me as an overstated in-your-face kind of materialism. But I have to admit I love their extravagant parties, where the food and the wine is decadently delicious.

I let myself in to the living room where at least thirty people were drinking wine and snacking on Elisa's famous hors d'oeuvres. Guitar music and raucous conversation floated toward me from the deck in back of the house. As I stood near the door checking out the crowd, I saw a tall woman with shaggy reddish-brown hair cross the flagstone patio to the front door. She wore a green silk shirt, white crop pants and sandals, and looked to be in her mid-thirties—just about my age. She hesitated, grimaced briefly, shrugged her shoulders and reached toward the doorbell. She looked vaguely familiar, and I was about to open the door and invite her in when she rang the bell. Elisa ran up, swung the screen door open and mashed her in an enormous hug.

"Sharon, honey! At last! We were afraid you'd changed your mind again." Elisa had on one of her more exotic outfits—a turquoise and silver dress with an intricate filigreed silver belt—that guaranteed she would stand out in the crowd.

"I've been watching for you, you know. I intend to personally make sure you enjoy yourself tonight."

"I told you I'm not sure I'm really up for a party," Sharon said, "but here I am."

"You'll be so glad you came once you meet Cleo," Elisa said, ferrying Sharon toward me. "Cleo, this is Sharon, at last! Sharon, Cleo. I'll leave you two to get acquainted while I run to the kitchen to check on the servers." Elisa darted off through the crowd, grabbing empty glasses and discarded napkins from tables as she passed by.

By then I had figured out how I knew Sharon. "You're Sharon from Shady Terrace," I said.

She had recognized me as well. "Right. I'm a social worker there," she said, giving me a small smile. "And your grandmother is Martha Donnelly. I don't usually work on the Alzheimer's unit, but we've met at Family Council meetings. I just never connected you to Elisa. I really don't know anything about your work, but Elisa's been nagging me about meeting you. You know how insistent she can be."

"Don't mind Elisa. She can be totally pushy, but she means well. Would you like to go out back on the deck where we can take advantage of the view?"

"Sounds fine." Sharon stopped for a glass of merlot at a long table that held several bottles of wine, juices and soft drinks in a large tub—then followed me through the double doors out to the deck. We sat on a short redwood bench near the railing where we could look out over the lights of the city of Boulder below.

"Actually, Elisa called me today to let me know she'd been pushing you to talk to me," I said. "She told me your husband died recently and that's why she wanted us to talk. I'm so sorry for your loss. How are you doing?"

"It's been three months, and I miss Adam terribly. Worse than that, sometimes I sort of forget that he's dead. I find myself thinking 'I have to tell Adam about this' and then I remember he's gone," Sharon said, leaning toward me with tears in her eyes.

I sat quietly with her for a few seconds, giving her time to collect herself. Then I spoke softly, acknowledging her feelings. "It's hard to accept that someone is gone," I said. "Especially when the death is sudden."

Sharon took a sip of her wine and sat up straighter. "Elisa says you're a grief therapist with an unusual project that can help me. What is it, and how does it work?"

"Yes, I'm a grief counselor. And everyone who is part of the project also does a lot of grief work. So, the project…the Contact Project…It's different and it's absolutely not for everyone. What it is…well it's a way of helping people make contact with loved ones who have died, which is why I call it the Contact Project."

I wasn't sure how much Elisa had told her about Contact so I decided to tread carefully. I spoke calmly, providing the information matter-of-factly with no indication that what I described was any more out of the ordinary than a new long-distance phone service.

Sharon choked up. "I feel like I'd try just about anything to be able to talk to him again," she said. "But—not to be rude or anything, I've always heard that these processes turn out to be fakes that get people's hopes up for nothing. Or, even worse, trick people out of a lot of money telling them they can reach someone they love, and then all they get is some taps on a table in a dark room. Adam was always so down-to-earth and sensible, it's hard to imagine him or his spirit or whatever hiding under a table in a séance room waiting to contact me."

I was used to this reaction and worse whenever I described the project, so I wasn't ruffled by Sharon's skeptical response. She didn't know my credentials, and I figured she thought I was one more New-Age flaky Boulderite, and maybe she felt irritated at Elisa for arranging this introduction without warning her about what the project really was.

"I understand why you say that," I said. "But this process isn't what you're expecting. There's no séance, no medium, no table tapping. You do it all yourself, and you do it alone. All I do is provide the setting and teach you how to make contact. And I can help you if you have problems."

"I don't know. How much would it cost to try this?'

"If you fit the project criteria, it won't cost you anything. But look—I don't want to even begin to push you into getting involved in the Contact Project. I just can't get Elisa to understand that it's not for everyone."

"I would so, so like to reach Adam. But I guess I'm sort of afraid to get my hopes up."

"It takes a lot of energy to make contact with someone who has died, and you have to be clear and focused to do it, and there are no guarantees," I said. "But some of the people in the project have had remarkable…"

"Hogwash! Total hogwash!" boomed a loud voice directly next to us. "Sharon, I know you've been in a bad state lately, but I didn't think you'd fall for this nonsense."

Sharon jumped up right in front of a broad-shouldered, stocky, balding older man whose jaw was tightly clenched. His red face and grim expression signaled a major temper tantrum on the way.

"Dad, this is none of your business—not as if that ever stops you from butting in," Sharon said. "Cleo, this is my father, Donald Waycroft. That's Dr. Donald Waycroft, the very important psychology professor from the university who always knows what's best for everyone—especially me."

"Dr. Waycroft. It's a pleasure to meet you. I've read some of your work." I stood, and extended my hand.

"And I've heard about your work—if that's what you call it." Waycroft responded gruffly. "Stay away from my daughter. She has enough problems as it is."

Ignoring my outstretched hand, he grabbed Sharon's arm, spilling her wine down the front of her silk shirt. "I need to take you home," he said. "Elisa said Maria just called to say Nathan has an emergency with his plants and needs you right away. My car's right in front. I'll drive you down, and we can get your car later."

Sharon yanked her arm back from her father's grasp, mopping her shirt with a napkin. "Dad, stop! You've ruined my shirt, and you're being rude and overbearing."

Sharon turned away from Waycroft toward me. "My dad's right about the plants. My son, Nathan—he's only eight. Those herb plants are everything to him right now."

"Sharon. We need to go NOW," Waycroft moved to face her again.

Ignoring her father, Sharon continued talking to me. "I'd better go. Maria, is babysitting tonight, but she's not at her best in a crisis. I'll talk to you soon."

I knew Sharon was right about Elisa's daughter Maria not being good at handling a crisis. I had been Maria's part-time nanny years ago, and we have stayed close. She's now a dreamy 16-year-old, who plays the violin exceptionally well but often isn't aware of much else.

Remembering Tyler's instructions to watch over Sharon, I decided I should stay in the picture. "I've known Maria since she was a baby," I said. "We're still close. Why don't I follow you down and give her a ride back here. That way Elisa and Jack can stay here with their guests, and you won't have to leave Nathan to drive her home."

"Thanks. That would be great," Sharon said as she brushed past her father and headed toward the living-room door with him close on her heels. "Dad, I can drive myself. There's no reason for you to come."

"I'll follow you home. Just to make sure everything is okay," Waycroft gritted his teeth and grabbed Sharon's arm again. I guessed Sharon was in no mood for the angry lecture she was likely to hear from him as soon as they got home.

I knew about those lectures. Listening to Waycroft's bluster, I flashed back to a time when I was 14 in Topeka and my father yelled at me for having gone with some friends to visit a psychic. My stomach twisted as I heard my father's words from long ago ringing in my ears. "Cleo, what did you think you were doing going into that part of town late at night? To see a psychic? They're all fakes—just after your money. You need to learn to think before you act!"

I returned to the present when Elisa popped up in front of us as we headed toward the door. She said she was sorry Sharon had to leave, but she appreciated my offer to pick up Maria.

Waycroft pushed her out of the way as he continued to propel Sharon toward the door. "Elisa, you are even flakier than I thought you were," he said. "You're certainly no credit to the Psychology Department, inviting guests like Miss Spirit Contact to your parties. Just who my daughter needs to meet! If you want to get tenure in the department, you're going to have to be a lot more careful who you hang around with."

Sharon ignored her father's ravings. "Thanks for inviting me and thanks for getting me hooked up with Cleo," she said.

"Donald, stop being a bully and let Sharon handle this herself," Elisa said, moving to step between Sharon and Waycroft.

She had time for no more as Waycroft hustled Sharon out the front door and toward his red Jeep Cherokee. But Sharon pulled away, striding toward her white Saturn parked nearby. "I'm in Martin Acres, 31st and Ash, just off Broadway" she yelled back at me. "It's 3122 Ash. See you in a few minutes."

She turned toward Waycroft. "Dad, I am driving my own car home, and I don't want to see you showing up there tonight. Why don't you just stay here and find someone else to annoy?" Sharon fished out her keys, unlocked her door, hopped in and drove off down the steep gravel driveway in a cloud of dust.

Waycroft stomped off to his own car muttering, "Stupid, stubborn girl." He got in, turned his Jeep around with a spray of gravel and headed off after Sharon.

I jumped into my Toyota and sped behind them down Old Stage Road to town.

$$4$$

Amazingly, I was able to follow right behind them down the winding road to flat but crowded Broadway. We all arrived at Sharon's house at almost the same time. Sharon made a sharp turn into her driveway and leaped out of the Saturn just as Waycroft pulled in behind her. They argued briefly in the driveway. Then Sharon dashed up the two wide wooden steps, crossed the covered porch and turned her key in the lock of the front door. Whatever she had said to her father made an impact. Instead of following her, he stood next to his car.

I parked on the street, got out of my car and walked cautiously toward the front porch. Waycroft glared at me. But I figured his anger was his problem.

The house was a remodel of a modest 1950-style brick ranch, with the living room right off the front door, which Sharon had left open. I could hear Nathan crying, "Mom! Mom! My plants are dead! That dog killed my plants, and now they're all dead."

I stood on the front porch looking in. The room was a mess. Dirty glasses and plates perched precariously on top of stacks of mail and newspapers that covered a table in front of a beige couch. A laundry basket piled with tee shirts and socks sat in one corner. And next to it near a large bay window, a sturdy brown-haired boy sprawled on the floor surrounded by dirt and broken flowerpots. His face was smeared with grime and tears.

Poor kid. Only eight years old, grieving for his step-father, and now his plants were smashed. I felt a strong desire to run over and give him a big hug, which of course I couldn't do since he had never met me. So I stood quietly watching.

I noticed Maria standing on the other side of the room holding a wiggly black puppy, trying to keep him away from the plants. Her head was bent toward the puppy, and as usual her long brown hair covered most of her face.

"I'm so, so sorry," Maria said, turning her scrunched-up face toward Sharon. "I only brought Gustav with me to keep him away from Mom's party. He is a little frisky, but I thought I could keep him out of trouble here. Usually he's fine as long as I'm with him. But he ran after Nathan's ball under the table by the window and somehow he knocked over the table and the plants fell on the floor. I told Nathan we could repot the plants but …"

"No, they're dead, dead, dead now and there's nothing we can do," Nathan sobbed. "I hate your stupid dog."

He had quite a bit of emotional energy invested in those plants. I figured they meant more to him than a potential source of cash.

"Nathan, it's not as bad as you think," Sharon said as she knelt in front of the crying boy and reached out to hold him in her arms. I felt relieved to see he would get that hug I knew he needed. But he rejected Sharon's comfort.

"No," he cried and jerked away. "If Dad were still here this never would have happened."

"Let me take a look," Waycroft spoke from the open front door right behind me, apparently having decided he had waited long enough. I was surprised at the warmth and concern in his voice. But his positive feelings didn't extend to me. He pushed past me into the room, without so much as an "excuse me."

"Hey, Dr. Waycroft!" Maria said, smiling at him. "Do you think we can save those plants?."

"Dad, I told you I can handle this," Sharon broke in. "Please give us a few minutes of privacy here."

Ignoring both Sharon and Maria, Waycroft squatted on the floor in front of Nathan. "Here's the thing, Nathan," he said calmly. "Plants are different than people. Plants have roots. See these roots," he said, cautiously fishing around in the dirt to show Nathan the spindly roots. "The roots are what keep the plant alive, not the dirt. As long as the plant is still connected to its roots, it can live in another pot. All we need to do is get more pots and dirt and put these plants in them and they'll be fine."

Nathan stopped crying and looked his grandfather straight in the eye. "Are you sure, Grandpa?" he asked. "Are you really, really sure?"

"I promise," said Waycroft. If your Mom can find some pots and dirt in this messy house, we can get your plants fixed up right now."

Seeing her dad with her son, Sharon put aside her impatience with Waycroft. "Okay, I'll get some pots from the carport," she said walking off down the hall. I decided to lay low and see how things went from there. Waycroft pulled Nathan onto his lap and talked quietly to him. Clearly a man who could control his mood when he chose to.

"Nathan, these pots are almost exactly the same as the ones that broke," Sharon said as she came back into the living room carrying a stack of clay pots and a bag of potting soil. "Do you want me to help you repot the plants, or do you want to do it yourself?"

"Grandpa's going to help," said Nathan, who looked much happier now. "Grandpa says he knows what plants like, and how to make them feel better. Did you know that one time Grandpa won a prize for a special flower he grew?"

I rolled my eyes. Waycroft, the gardener? I flashed on an image of him yanking out any plants that didn't meet his standards.

"Ok, here's the stuff. You go ahead," Sharon said putting the pots and the dirt right on the living room floor in front of Nathan and Waycroft. "But let's be sure to keep Gustav away from this dirt."

I stepped into the living room. "I'm going to take Maria and Gustav home as soon as she's done here," I said.

Maria looked startled. "Cleo, hi," she said. "I didn't know you were here. Isn't this a mess?" She leaned toward Nathan while keeping a firm grip on the wiggly Gustav. "Nathan, I'm really, really sorry about your plants," she said. "I'd help you clean up, but I think I'd better get Gustav out of here before he causes any more trouble."

"That's OK. We can clean it up. You go ahead," Sharon said. "And tell your mom I really appreciate her introducing me to Cleo. I think her project sounds really interesting."

"Sharon, did you hear anything I said?" Waycroft said frostily. "I told you to forget about that. If you get involved with this Cleo woman and her crazy project, there will be unpleasant consequences for you and Elisa and Cleo. I promise you that. "I felt my body tighten as I absorbed the tension in the room, but Sharon didn't react at all.

"Mom, why can't you be nice to Grandpa? I need him to help me now that Dad is gone," Nathan cried.

I didn't want to give Waycroft the satisfaction of thinking he'd chased me off, but I was more than ready to get out of there. "It's time for us to go," I said, turning to Maria. "Do you have all your stuff?"

"Can you get my backpack in the corner?" she said.

I grabbed it and we were on our way. Maria took a few minutes to get Gustav settled, but he quieted down quickly once the car got going. "I probably shouldn't have brought the puppy," she said. "I thought Nathan might enjoy playing with Gustav, but he's totally obsessed with those plants. He talks to them every day. He thinks he can get rich from them if they grow. He totally worships that soccer player David Beckham, and he wants to get enough money to go to England to see him play. I'm a little worried that it won't work out and he'll be majorly disappointed."

I figured Nathan felt like his life was out of control, and the plants could be good therapy. But I didn't want to analyze Nathan's behavior for Maria, so I said, "I expect Sharon is watching out for him."

Then, curious about the enthusiastic welcome she had given Waycroft, I asked, "How do you know Dr. Waycroft?"

"We both play in the Boulder Symphony," she said. "He's an awesome trumpet player. I don't know him that well. I've seen him a few times at Sharon's when I was babysitting, and he came to pick up Nathan to take him somewhere. Nathan relies on him a lot since his dad died, so I was glad to see him there tonight."

For the rest of the ride, Maria filled me in on her progress with the Boulder Symphony. I listened with half an ear, while I thought about the two faces of Waycroft. His threats had me nervous about what sort of trouble he might stir up. I'd heard horror stories about the difficulty of getting tenure at the university. Could Waycroft find a way to keep Elisa from getting tenure just because he disapproved of her introducing Sharon to me? And what about Sharon? Would he be able to keep her from even trying to contact Adam?

I wasn't inclined to worry too much about what Waycroft might have in mind for me. After a lifetime of arguments with my own father, I've learned not to be intimidated by bluster and demands. If anything, Waycroft's pompous assumptions that I was a flake or a fraud made me more interested in helping Sharon, just to show him how wrong he was.

5

On Monday morning, I thought about Sharon as I stepped out of my dusty green Toyota into the sweltering parking lot of Shady Terrace Care Center. Belying its name, the ranch-style nursing home was bathed in fiery Colorado morning sunlight, even though it was only 9:00 a.m. No wonder the residents keep their blinds closed, I thought. The drought had reduced Shady Terrace's attempts at landscaping to toast, so there wasn't much to look out at anyway.

As I walked into the main lobby, the air-conditioning hit me with a cold blast. I've never liked air conditioning, which is another big reason I've always favored Colorado over Kansas in the summer. Like the temperature, everything in the Shady Terrace lobby is artificial—plants, flowers, fake store fronts that have the look of an old-fashioned barber shop or ice cream parlor. The theory is that the old people will feel more comfortable in the cozy environment of their past, but to me it has always felt like a stage set without a play.

I crossed the lobby to the Alzheimer's unit, punched in the security code on the number pad next to the door, and walked in. As usual, I felt like I had fallen through the looking glass to an alternate reality, where the people tuned in to some far-off frequency I couldn't receive. In the unit's main room, called the Fireside Lounge because it has a fake fireplace in one corner, Maxwell Kohn paced in circles singing "Row, row, row your boat," while making vigorous rowing motions with his arms. Dianne Amball slumped in her wheel chair in front of the TV and stared open-mouthed at a commercial featuring Dealing Dan Your Mattress Man. Her expression remained impassive as Dan pointed his finger at his viewers and ranted on about "the deal of a lifetime."

Flora Gypsum, always dressed as if for a party, wore a red and black paisley skirt with a purple sweater and silver high-heeled shoes. A hat with pink roses perched crookedly on her tightly curled white hair. She sat on a small blue plastic-covered couch reading the daily paper upside down.

I try hard to respect the dignity of these residents by learning their complete names, finding out a little about who they were before they came here, and having conversations with the ones who are able. It's the way I hope other people will treat Gramma.

Hey, Flora, any good news today?" I asked.

"Same old stuff," she replied. "My father will be very upset about the economy."

Since I figured Flora's father, if alive, would be at least 110, I didn't explore this further.

"My father's planning to buy this place, you know," Flora went on.

"Do you think he'll change it much?"

"Well some of the people here are pretty crazy. I think he'll be able to bring in a better class."

I suspected my 87-year-old grandmother Martha, whose Alzheimer's disease is more advanced than Flora's, was one of the crazies Flora wanted to get rid of. My grandmother is more and more confused and disoriented these days. Sometimes she thinks I am her sister, Gail, who has been dead for 20 years. In the beginning that was hard for me to deal with, but I now respond to any name she calls me. I've come to realize there is no use in trying to set her straight on who is who. Besides, what does it matter? She is still my Gramma, and always will be.

When I visit, I try to find ways to connect like we used to. My grandmother was quite a movie buff and sometimes when I play a video of an old movie for her, she perks up.

As I headed down the hall, I saw Tanya, one of the unit nurses, leaving Gramma's room. Tanya's easy to pick out from a distance. She's short, and wide, and walks with a rolling gait like she recently got off a ship. She usually wears bright multicolor-flower-patterned scrubs that I personally think are a bit intense for the agitated residents.

"Cleo, could I talk to you a minute?" she asked frostily.

My stomach did a quick flip. The last time Tanya had a talk with me, it had been about my grandmother's habit of collecting any stray pair of glasses she came upon and hiding them in the back of her closet.

"Sure. What's up?"

"Could we talk down at the nurse's station?"

Another stomach flip.

"Sure." I followed along down the hall

Tanya said nothing until we got to the nurse's station, where she was all business as usual, standing behind the station counter. Did this woman ever smile? "Your grandmother's not having a good day today, Cleo," she said. "And she's been upset all weekend. She's been wandering at night instead of sleeping. Last night she wandered into Flora's room and tried to climb into her bed. You can guess how that went down with Flora. She started screaming, and your Gramma burst into tears. It was a mess."

Ouch! This was so what I didn't want to hear. Gramma's decline and my inability to stop it is a continual lesson in coping with having no control. That's one of the reasons I'm studying meditation with Masuka. But I still find it hard that I can't help her more. "I wish we could figure out what's bothering her," I said with a big sigh....

"I think she still misses Jenny. She asks for her." Jenny, Gramma's favorite nurse, had died tragically on a backpacking trip the previous fall.

"But Jenny died almost a year ago," I said. Standing on the other side of the nurse's station counter, I felt like a kid arguing with a teacher, but I went on. "With Gramma's memory problems, I can't believe she even still remembers her."

"These Alzheimer folks can surprise you sometimes," said Tanya.

She was too busy going through a stack of papers in front of her to even look at me. "Anyway, I'm wondering if we should talk to Dr. Ahmed about changing her medications."

"Let's give it a couple of weeks," I said. "Every time she gets new meds, she loses a little more of who she is."

Tanya kept her face down and began writing. "OK. We'll watch her for now," she said, dismissively. "I put on that Cleopatra movie she likes so much—maybe that will help her stay calm for a while."

That Cleopatra movie—the mega-blockbuster starring Elizabeth Taylor and Richard Burton—was one of Gramma's favorites. It came out a few years before I was born. My mother loved it too, which is how I got the name Cleopatra. I'm proud of my name and I take it seriously. Cleopatra VII was an amazing and inspiring woman. She was Queen of Egypt when she was only 17. She was quick-witted, fluent in nine languages, and a shrewd politician, who fought to save her county from absorption into the expanding Roman Empire. Her life gives me a lot to live up to and she was only two years older than I am now when she died. She killed herself at age 39 in order to avoid the humiliation of being marched through Rome in chains. Sometimes when I feel my life is too difficult or out of control, I remind myself of what she faced trying to save her country.

But when you grow up with a name like Cleopatra, you develop a thick skin for jokes and insults. I've heard all the "Where's Anthony?" comments you can think up, and don't even get me started on barges.

When I walked into her room, Gramma greeted me with her usual questions. "What time is it? Where's James? I haven't seen him all day." This is a hard one for me. At first, I used to gently explain to her that Grampa had died, but she would refuse to believe me and I didn't feel comfortable arguing the point with her. So now I just say, "He went to a conference in Boston," or "He had to give a paper in San Francisco." She remembers him doing those things, so she accepts the explanation.

I diverted her attention to the video, and sat with her for about half an hour watching it. When it came to the part where Julius Caesar was murdered, Gramma lost interest and dozed off. I had an appointment at my office downtown, so I turned off the video, gave Gramma a quick kiss and headed down the hall toward the front door.

When I let myself out of the Alzheimer's unit into the main hall, I saw Sharon absorbed in conversation with a muscular, dark-haired thirty-something guy. He wore royal blue gym pants and a matching sleeveless sport top—the fancy micro-fiber kind with the black side panels. I could barely take my eyes off his bulging muscles long enough to look at Sharon. It took her a minute to notice me as well.

"Cleo, I was just telling Erik about your project. This is Erik Vaughn. He's a fitness trainer and nutritionist. He comes over here twice a week to work in our Wellness Center with some of the residents of our Senior Apartments. Erik was one of Adam's best friends, and he's been helping me and Nathan out a lot since Adam died. I don't know what we would have done without him. He's the one who gave Nathan the plants that had the unfortunate accident the other night." Sharon gave Erik a big smile.

"Good to meet you, Cleo." Erik shot out his hand for a handshake, which I have to admit left me sort of tingly. His eyes and hair were brown, nothing spectacular, but somehow I felt myself drawn to his straightforward gaze.

"I think that's a great idea for Nathan to have those plants to grow," I said. It probably helps him to have a positive focus like that."

"Maybe that helps," Sharon broke in, "but I think it's mainly the money Nathan is thinking about with those seeds."

"It's actually a business," Erik said. "I'm working with the Natural Herbal Remedies Company to find people willing to grow herbs at home, dry the medicinal parts and sell them back. Right now we're getting people to grow valerian plants. The home growers invest $500 for the seeds, and stuff like containers, peat pellets, and a greenhouse dome. They're slow-growing, but eventually you can make about $5000 selling back the roots. I gave Nathan a set a couple of months ago, and he's really excited about the whole thing."

"Interesting. What is valerian used for?" I asked. Boulder being a center for natural foods, supplements, herbal remedies and so forth, I figured I was showing my ignorance by not already knowing about valerian.

"Some people call it an herbal valium," Erik said, "because it's relaxing and sleep inducing, relieves spasms, calms the digestion, and lowers blood pressure. It's especially useful for severe insomnia because it can bring on a restful sleep without morning sleepiness or other side effects."

"Sounds like an unusual business," I said, "growing medicinal herbs at home."

"Your business sounds more unusual," Erik replied. "Talking to people who have 'crossed over,' or whatever. It would take some convincing to get me into that."

"I'm thinking about trying it," Sharon said.

"Hmm…," Erik said. "Good meeting you, Cleo. I have to get over to the gym. Let me know if you're interested in getting in on the herb-growing business. See you later, Sharon." He loped off toward the Wellness Center.

Turning to me, Sharon asked, "Do you remember Jenny, the nurse who worked here and died last fall? She was Erik's wife. It was so tragic what happened to her."

"I certainly remember Jenny. She was my grandmother's favorite nurse. Didn't she die of an asthma attack on a backpacking trip?"

"Yes, she forgot her inhaler. Erik hiked out as fast as he could to get help, but by the time he got back Jenny was dead. It was awful. Erik has had a tough time, feeling guilty and all. I told him that maybe he could look into your Contact Project to try to reach Jenny. I'm sure she'd forgive him for not being able to get help fast enough. And he'd probably feel more at peace with the whole thing. But Erik has pretty much the same take on it as my dad does."

"Never mind. I'm more concerned about you right now," I said.

"Me too. Do you have a couple more minutes to talk about it?" she asked.

"I have an appointment downtown in about 15 minutes. Could we set up a time for you to come to my office and talk? We can talk about the Contact Project and see if it's a good fit with what you're looking for."

"OK. When can we do it?

"Could you come after work today? I'm free anytime after 5:15."

I don't usually provide appointments on such short notice, but Tyler's warning was still bothering me.

"I could be there by 5:30."

"Sounds good. I'm at 736 Pearl. Unfortunately I don't have a parking lot, so you'll have to find parking on the street."

As I rushed out to meet my client, I found myself thinking about Erik. I was curious as to whether his herbal remedies might be able to help Gramma calm down and get some sleep at night. I also wondered whether Adam had told him anything about what he'd been so worried about.

6

Pearl Street has become the place to be in Boulder. Maybe you're wondering how I could afford an office there, and how I could offer Sharon free participation in my project. Am I rich or do I owe my soul to Visa and MasterCard? Well, here's the deal—to my amazement, the Contact Project is an actual funded project. I have an endowment from a man who was able to contact a family member and wanted to help other people do the same. His first name is Bruce. I can't tell you his last name because, even though he's very high on the project, he doesn't want to be publicly connected to it. Go figure.

Anyway, a friend referred Bruce to me for grief therapy not long after I first set up the apparition chamber. His daughter had died from a drug overdose. He was devastated because his relationship with her had been stormy for several years before she died. I'm not sure he knew how much he loved her until she was gone.

The first time Bruce came to see me, he cried, which I've since learned is way more open than he usually is. He sat in my counseling room with tears running down his face and said, "I wake up every morning with this horrible feeling that something is wrong. Then I remember my daughter is dead and I'll never be able to make it right with her. How can I live with that?"

It only took a couple of sessions with him for me to realize that although he's brilliant, his feelings are mostly unspoken and generally unknown to him. He's the kind of guy who's probably never even told his wife he loves her. But when his daughter died, it was like he rammed full force into a stone wall. At a very deep level he got that she was gone for good, and he'd never be able to make peace with her. He's not used to problems he can't solve and he hates unfinished business, and there he was in a situation where he felt like there was nothing he could do. He was desperate enough to come for grief counseling, even though he doubted it could help him.

By our third session, I realized he would be a good candidate for the contact process, so I screwed up my courage and asked him if he wanted to try. Once he got over thinking it was spooky, he was enthusiastic. He was able to reach his daughter. It was only once—but he felt immensely better afterward. He told me they had each acknowledged their mistakes, forgiven each other and made up. He was able to say goodbye to her and feel okay about that. He was almost floating around the room when he told me about it—like he'd gotten free from a heavy chain that had been weighing him down.

Bruce's contact with his daughter changed him. He went from feeling isolated and alone with his bottled-up grief, to being able to remember and talk about the good parts of his relationship with his daughter and the love he felt for her. He wanted other people to have the opportunity to benefit from the process the way he did. So he decided to use some of the fortune he'd made in high-tech businesses to fund the Contact Project. There are some conditions as to who qualifies and what kind of records I keep, but basically it's my show to run. Which, I admit, is mind-boggling—and a lot of fun.

I moved into the Pearl Street office last year, after a Buddhist bookstore vacated the property in Boulder's pricey west end to move to a more harmonious location. Aside from the lack of parking, I love everything about the place. It's a pinkish flat-roofed stucco building that was once a house, but later converted to retail use. An earlier owner enclosed the front porch, making it two front rooms with large rectangular windows on either side of the front door. The building is finished with brown wood trim, and has masses of ivy growing up one side. A gigantic maple tree provides summer shade and fall color.

Inside I have four rooms and a bathroom. I use one of the front rooms as a waiting room, and one as my office. In the back, I have a counseling room, and a smaller room, which I use as an apparition chamber. My funding covers the steep rent and stretched to pay for new furnishings as well. I decorated the rooms with a southwestern look, using shades of burnt sienna, gold, cream and dark turquoise. I bought a wool hand-woven Mexican rug down the street at Marisol Imports for my waiting room floor and stuck a fat cactus next to the window. I have three of Gramma's colorful paintings on the walls in the counseling room, which makes my insurance company nervous because they're so valuable. But I enjoy the artwork every day so it's worth the risk to me.

At 5:30, Benita, a client whose brother had disappeared while hiking in the national forest was on her way out of my office.

"He's likely to show up at my door tomorrow and ask me why I've been seeing a grief counselor," she said.

"That's certainly a possibility. How do you feel about that?"

"My brother always drove me crazy and he's still doing it is how I feel. Why couldn't he either die or not die? That sounds like a simple request, but not for Darren. He always finds a way to make everything my problem."

"Maybe you could focus on what he added to your life and what you miss about him." I suggested.

"Well, maybe. I'll think about it." Benita said as she headed out into the waiting room.

"See you then." As I waved goodbye to Benita, I saw Sharon hurrying along the sidewalk toward my office.

"Parking in this town is impossible," Sharon said as she dashed through my front door, wiping sweat from her forehead.

"Sorry you had to rush," I said, beckoning her inside. "The sun is wicked at this time of day. Would you like some water or iced tea?"

"Tea would be great, thanks," Sharon said as she plopped onto the chocolate-brown sofa in the counseling room. "Before we get started, I want to apologize again for my father's rude behavior the other night. Sometimes I think he deliberately tries to embarrass me."

"You and your father do seem to have some disagreements," I reached for the pitcher of sun tea in the under-counter refrigerator on the back wall. I grabbed two tall glasses from the cabinet above, added ice cubes from my tiny freezer compartment and filled the glasses with tea. I handed Sharon a glass and sat across from her in a tan leather armchair.

"Thanks," she said. "Maybe I'm too hard on Dad. I have to admit I'm grateful to him for the help and support he gave me in the weeks and months after Adam died."

"It's good that he could be there for you. Sudden death is such a shock that the details of daily life can be overwhelming."

"That's for sure." Sharon paused, took a deep breath, and continued. "I got this horrifying phone call about Adam's accident and I had to fly to Las Vegas because that's the closest airport to the Grand Canyon. I was in complete shock. My dad happened to be in Vegas at the time at a professional conference. So he met me at the airport and drove me the five hours to the Grand Canyon. He was amazing with all the gruesome details of picking out a coffin and a burial site, and arranging the funeral." Sharon swirled the tea around in her glass, staring at it as if she could see those miserable memories floating by.

I sat quietly, giving her time to experience her feelings and collect her thoughts. After a few minutes, she looked up and said, "Lately, though, I've been getting fed up with Dad's bossiness. It takes me back to when I was a teenager. Sometimes I'm not sure whether I'm making my own choices, or following his single-minded plans for my life.

Sharon didn't exactly seem like the passive type. And I had seen her stand up to her father at least for a short time. I wondered if sometimes he managed to gradually wear her down. "Do you often go along with his plans?" I asked.

"No, I don't. In fact sometimes I think I react against his plans just to show him he can't tell me what to do."

I sure could relate to that kind of reactance, but I merely nodded to encourage her to go on. "He likes to call me stubborn and selfish," she said, "but I see it as determination and backbone. I think of myself as a 'can-do' person. When I set my mind in a certain direction, I sort of mow over the objections and keep going until I get there. I think that's why I became a social worker, and it's a good fit. The people I work with need someone on their side who doesn't give up easily."

"But it doesn't work as well with your father?"

"Well, you know he's a big deal psychologist," Sharon said, taking a big drink of her tea.

Probably not as big a deal as he thinks he is, I thought as I nodded to show I followed Sharon's story.

"He studies behavior, which he sees as pretty much determined by what gets reinforced and what doesn't."

"Yes. I knew that."

"So, when my brother and I were growing up, we lived in what the behaviorists call a token economy. My father set up charts of everything we were supposed to do—all broken down into small steps—and then added a point system for each step we got done. We could turn in the points for spending money, TV time, use of the car, stuff like that." Sharon set down her glass to tick off on her fingers the prizes available for points.

"Hmm…could make you feel more like a pet than a daughter."

"I'm not saying it ruined my life, but even now I find myself thinking I should get points for washing my car or cleaning my house," Sharon said. "Which I expect is why those parts of my life are so disorganized. Why do that stuff if you don't get any points for it?"

"How did your mother feel about that?"

"My mother died when I was only four," Sharon said, staring off at one of my grandmother's paintings on the far wall. "Dad never talked about her. Most of his energy went into his work. Not that he neglected us—everything was organized at home. We had our charts of jobs and our point system."

"And you didn't get any points for talking to him about your feelings."

"Actually, I don't even remember wanting to. As soon as I was old enough, I put my energy into sports. I've always been athletic. I played tennis, soccer, and basketball. And I skied and hiked whenever I could. I still do." Sharon perked up as she mentioned the sports.

"So you got out of the house and into a different point system."

"Yes. And after that I couldn't wait to get out of there and go away to college."

I could easily relate to her desire to escape an overbearing father. But as a therapist my job was to listen, not to share my personal experiences. So I nodded, and asked "So you did go to an out-of-state school?"

"Absolutely. Dad's a sucker for education, so as long as my grades were first-rate, he was willing to spend the money to send me to an expensive school. I went to Stanford, and I loved Palo Alto and the school. But I missed Colorado, so after I graduated, I came back and got my Masters degree in social work at the University of Denver," Sharon said, clinking the ice cubes around in her empty glass.

"Is that where you met Adam?" I took a few notes on a yellow pad, beginning a social history on Sharon.

"No, I met Adam three years ago here in Boulder. We were only married two years. He's not Nathan's father. They were really close, though, and Nathan started calling Adam 'Dad' after we got married. And last fall Adam adopted Nathan. That was Nathan's choice. You can imagine how Adam's death has hit him."

"What about Nathan's father?"

"His name is Joel," Sharon sighed. "He left when I was pregnant with Nathan. I was 26 and we'd been together for two years. We weren't married because Joel always said it would be unfair to both of us if he made a long-term commitment before he really knew himself."

"So he left when he found out you were pregnant?"

"No, at first Joel got into the idea of being a dad. We planned to get married. But one day I came home from work to find him gone, his things cleared out. He left a long letter explaining that he had been having nightmares where he found himself trapped in a small space, desperately trying to escape. He wrote that as much as he wanted to stay with me, he knew these dreams were a sign that he wasn't ready."

I hoped Joel had been at least an absentee father to his son. "Has he kept in touch with Nathan?"

"No, we never heard from him at all—until last February when he called out of the blue and said he wanted to come and visit and meet Nathan. Right!! After eight years, he's finally ready! I told him to forget it. He never cared before, and now Nathan had finally found a dad in Adam. We didn't need Joel showing up and complicating our lives."

"What about child support?"

"I never tried to get anything from Joel after he left. In fact, since he left so early in my pregnancy, I didn't even put his name on Nathan's birth certificate. I figured I could raise Nathan on my own, and if Joel didn't want to be involved, that was his choice. But that also meant he couldn't just drop back into our lives at his convenience."

"It sounds like you've had a lot of loss earlier in your life—and now Adam. I know you said you really want to talk to him again. Is that mostly because you miss him so much? Or is there something specific?"

Sharon leaned forward and looked me in the eye. "I just can't believe that Adam would fall accidentally like that. In the first place, the canyon rim isn't even a hike. Adam saw it more as a walking meditation. But he was so fanatical about hiking safety—reviewing maps, preparing for weather fluctuations, carrying food and water—that I can't imagine him falling accidentally. When he was a teenager he went off a trail, slipped on some wet rock next to a mountain waterfall and fell into the rapids. He was lucky he didn't drown. Instead, he got tossed onto a rock that was right in the middle of the waterfall. But he had to be rescued, and he had a fractured skull and concussion. So he's been extra careful ever since."

"I can see how that would bring on an attitude shift," I said. "So what do you think happened at the Grand Canyon?"

"The rangers said he went off the trail, stood too close to the edge, slipped on some icy rocks, lost his balance and fell off. They told me Adam fit the profile of the person at the highest risk of a fatal canyon fall—a young male hiking alone. But Adam was the opposite of a reckless tourist. You can see why I don't think it sounds like him."

Did Sharon think someone had pushed Adam over the edge or he had jumped? I didn't want to be the first one to say it. So I asked, "Do you have any reason to think Adam was in some kind of trouble?"

"Lately he had been working long hours," Sharon said. "His office was in the remodeled garage next to the house, and he was out there all the time. When he did come back into the house, he was so tired he hardly talked to me or Nathan. Since he died, I've found out that his web-design business had financial problems. I'm sure he didn't want to tell me about it. My dad always thought Adam was a goof-off, and Adam desperately wanted to prove him wrong."

"Your father and Adam didn't get along?"

"Well, Nathan's father, Joel, was one of my father's graduate students in behavioral psychology before he dropped out and left. Dad was furious at Joel for leaving, but still kept hoping he would come back. Even though we never heard from him and had no idea where he was. When Adam adopted Nathan, Dad took it hard. We had to run notices of intent in the paper and try to find Joel before the adoption, so he had a chance to respond. Dad thought for sure Joel would show up and stop it. But he never did, and the court let Adam adopt Nathan."

"So your dad saw Adam as taking the place where Joel should be?"

"Yes. But Dad was wrong about Adam. He thought that because Adam was a high-school dropout who got a GED and went to community college, he would never amount to anything. As you can see, Dad doesn't exactly give anyone a break. But Adam was smart and worked hard, and his business had been doing well. In fact, I still don't understand how he could have been in debt."

"You say you think the financial problems were part of what was preoccupying him. Do you think there was something more bothering Adam lately?"

"I do. He looked worried. And he sort of seemed to be somewhere else a lot of the time. I'd be talking to him, and he'd be staring off into space over my head. I don't know what was going on with him. He said he had a lot of things to think about. He'd go out and hike up Mt. Sanitas to clear his mind, but when he got home he wasn't any calmer. That wasn't like him. Usually getting out into the mountains by himself was all he needed."

"Is that why he went to the Grand Canyon?"

"Yes. Somehow he got it into his head that if he could go there and hike around the rim, he'd feel much better. I didn't really want him to go—it's so far and it was April when you can run into some major snow storms in the mountains. But he was dead set on it. He started telling everyone he knew that he was going on a 'midlife crisis trip.' Which was really dumb because he was only 37.

"So are you thinking that if you contact Adam you can find out what really happened?"

"It's the only thing I can think of to do now. Nobody believes me that it wasn't just some stupid accident. The rangers didn't exactly say it but I could tell they thought it might be suicide. But I don't think Adam would decide to leave me and Nathan without even saying goodbye. Now no one will do any more investigating. I can't afford a private detective. But I have to find out."

"I think the Contact Project sounds like a good possibility for you. But I have to tell you that you may not reach him. Or you may reach someone else."

"In a way I feel like I already made contact," Sharon said, leaning forward in my direction. "I had this really vivid dream about Adam just before I woke up this morning. He seemed so real and he was trying to tell me something—but then he faded away and I woke up. But it felt like he was still in the room somehow."

"What happened in the dream?"

"I was lost in a maze of long halls," Sharon said, "and I was feeling really scared because I had no idea how to get out or to get where I wanted to be. I ran around trying different paths. Some of the halls were dead ends, others led further into the maze. There were people around—sort of gliding by–but they ignored me. Every time I thought I was almost at the end of a hall, I came to a bend where it stretched out farther in front of me. Then I saw Adam at the end of a hall. He was on a sort of spinning platform with two other people.

I ran toward him as fast as I could, but the air felt thick and it took me a long time to get close."

Caught up in the telling of the dream, Sharon got up from her chair and walked around my office.

"I reached out to try to get his attention," she continued, extending her arm, as if reliving the dream. "The floor where he stood was spinning very fast. He stopped and got off. He was very real and alive to me, and I felt like it had all been some sort of mistake, that he wasn't really dead."

Sharon stopped pacing right in front of me, but looked past me into the distance. "So I said 'Adam—they told me you were dead. Where have you been for the last three months?' And then he started to get blurry and fade away, like the Cheshire cat. I yelled out at him, 'Adam! Don't go!'"

She sobbed as she resumed her walking and continued relating the dream. "And then he looked straight at me and said, 'There's danger for you and Nathan. Don't trust….' And then his voice faded away with the rest of him. I ran toward the spot where he had been and jumped and reached out to grab him, but I felt myself falling forward into a foggy hall in front of me. And then my alarm rang and woke me up."

She blew her nose and went on. "I'm so ready to try to reach Adam. Especially because of that dream. Adam seemed so real talking to me and then he faded away before he told me who not to trust. I know it was a dream, but it feels like more than that. I feel like I need to find out what he was saying." She came back over and sat in her chair.

I sat silently, not wanting to interrupt her mood. She shook her head, as if to banish the dream, then looked at me. "His presence was so strong in my mind all day that I kept looking over my shoulder for him and listening for his voice. Now I feel like I'd try just about anything to be able to talk to him again. You said I might be able to do it at no charge? I don't have much money right now."

"Yes, I have funding available, and you're a good candidate." I thought about Tyler and his message for Sharon, but decided it was too soon to bring that up. Maybe after she contacted Adam. I wondered how easy that would be for her. Some people have more success with the process than others do. It seemed like a good time to find out.

"The contact process takes a good part of a day," I said. "I keep Fridays free for that and the person I had scheduled for next Friday cancelled yesterday. Could you get the day off?"

"I have some comp time I need to use this month. Friday will work," Sharon said.

"OK. We'll need to start at your house so we can look at photos of Adam, and mementos, like a favorite shirt or jacket of his, tools, stuff in his office, whatever you have that is closely associated with him. Can you arrange for Nathan to be somewhere else?"

"He's leaving at 1:00 for a friend's birthday party and won't be back until about 8:00. Will that work?"

"That's perfect. After we get done at your house, we'll come over here and walk outside a little to relax—somewhere along the creek path. Then you'll be ready to try to contact Adam. And after that, we'll talk about how it went, and where you want to go from there."

"OK, you know where I live," Sharon said. "So I'll see you Friday at 1:00?"

"Sounds good. And try to avoid caffeine or heavy food that day."

7

I went home, made myself a turkey-avocado wrap with lettuce and leftover curry rice, and headed out to my studio to paint while there was still some daylight left. I love the studio. It's built from rose-colored natural stone like the main house, and lit by north and south facing windows and a skylight, enhanced by daylight fluorescent tubes. The floor is ceramic tile for easy clean-up. I have plenty of room for oils, watercolors, pastels and gouache, and I have blank stretched canvases stacked along one wall. It's a luxury to spend quiet time there after hours of seeing clients.

My latest project was an abstract series of Tyler, depicting him in both this world and the afterworld, but progress had been slow. Gramma taught me a long time ago that when these lethargic times come, I need to keep working and push through the fog. Because she shared the ups and downs of that process with me so openly, I know how important it is to persevere even when I feel like I am slogging through mud in heavy boots that are sapping my energy.

She was a marvelous example herself—focused, creative and productive. She would typically complete about fifty paintings each year. And they were first-rate. Her work was selected for nationally and regionally juried exhibitions, where she won loads of awards. Her paintings were bought by private collectors nationally and internationally, and by several Fortune 500 companies. In 1960, she was elected to the National Association of Women Artists. It was a lot to live up to.

Painting is what I do to balance my life, and to stay connected to my creative inner core. I take my art seriously, but it's not how I want to make my living. I don't share Gramma's discipline and love of the artist's solitary life, but thanks to her, painting for me is usually an adventure with lots of excitement. Except when it isn't.

Like on that Monday evening. I couldn't stop thinking about Sharon long enough to focus on painting. As the sun went down I was at my easel, gazing off at a dark window at the end of the room, when I saw Tyler walking toward me. Seeing him blew me away as usual. After all, he is dead!

"Yo, Cleo."

I grabbed my brush to take advantage of having the actual—if not in the flesh—model for my painting. But my questions took priority over painting.

"Tyler! I need some help! What's going on with Sharon? Is she right? Did someone push Adam or make him fall? Do you know who it was?" I waved my brush in the air like a frantic orchestra conductor.

"Chill, Cleo. Sharon has some issues. I'm not the one with the answers. I told you, it's you. You play Nancy Drew."

"But I'm a therapist, not a detective," I protested—even though I knew from experience that Tyler is always in charge of the dialogue between us, and never gives me specific answers to questions like the ones I'd asked.

"That's all make believe. Just ride the wave," Tyler said, and vanished with no warning as usual.

I decided to clean up and go back to the house, even though it was only about 8:30. Just as I turned off the studio lights, my cell phone rang.

"Hey, Cleo. This is Erik Vaughn. We met over at Shady Terrace this morning."

"Sure. I remember you. You're the fitness trainer who grows herbs. How are you?" I cursed myself for babbling. As Tyler would say, I needed to chill.

"I'm good. I was just wondering if you'd like to get a drink somewhere and talk more about herbs and spirits and stuff."

Hmmm…interesting, I thought. I figured I might get some useful information—and Erik wasn't exactly hard to look at—and I needed a change from Pablo—so why not? "That sounds great. I was feeling a little restless. How about Rhumba at 9th and Pearl? It's not usually too crowded on a Monday night. I could meet you there about 9:30."

"See you then."

It was my favorite kind of Colorado summer night—warm and pleasantly dry with a light breeze that whispered over my skin. We got two of the high turquoise seats at the long stone bar at the edge of Rhumba's patio, not easy in this popular spot. The terrace is a combination of bricks and flagstones carefully arranged around three trees whose leafy branches provide shade in the daylight and twinkle with strings of lights after dark.. With its ceiling fans, Latin music and island ambiance, this place is about as close as you get to the tropics in this mountain community.

It had been a long day, and I was ready to play. I had taken time to change into a lavender halter sundress to match Rhumba's Caribbean décor. Erik wore khaki shorts with a silky black tee shirt that fit snuggly over his bulky shoulder muscles, Yum!

The bar there offers a selection of fifty rums, but I usually get their most popular drink, the Mojito, made with silver rum, mint, lime, soda and powdered sugar. Erik had a Dark and Stormy—dark rum and ginger beer with a lime wedge perched on the edge of the glass.

As usual the place was packed, and the noise level was high, which oddly makes it easier to have a private conversation. Erik's intense gaze—as if I were the only woman in the room—was more intoxicating than the drink. But I needed to get some information before I started having too much fun. So I took a long sip of my drink, and said, "How long did you know Adam?"

"About two years. We met at the gym, and it didn't take us long to see a good opportunity to barter our services. I provided some personal training for him in exchange for a website he designed for me."

"Sharon said you were close friends." I decided to probe a little. "If you know what was bothering Adam, it could help her."

Erik leaned forward, still looking intently into my eyes. "Here's the thing, Cleo. I think Adam jumped. That's why I wanted to meet with you."

Erik's declaration jarred me out of my tropical trance. Why hadn't Sharon mentioned Erik's theory? "Have you told Sharon that?"

"No. I don't think it would be good for Sharon and Nathan to find out any more about what happened. Let them think it was an accident. Sharon will be better off if you just help her with her grieving and forget about this contact stuff."

"But she doesn't believe it was an accident. And I think she'll be better off knowing as much as she can."

"How are you two on drinks?" A sweaty waiter on the restaurant side of the bar eyed Erik's nearly empty glass.

"I'll take another one of these," Erik said.

"I'm fine," I said, preoccupied with thinking about how to get Erik to be more forthcoming about Adam's problems.

I waited until the waiter was out of earshot, and asked, "Why would he have jumped? Was it business troubles?"

Erik gave me a conspiratorial smile.. "Look— there's a lot Sharon doesn't know about him. They were only married two years, you know. And I think they were only together about a year before that." Erik leaned closer and spoke softly. "I wouldn't want Sharon to know this. But Adam had gotten into internet gambling. He lost a bundle, kept thinking he'd make it back, but it got worse instead of better. He borrowed on his business to pay the debts."

"I didn't know Adam," I said, "but from what I've heard about him, he doesn't sound like the type of person to jump off a cliff and leave Sharon and Nathan without a note explaining why. And if he was going to kill himself, why drive all the way to the Grand Canyon to do it?"

He sighed, and took on a pensive look. "I don't think he was planning to jump when he went there. In fact, I was originally going on the trip with him."

"You were going with him?"

"Yes, but it turned out that I had to visit my brother for an important family thing. I tried to talk Adam out of going by himself. But he said he couldn't wait any longer to get some clarity to come to a decision on what to do. He thought an answer would come to him at the Grand Canyon, but it didn't, so he panicked and bailed out."

The waiter came back with Erik's drink, which gave me an opportunity to look away and collect my thoughts. This was turning into a very curious evening. I know it sounds odd, but in a way Erik's mysteriousness added to the strong attraction I felt for him. At the same time, I felt annoyed that he'd kept all this from Sharon.

As soon as the waiter left, I continued my questions. "So you're not going to tell Sharon any of this?"

"No, I'm not. And I don't want you to tell her either." Okay, that was a little bossy, but I didn't feel bound by what he wanted me to do or not do, so I didn't argue with him about that. But I did want to convince him to be honest with Sharon.

"Don't you think she deserves to know what was really going on with Adam? All her questions and doubts are so troubling, the truth might be a relief—even though it's not news she'll want to hear."

"Look, Cleo," Erik paused until I returned his intent gaze. "I know you want the best for Sharon. But I know her better than you do. I've been taking good care of her and Nathan. I have them on dietary supplements that will boost their immune system cells and improve their energy levels. And I'm making sure they get plenty of exercise. This is what they need to help them let go of the past and move on. Trust me, I've been through this after my wife died, and I know what works. You'll be doing Sharon a big favor if you discourage this idea of contacting Adam, and encourage her to focus on her future."

I have never subscribed to the just-let-go-of-the-past-and-move-on approach to dealing with grief. It's the old time-heals-all-wounds myth.

I've found people do much better when they actively work through their grief, much of which involves looking honestly at the relationship they had with the person who died, and seeing what they need to do to feel complete with that relationship. I didn't want to debate theories of grief recovery with Erik, but I did want to acknowledge his backhanded mention of Jenny's death.

"I know you have some personal experience with grief, since your wife died less than a year ago," I said quietly. "I knew Jenny. She was my Gramma's favorite nurse. You must miss her terribly."

"Look, she was careless. It's caused me a lot of grief, but I've had to get over it and take care of myself. Life is short." Erik gulped the rest of his drink and motioned for the check.

I was too stunned to answer. His rapid jump from sensitive to callous gave me whiplash.

He got out his credit card. "I need to get home, it's late," he said. "Hey! Maybe you'd like to check out my website." Erik gave me a sweet smile that reminded me why I had worn the lavender sundress. He handed me a card that read "Vaughn's Holistic Healing….innovative and affordable products for your journey to optimal wellness."

At this point I felt a little bit jerked around by Erik's emotional volatility, so I jumped off my barstool and said, "Thanks for the drink. Talk to you later." I ducked out to Pearl Street and began walking west toward my house eight blocks away.

Walking along the quiet, dimly lit sidewalk, I thought about Adam. Could Sharon be wrong about him? Had he gotten himself into deep gambling debt and jumped over the edge of the canyon? It didn't fit with my image of the loving husband and step-father who had adopted Sharon's son. I did know gambling addicts often leave loved ones alone and poor. Still, I didn't think Tyler would be telling me to "play Nancy Drew," if Adam's death was suicide. But I couldn't figure why Erik was so convinced of this explanation.

I was so deep in thought that I tripped on an uneven piece of paving when a sprinkler system started in the yard next to me. As I picked myself up, bruised, annoyed, and wet, I gave new credence to the accident possibility. Even a cautious person in familiar territory can get distracted and stumble. I decided I should definitely encourage Sharon to be open to all the potential explanations.

8

On Wednesday morning, I had planned to get to Shady Terrace in time to visit Gramma before I went to her quarterly Care Conference. But I stopped at the gym to work out and got held up for 15 minutes by the road construction on Broadway, so I barely made it in time for the conference. When I rushed in to the tiny windowless conference room, most of the interdisciplinary team members were already gathered there. Betsy, the sweet twenty-something social worker for the Alzheimer's Unit was talking on her cell phone to someone who was looking for a nursing home for a parent. She twisted a lock of her long curly blond hair with one finger as she earnestly recited the benefits of care at Shady Terrace.

Susanne, the gray-haired slightly overweight dietary technician, made notes in a bulging day-planner notebook, highlighting some of them in yellow. Tanya, my adversary from nursing, munched on a cinnamon roll as she chatted with Alicia, the bubbly long-legged activity director. I wondered how much of Alicia's boundless energy came from the grande-sized Starbucks paper cup in front of her.

They all stopped what they were doing when the medical director, Dr. Ahmed—a slightly-built dark-skinned man in an impeccable white lab coat—darted in and took the seat at the head of the table. He placed a stack of residents' medical charts on the table in front of him, nodded a brief greeting to the group, opened the top chart, and said, "Martha Donnelly, age 87."

This no-nonsense beginning to Gramma's care conference was typical. The schedule is always tight, and staff members are in a rush to get back to their routine tasks. As usual, they did a quick round where each member described Gramma's recent ups and downs in their area of expertise. I'd been coming to these conferences for years, so by now I could recite nearly all their lines on my own. Gramma spurned most group activities, especially bingo. She would attend musical performances, which she usually enjoyed. She refused to eat anything that required much chewing, didn't drink enough fluids, and didn't sleep well at night. It was the nighttime activity that was the issue today.

"I told you about the behaviors, Cleo," Tanya said, leaning across the narrow table in my direction. Her face was so close I could see bits of partially-chewed cinnamon roll as she spoke. "We had a tough time calming her down after she tried to climb into Flora's bed, and Flora was furious. We've tried everything to keep Martha settled in the evening, but it's not working. I really think she needs new medications. What do you think, Dr. Ahmed?" She finally looked away from me, as she turned her face in his direction.

He flipped through Gramma's chart, without looking up. Dr. Ahmed isn't much for social skills. "We could try Ambien," he said, writing in her chart—no doubt already ordering the sleeping pills. "We can start with a low dose and see how she responds. She might actually be more alert during the day if she gets more sleep at night."

I frowned and shook my head. I remembered the problems Grampa had with Gramma wandering out in the evenings and nights before she moved to Shady Terrace. Alzheimer's patients are at their worst after the sun goes down. In fact, it's called sundowning. So I knew what the staff were up against. But I didn't want to dope her up and lose even more of her essence. And in my mind, Dr. Ahmed was all too willing to sedate the residents.

"Cleo, I understand that you don't want her medicated," Tanya said. "But we have to try something to change her nighttime behavior. I don't want to wait until another resident gets upset and hits her. We know she doesn't mean any harm, but there's no way to explain that to them."

I tried to make eye contact with Dr. Ahmed as he continued to page through Gramma's chart. "What about trying some herbal products?" I asked, thinking of Erik's roots. "That fitness trainer and nutritionist who works in your Wellness Center—Erik Vaughn—tells me that valerian helps people sleep without drugging them."

"We can't use herbs like that here," Dr. Ahmed said, finally looking up. "They're not FDA approved, and we have no idea what side effects they might have. And it makes me a little nervous that we have some nutritionist going around here, making suggestions about medicating our residents with herbs."

"He didn't suggest valerian for Gramma or any resident," I said. "He talked about growing it, and I asked him what it was used for, and he told me. If I sign something waiving liability, couldn't we at least try it? I think Gramma would want to if she could decide for herself. You know my grandfather was very interested in herbs. He grew lemon balm, and mint and chamomile, and made teas that they both drank. I wouldn't recommend those teas for taste—personally I prefer coffee—but they both swore by them as a daily tonic."

Suzanne from Dietary rolled her eyes. "Cleo, if you want to feed your grandmother herbal tea we have no problem with that. In fact we have a selection in the kitchen," she said..

"We'll start her on Ambien and see how it goes," said Dr. Ahmed, closing the chart and the subject.

"Do you have any other concerns, Cleo?" Betsy asked, giving me a sympathetic look..

"No, that's all I have, Betsy," I said. I knew she was trying to validate my concerns, but I was fed up with Ahmed and Tanya by then.

I knew there was no point in arguing with them further, so I got out of there as quickly as I could and headed over to the Alzheimer's unit to visit Gramma. Some of the residents were already seated in the dining room even though lunch wouldn't be served for at least 20 minutes. Others were parked in front of the TV in the main room or pacing in the vicinity of the dining room door. Dianne Amball, slumped in her wheel chair, called out over and over, "He-el-p me! Somebody hel-l-p me." This was her standard refrain, which wasn't a cry for help in the usual sense, but rather her way of making contact. Nothing anyone did ever got her to stop for more than a few minutes, so no one rushed to her aid.

Loretta, one of the newer residents on the unit, shuffled slowly over to Dianne. "I can't stand whiners," she said. "I'm a school teacher and I expect adult behavior." I thought to myself as I often do when I hear the confused residents speak out this way that dementia frees people to say what most of us merely mutter to ourselves.

Dianne ignored her and continued calling out for help. Soon an aide appeared and wheeled her into the dining room. Meanwhile some of the residents who had been seated in the dining room drifted out into the main room, perhaps forgetting lunch hadn't been served yet. The aides gently directed them back into the dining room, as if they had simply taken a wrong turn. I reminded myself that taking care of these confused people is a hard job, and I should be more patient and understanding of the staff. As nursing homes go, this one provides pretty decent care.

I saw Gramma coming along the hall. She looked pretty, dressed in a loose lavender dress. with her white hair freshly brushed. Her eyes looked worried, but she smiled when she saw me. I gave her a hug, walked with her into the dining room, and sat with her until the food came out. Her meal was mostly pureed since one of her Alzheimer's symptoms is that she doesn't like to chew—or maybe she has forgotten how to do it. The multi-colored mounds of mush took my appetite away, but she began spooning it in. I said goodbye, leaving her to her lunch.

In the parking lot, I ran into Sharon. "Hey, Cleo. I was just going out for a quick lunch. Want to join me?" she said. "We could grab a salad at Wild Oats."

"Sounds good. I have to be at the office by 1:00," I said. "I'll meet you over there."

We sat on the covered patio outside the Wild Oats grocery and café on Broadway and Arapahoe, munching our salads of assorted baby greens, veggies, sprouts, tofu and sunflower seeds, and enjoying the mountain view. At the next table, a man in his late 50s with thinning gray hair in a pony tail shared a sandwich with a black Labrador retriever, while pretending not to stare at a 20-something girl in a low-riding sheer ruffled raspberry-colored skirt, bare midriff and a pink slip-like top, as she walked past us into the store. She didn't look in his direction, but I figured she knew the effect she had. I never dressed like that in my twenties, but now that I'm 37 I kind of wish I'd tried it out back then.

"I hope I didn't get Erik in trouble today," I said, as I tried to spear a cherry tomato with my plastic fork. "At Gramma's care conference, I asked Dr. Ahmed to consider valerian to help her sleep at night, but he got kind of huffy about Erik and the whole herb thing."

"Ahmed's a strange one," Sharon said, breaking off a piece of her whole-grain roll. "He does a lot of his work in nursing homes. Some of the residents on other units, who aren't confused, have complained about him—don't want to take the medications he prescribes." Sharon absently rolled pieces of bread into pea-sized balls as she spoke. "When I talked to him last month about their right to refuse treatment, he told me that grief was clouding my judgment. Then he offered me drugs. He gives out samples to the staff whenever they ask—which makes him pretty popular with some."

"I don't like him myself," I said. "So does that mean I can ask for him not to see Gramma anymore?"

"You should talk to Betsy about it since she's Martha's social worker. But, if you can find another physician to see her, you can switch. I shouldn't really get into this with you, but confidentially I thought last year that Ahmed might be ripping off Medicaid."

"Really? How come?"

"He prescribes so many meds that come from the pharmacy next to the pain clinic he owns. Would you believe they call it the We Feel Your Pain Clinic? He prescribes oxycontin and a bunch of other drugs to everyone who goes there. I know about that because he hired Adam last year to put up a web site for him, and Adam spent some time over at the clinic. He thought Ahmed was kind of a shady character."

I wanted to get more information from Sharon about Dr. Ahmed, but before I could come up with an appropriate question, she choked, spraying iced tea all over the table. Color drained from her face as she jumped up to face a slim, tan, young man with dark wavy hair and what looked like a three-day growth of dark beard. He wore khaki shorts, Teva sandals, and a black tee shirt with a red and gold elephant on the front. And he grinned from ear to ear.

"Joel?" Sharon gasped. "What are you doing here?"

Did she say Joel? As in Nathan's father, Joel? The guy she said she hadn't seen for years?

The smiling guy standing directly in front of Sharon reached out to hug her, but she backed away. "Sharon! I was just going in to get some groceries. I wasn't expecting to run into you here, but it's so great to see you."

"I told you last year that I didn't want to see you. How can you just show up like this after all these years?" Sharon still looked stunned.

Joel's smile gave way to an intense, brooding look. "I wanted to see you and our son. I've changed, Sharon. I wanted to tell you that when I called last winter, but you wouldn't listen. When you told me you'd gotten married and your husband had adopted our son, I thought it was too late for me, so I didn't come. But then I heard your husband had died in an accident, so I decided to come back to Boulder after all." Joel reached out to touch Sharon's arm, but she backed off again.

"How did you find out that Adam died?" Sharon asked. "Did my dad call you?"

"No, I haven't talked to him in years," Joel said.

I stared at Joel's elephant tee shirt, a clue that he was into meditation and yoga, and wondered whether he'd changed much since Sharon saw him last. All at once I realized I was the third wheel in this reunion. So I collected my trash, stood up and said, "I need to get to my office."

"Oh, Cleo. This is Joel. Joel, Cleo." Sharon said, too flustered to add any identifying information to the introductions. "We're still set for Friday, right?"

"I'll be there at 1:00," I said, "unless you change your mind." I thought Sharon might not be in the best frame of mind for the contact project, given the reentry of Joel into her life, but now certainly wasn't the time to discuss that.

9

After a busy afternoon with grief therapy clients, I went home and worked in Grampa's garden, untangling and pulling out bindweed that had twined itself around some rose bushes. Gardening got me thinking about herbs again, so I went in to look up possible non-toxic herbal sleep remedies. Poring over Grampa's collection of old herb books, I had just found an intriguing note about rose water and rose vinegar in an old book called The English Physitian, when the doorbell rang.

I was surprised to see Erik standing on my front porch, looking relaxed in shorts, a tank top and flip-flops, and holding a large white cardboard box. "Erik! How did you know where I live?" I blurted out before I thought about what I was saying.

I've kept the phone book listing for my house phone in my grandparents' name because I don't want to be surprised at home by discontented or needy clients. Most of my friends call me on my cell phone, which I also use for my business. And I don't give out my home address casually.

"I'm good at finding people—nobody can hide from me," he said with a laugh. "I wanted to bring you this starter kit for growing the valerian plants. We usually charge $500 for them, but I'll give it to you for $250." He stood there oozing boyish charm, waiting to be invited in.

I figured he was the kind of cute, sexy guy who usually got

whatever he wanted from women and I didn't plan on falling for that. No way would I be buying any herb kits or whatever else he might be selling. But his winsome smile melted my initial resolve to send him away. And I figured I could use his help with the herb thing for Gramma, so I asked him in.

"Thanks for the offer, but I don't think I have time for another project," I said. "But I would like to get your ideas on an old remedy I found. Do you have time for a beer?"

"Sounds great," he said, and followed me out to the kitchen.

I grabbed a Fat Tire for each of us from the refrigerator. We settled at the old maple kitchen table where I had been looking through the herb books. "Here, read this," I stuck *The English Physitian* in front of his face, pointing out the section that read:

> Vinegar of Roses is of much good use, and to procure rest and sleep, if some thereof and Rosewater together be used to smel unto, or the Nose and Temples moistned therewith, but more usually to moisten a piece of Red Rose Cake cut fit for the purpose, and heated between a double folded Cloth, with a little beaten Nutmeg and Poppy Seed strewed on the side that must lie next to the Forehead & Temples, & so bound therto for al night.

I noticed Erik frowned as he read, so I said, "Well, okay, the book was written in 1652, but maybe they knew more about natural remedies than we do now. I have roses, and I'd like to maybe try that for Gramma, but I need some help knowing how to make this stuff. What's red rose cake?"

Erik wasn't too impressed with my rose water idea. "Cleo—hello—this is the 21st century not the 17th. You don't have to make your own potions anymore." He closed the book and pushed it away. "Have you gone on my website? We have concentrated valerian root available in capsules, or you can get tablets with valerian and chamomile and passion flower."

"But Dr. Ahmed won't let her take those. Because they're not FDA approved, and so on. I thought the rose potion would be acceptable because she wouldn't be taking it internally, just breathing it in."

"Ahmed's a jerk! That guy always has his head stuck where the sun doesn't shine," Erik exploded, banging his hand on the table for emphasis. "I can't help you if you want to listen to his advice."

Wow! He didn't seem so relaxed anymore. But as a therapist, I see lots of angry outbursts. I know how to meet a strong emotion with a calm voice and a bland face. So I said quietly, "It's not exactly that I want to listen to him. But right now, he's her doctor."

"Well, let me know when he's out of the picture, and maybe I can help. Meanwhile, what's up with Sharon? Were you able to talk her out of trying to reach Adam?"

"Erik, you'll have to ask Sharon if you want to know what she plans to do. I can't tell you that."

Erik leaned across the table toward me, and put his hand over mine. He looked me straight in the eye. "Cleo, we both want the best for Sharon and Nathan. Do you really think this is going to help them? I'm afraid your project could destroy them."

Angrily, I yanked my hand out from under his and jumped up. I'd had more than enough of his attempts to interfere with my work with Sharon. "Erik, I'm not going to talk about this with you. You need to go now. I have some work to do."

Erik laughed, chugged the rest of his beer, and lazily got up from the table. "Ah, Cleo. You're even cuter when you're mad. I know you'll eventually see that I'm right about this. I just hope it's not too late."

I ignored his condescending remark. I just wanted to get him out of my house. I headed straight to the front door and stood there, holding it open.

"OK, Cleo. See you around." He flashed me a smile as if we were saying goodnight after a friendly visit. Then, finally, he left.

After he was gone, I noticed he had left the starter kit on a table in the living room. I hadn't paid him anything, but I figured he owed me at this point for trying to push me around, so I opened it up. Inside was a letter that read:

Congratulations! You're going places. By taking advantage of this special offer, you've shown that you're the kind of person who charts your own course. Your decision to invest in this starter kit says a lot about you. You set high goals for yourself, and you recognize a genuine opportunity when you see it.

You already know that your investment will pay big dividends. You'll make ten times your original outlay, just by letting your plants grow while you go on about your life. But that's not all!

We're going to let you share this offer with special friends, family, and co-workers who would appreciate an incredible money-making opportunity. And for every potential investor you suggest who decides to join us, we'll reward you with a $50 bonus. You win, your friends win, we all win. You can't beat that!

We'll be calling you in the next few weeks to see how you're getting along with growing your herbs. That will be the perfect time for you to give your friends and family the chance to benefit from this remarkable opportunity. But make your list today, so you'll have it ready. We'd hate to run out of starter kits before your people get theirs.

The letter was signed by Erik Vaughn for the *Natural Herbal Remedies Company*. I wondered whether this was a subsidiary of *Vaughn's Holistic Healing* or a completely different company. The whole thing began to feel more than a little shady. Pyramid scheme, anyone? I started thinking Dr. Ahmed might be right about Erik. But what about Sharon's questions about Ahmed? And she thought Erik was great. I wanted to look up Erik's website, but my home computer had some new problem connecting to the internet, and I hadn't had the patience to sit on hold waiting to talk to a technician about it. I made a mental note to check Erik's site at the office the next day.

I stuck a frozen organic spicy Kung Pao chicken bowl into the microwave, cut up some fruit, and took it all out to my studio. I needed a break from the intrigue. While I ate, I contemplated my Tyler abstracts. Something about them had been bothering me, but while I ate I got an insight as to how to move on. I painted, deeply engrossed, for several hours without noticing the time until I heard a knock on the studio door.

10

Had Erik returned for his starter kit? The thought of having to deal with him again left me cold. When I opened the door to Pablo, I was so relieved I forgot I was mad at him and jumped into his arms. I guess he forgot too, or else he'd decided to let it go. So we sort of made up without any discussion. That's one of the best things about our relationship. We've been together off and on for so long we know each other like family. A look, a kiss, or a hug can say it all, when we want it to. Of course the downside of this familiarity is that we can set each other off as fast as a spark in dry pine needles, which unfortunately happens all too often.

I didn't want to discuss my paintings of Tyler with him—Tyler being one of those sparky issues between us—so I sent him over to the house to get himself a beer while I cleaned up the studio. When I got over there, he was stretched out on the couch with his beer watching Larry King interview Cameron Diaz. Pablo looked at least as entranced as Larry did. "Hey, Cleo. Did you know Cameron Diaz left home at 16 and lived all over the world? And she hadn't even had any acting experience when she got that part in Mask."

"Hmmm, interesting," I said, admiring Pablo's thick dark hair and fit body. He's over six feet tall, played football in high school, and works out to keep himself in shape. I could imagine even a celebrity like Cameron Diaz finding him as appealing as he found her. I grabbed myself a beer and joined him on the couch, snuggling into his solid body. We cuddled on the couch, watched the rest of the show and finished our beers. I felt mellow and close to him, so I leaned my head over until our lips met. We were engrossed in the intense kisses that come with making up, when Pablo's cell phone rang. He jumped, grabbed the phone from his pocket and flipped it open. "Gomez," he barked. "Yeah. Right. How long ago? Okay, I'll be there in about half an hour."

He untangled himself from my arms and stood up. "Sorry sweetie, I have to get out to a drug bust in an apartment in Longmont." He gave me a goodbye kiss, and turned toward the door.

Suddenly I remembered I had wanted to ask Pablo about police investigations after hiking accidents. "Hey, before you go can I ask you a question?"

He stopped. "I'm in a rush. Can't it wait?"

"No, I need some information right away." I stood up and walked over to stand in front of him. "When someone falls in the mountains and dies, how do the police or sheriff or whatever know if it's an accident, or suicide, or maybe someone pushed the person over a cliff?"

"Hmmm…they look for a note? Ask witnesses what happened? Check out the hiker's state of mind. There's no simple answer to that question, Cleo. We can talk about it more when I have more time." He turned and opened the front door.

"Well what kinds of things might make them suspicious that it wasn't an accident?" I wasn't going to let him blow me off, even if he was in a hurry.

"Give me a break, Cleo." He walked out onto the front porch and turned back in my direction. "I don't have time to talk about this right now."

"Come on, Pablo, another few minutes won't make that much difference. Just give me a quick picture of what the police would think was suspicious."

"I have to go. Can't you learn to be a detective some other day?" I heard his I-have-important-police-work-to-do-don't-bother-me-with-stupid-questions voice. All of a sudden I remembered I was mad at him.

"Okay, never mind," I said, with an ever-so-slight edge to my voice. "I'll ask someone who's not too busy and important to answer my questions."

"Hey, maybe you could ask that Tyler dude. He can look down from the afterlife and tell you what happened." Oops—Pablo had remembered he was mad at me, too.

"Didn't you say you had to be somewhere? I wouldn't want you to be late," I wasn't even trying to be civil anymore.

"Okay, Cleo. Goodnight." He walked across the yard, got into his car, slammed the door, and drove off.

Wow. My karma was really off for males that Wednesday. Dr. Ahmed, Joel, Erik, Pablo. And of course Tyler, who I hadn't seen that day but who I was sure could give me some answers if he wanted to. I was definitely hoping Sharon would make contact with Adam at our Friday session, and that he'd be one male who would actually help.

11

I woke up on Friday to one of those gorgeous sunny summer days that brings tourists flocking to Colorado in July to escape the heat and humidity back home. I took a cup of freshly brewed Columbian coffee out to my back patio to enjoy the sweet peas, delphiniums, and columbine sparkling in the sunlight. A fabulous day—but to be honest, I couldn't sit still. A lot was riding on today's contact session. If I could believe Tyler, Sharon was in danger. But I had no idea what sort of danger, or from whom. I didn't even know what had happened to Adam. This is a lot of pressure for a contact session and not the way I usually set them up.

I decided to take a short but steep hike up a trail in Boulder Canyon's Settler's Park behind my house to a rocky ridge that overlooks the whole city of Boulder. Tourist photo-ops everywhere I looked. Our most famous landmark, the Flatirons—1,400 foot tall sandstone formations that jut up from the tree-covered foothills at Boulder's west end—glowed red against a brilliant blue sky. That view always refreshes me and restores my perspective. And it worked its usual magic that day, so when I arrived at Sharon's at 1:00, I felt relaxed and ready to start preparations for her contact session.

Nathan answered the door wearing a grubby Beckham 23 white tee shirt and dark shorts. He was grinning, but his face fell when he saw me. "Mom, that woman Grandpa doesn't like is here. You'll be in big trouble if he finds out," he yelled into the house at Sharon. I was sorry Nathan had already decided I was trouble.

"Come in, Cleo," Sharon yelled from a back room, and Nathan backed off so I could. In the daylight, I was able to take a closer look at Sharon's house. The windows had all been redone to let in the maximum light, which was enhanced by faux painted walls in shades of copper, crimson and amber. The contemporary furniture looked new. Someone had put a lot of energy into remodeling and decorating this house.

But the living room was as big a mess as it had been on Saturday. The hardwood floors sported large dust balls. A pizza box lay in one corner, with three shoes and a baseball glove on top of it. Newspapers, mail, and dirty glasses covered the round glass-topped coffee table. Sweatshirts and jackets were strewn over the couch, and a black leather camp chair was draped with a couple of light brown towels. I wondered whether Sharon kept her house this way to show Waycroft his training didn't take, or whether she liked it this way, or whether maybe she just didn't notice the mess.

However, I noticed Nathan's herbs had been repotted and were neatly arranged on a tile table by the window. "How are your plants doing, Nathan?" I asked hoping I could get him to soften toward me a little.

"They're okay," he said looking down to avoid meeting my gaze.

"Erik wants me to grow some, too," I said. "Do you have any advice?"

He perked up. "I gave them all names—and I talk to them every day. I heard that makes them grow faster."

Just then a car honked out front. Sharon ran in from the bathroom wearing a white terrycloth robe, her hair wrapped in a towel. "That's Jeanne. Do you have all your stuff packed, Nathan? Don't forget sunscreen."

"I've got everything you told me to put in there, Mom," Nathan said impatiently, grabbing his backpack as he rushed out.

Sharon waved to the driver, and turned toward me. "I'll be ready in two minutes, Cleo. I just got out of the shower." She dashed off toward the back of the house.

I noticed some framed snapshots on a bookcase, so I walked over to take a closer look. One was of a younger longer-haired Donald Waycroft with a toddler in his arms, standing next to a dark-haired young woman in a long skirt holding a baby. Looked a lot like my own late-1960s baby pictures.

Next to that was a shot of Sharon, her dad, and a toddler-sized version of Nathan at a mountain lake that looked like Bear Lake in nearby Rocky Mountain National Park. A more recent picture showed a smiling Nathan in a soccer uniform, standing next to a broad-shouldered man in a gray sweatshirt who gazed at him proudly.

"Adam coached Nathan's team. Did I tell you that?" Sharon said, coming up behind me, now dressed in white shorts and a turquoise tank top. Her shaggy auburn hair fell from its side part to frame her face as it dried. It looked like an expensive cut.

"Adam was such a great dad to Nathan," she went on. "It's so unfair to both of us that we lost him."

"It is unfair," I said, recalling one of my Grampa's adages. When I would rail against an injustice, he would say, "Nobody ever promised that life would be fair, Cleo." As a child even saying that seemed unfair to me. But he and Sharon were right—we don't always get what we deserve. Certainly she'd scored very high on the unfairness meter lately.

"I know we need to look at Adam's things and focus on him," Sharon said. "But it's hard for me. Mostly I'm trying not to think about him, because it's so painful, and I miss him so much, and everywhere I look there are memories of him."

"Sharon, maybe you'd like to put this off for a while. We don't have to do this today."

"No. I want to go ahead. Here, this album has a lot more pictures." She handed me a fat blue photo album, walked over to the couch, and tossed the clothes over on top of the towels so we could sit. We looked at pictures of their wedding, held at a rustic outdoor theater made from local stone, located at the top of Flagstaff Mountain. Sharon and Adam looked radiant, Nathan grinned, and even Waycroft smiled in a couple of pictures.

"We had a wonderful wedding," Sharon said. "Of course, my dad wouldn't pay for any of it. I think he said something like, 'Why would I want to reward you for making a foolish choice?' So we used our savings. But it was worth it. After waiting this long and finally finding Adam, I wanted to celebrate with a fantastic party. And Adam didn't really have a wedding for his first marriage, so he wanted to do it right this time."

"Adam was married before?" I asked, running through details in my mind to see whether I'd glossed over that one.

"Yes, didn't I tell you about crazy Natalie?"

"Um…not that I recall."

She stared off into the distance. "Where do I begin? He was 20 and she was 18. Five years later they were divorced. Her looks and athletic ability were what attracted him. Her craziness was the problem. She was on a lot of anti-depressants and tranquilizers—fighting battles from growing up with an alcoholic mother and stepfather. Adam wanted to help her, and he thought he could. He supported her for a year in massage school so she didn't have to take out any loans, and he paid for a lot of therapy, but I guess it didn't do much good. One day a woman called him and said, 'Your wife is in a hotel room with my husband right now.' It turned out she had been cheating on him for almost a year with several men."

"He must have felt very betrayed," I said, thinking to myself that for all his sunny smiles, Adam had a bunch of bad karma.

"Oh, it got worse," Sharon continued. "Adam didn't want to give up on the marriage, so they went to couple counseling. But she kept on lying. She had more affairs and hid them from him. Then, after he left her, Natalie was abusive and nasty, even threatening to hurt him—showing up where he was—shouting, throwing things, calling him horrible names. Once she tried to run him over with her car. He had to get a restraining order. And then she finally left town."

"Where is she now?" I asked, adding Natalie to my mental list of Adam's possible enemies, which now also included Joel, Erik, Donald Waycroft, and Dr. Ahmed, not necessarily in that order.

"Actually, she's here in Boulder—been back for about two years.

She goes by the name of Narmada—maybe you've heard of her. She's a massage therapist and psychic, does aura cleansings, past life readings, and Chakra balancing. After she left Boulder, she studied in India. But in my opinion, she needs her own aura cleaned or whatever, because she's still a nutcase.

"So you've met her?"

"Oh, yes. Not long after we got married and Adam's business was doing well, she showed up all pissed because Adam had made money after their divorce, and she had missed out. She saw me as getting all the benefits and wanted her share. Had the nerve to tell him he owed it to her to give her money to get her business started here."

"I'm guessing he refused and she didn't take it well."

"Exactly. And she's still mad. She called me after he died and said, 'That bastard finally got himself into a hole so big it swallowed him up. Mother Earth knows when to take revenge.'"

By then, I realized this focus on Natalie—Narmada, whatever—wasn't doing much to get Sharon into the frame of mind to contact Adam. So I said, "Do you have any of Adam's clothes? Like a favorite sweatshirt or jacket? The feel and smell of his clothes can help you move into his space."

"In here," Sharon said, walking down the hall to a bedroom with carpet and walls done in various shades of beige, oatmeal, and off-white—reminded me of a mushroom patch. Most of the room was taken up by a king-sized bed, covered with rumpled sheets, multi-striped in various shades of red, copper and brown. Pillows in similar shades lay on the floor next to the bed. Sharon opened the closet door and pulled out a red fleece jacket with a front zipper, and a long-sleeved Bolder-Boulder 10K white tee shirt with a picture of the Flatirons on the front.

"I can almost feel him when I touch these. Sometimes I wear that tee shirt to bed when I'm having trouble sleeping. It's like having his arms around me."

"Good. Let's take those with us. Now, could we go out to Adam's office?"

"Sure. It's pretty much the way he left it." She led the way through the kitchen. Above the sink, an amazingly long sheet of glass served as a see-through backsplash, revealing a stone patio shaded by maple trees. Adam's office was in back of the patio, connected to it by a floor of the same rosy stone, which extended through glass doors into the office. Sharon unlocked the doors and we went in. The sound of falling water from a fountain at the edge of the terrace carried into the office.

Like the house, the old garage had been carefully remodeled to let in light and connect to the garden outside. Bookshelves lined the walls below the windows. A sleek desk held a computer monitor and a combination printer-scanner-copier. The computer tower sat on the floor under the desk, next to a bank of file cabinets. The computer somehow drew us in its direction, although its screen was dark.

"Have you found anything on his computer that gave you any clues as to what had been bothering him before he died?"

Sharon sat in a wicker chair next to a round table and motioned me toward the ergonomic computer chair. "Actually we haven't been able to boot up Adam's computer," she said. "He has it password protected. I used to know the password but I guess he changed it. Both my dad and Erik have tried to boot it up. We've tried every password we can think of."

"Is it possible he wrote it down somewhere?" I asked, pointing to the file cabinet next to his computer.

"We've looked but I never did think he wrote it down. Adam used what they call 'strong passwords,' which are at least eight characters combining upper case and lower case letters with numbers or symbols. He would remember them with a passphrase—a sentence where the first letter of each word, combined with numbers or symbols makes the password." She grabbed a piece of paper, wrote Il2hMSdy?, and handed it to me. "This was his last one—'I love to hike Mt. Sanitas, don't you?'"

"Wow, that opens a lot of possibilities. How will you ever figure it out?" I twirled around in the chair, checking out the rest of the office.

"I doubt we will. Erik looked into other solutions, and found out that we can get some kind of emergency boot disk to boot it up and somehow change the password but he keeps forgetting to get it. I reminded him again this week, so I'm hoping he'll bring it in the next few days."

Just then the office phone rang. We both jumped and looked over at it. "I'll let the machine get it," Sharon said. "I've kept the phone connected with a new message because I didn't know who his customers were, and I need to get word to them if they haven't heard."

The machine picked up and played the message, in Sharon's voice. "Adam's Web Search and Design is permanently closed. If you have pending business, please leave a message and someone will call you back."

We heard the beep, followed by a man's slurred voice. "Adam, you son of a bitch! I'm still waiting for the stuff. You said you'd have it by July. Don't think you can just leave town or whatever. You know I'll find you. So you better call me back. You know where." He banged down the phone.

Stunned, Sharon and I looked at each other and ran for the phone to check the caller ID. "Oops, it says 'ID blocked'" I said. "Do you recognize the voice?"

"Nope," she said. "I have no idea who that was or what it was about."

We left and drove separately across town to my office. As I drove I thought about the phone message and wondered if it had any connection to the internet gambling debts Erik had mentioned. I didn't want to bring that up with Sharon now—especially since I wasn't even sure it was true.

I realized I was counting on Sharon contacting Adam, and possibly me getting new information from Tyler to find out more about any danger facing Sharon. And then I asked myself what it said about my faith in the law enforcement system that I relied on ghosts to tell us what was going on. Hmmm….maybe I mistrust Pablo's way of working as much as he mistrusts mine.

12

Once at my office, Sharon and I shared some lemonade and then went for a short walk over to the Boulder Creek Path to relax and clear our minds. The creek flows down the canyon from Nederland, splashing along a rocky bed that creates a series of tiny waterfalls enjoyed on hot days by kayakers and kids in inner tubes and rubber boats. We walked along the adjoining dirt trail to a shady bench that sits just off the path, on a promontory jutting out into the rushing water below. It's one of my favorite calm places. Four large trees on the outcrop create a sense of privacy, and the soothing sound of water gurgling over the rocks masks the traffic sounds from nearby Canyon Boulevard.

We sat there a while and talked more about Adam—the sort of person he was and the relationship he and Sharon had. When we both felt relaxed, we ambled back to the office.

The apparition chamber at my office is the same as the one at home—a four-foot square mirror on the wall, surrounded by a black velvet curtain that creates a small booth. Inside the curtain, an easy-chair is inclined backward so the sitter can gaze into the mirror and see only darkness. I had Sharon remove her watch so she wouldn't be focused on the time, then took her in and got her situated in the chair with Adam's shirts on her lap. I told her to relax, clear her mind of everything except thoughts of Adam, and gaze into the mirror.

"Don't try to rush it or make something happen, I cautioned her. "Just be here. You can stay as long as you want. I'll be right across the hall in my office if you have any problems."

I left her there and went to my desk to catch up on paperwork. Quite a few of my grief therapy clients are covered by insurance, which means I have to justify and label everything we do together so some bureaucrat can decide whether or not it's appropriate. It's a confusing system, but I've learned how to jump through the hoops and code my clients into insurance-approved categories.

After about an hour had gone by, I felt quite a sense of satisfaction at my shrinking pile of paper. When I heard the apparition chamber door open, I got up and walked to the door, just as Sharon came out slowly, blinking in the sunlight. She looked dazed. I led her into the counseling room, sat her in a chair and handed her a big glass of water. I sat in the chair across from her.

She gulped some water, put down the glass, looked me straight in the eyes, and said, "Cleo, you'll never believe what happened."

"Tell me about it."

"I sat there a long time and nothing happened. I was almost ready to give up and come out, when I started to notice color patterns and light flickers in the mirror. Then a big mist, like a fog, filled up the mirror, and I could see a light off in the distance. I saw a path, and I knew I should follow it. I don't think I got out of the chair, but at the same time I went down the path and at the end of it, I saw a woman. At first I didn't recognize her, but then I knew it was my mother! She didn't look much like her pictures, but I was sure it was her, and I felt so happy to see her, and I knew she felt happy, too." Sharon stopped for more water. I stayed quiet so as not to disrupt her recollection.

"She talked to me," Sharon went on. "She said, 'Sweetie'—that's what she used to call me—I'd forgotten that, but as soon as she said it, I remembered. I wasn't touching her, but I felt like she was hugging me. She said, 'Sweetie, I came because Adam couldn't come yet.' Then we walked along the path together and talked about a lot of things. She told me she's proud of me and Nathan."

"Were you able to ask her about what happened to Adam?"

Sharon pulled out a tissue and wiped some tears from her eyes. "Well, I know I said we talked, but it wasn't exactly like talking. I think I just said things in my mind, and she did too. But she didn't talk about Adam after she said he wasn't able to come. She did answer a question about Dad, though. I asked her why she let him raise my brother Will and me in such a rigid way. She said, 'Sweetie, I had no choice. You know your father. When he sets his mind to something, nothing gets in his way.' Then she reminded me that I can be a little bit that way myself—which I guess is true."

"So how did it all feel to you?"

"Oh, Cleo, it felt wonderful," Sharon jumped up and hugged me. "I've had dreams about my mom, but this was so different. She was really there."

"How do you feel about not reaching Adam?"

"Well, you did warn me I might reach someone else. I still want to reach him, but now I know I can't just order him up like a television program on Tivo. I'd like to keep trying, though. When can we do this again?"

We set up an appointment for the next Friday afternoon—the time I have set aside for the Contact project—and Sharon left.

13

It was after 6:00 by then, so I decided to close the office and walk to the Pearl Street Mall to unwind. Six blocks of Pearl Street in downtown Boulder have been a pedestrian mall since 1977. The trees in the middle of the brick mall have grown taller than the two-story buildings and provide plenty of shade for the benches that dot the bricks here and there. Large raised garden areas and planters are filled with colorful impatiens for the shady areas, plus petunias, snapdragons, marigolds and such in the sunny parts.

I knew the mall would be crowded with tourists on a warm Friday evening in July, but I always find it relaxing to stroll around and people-watch there. Three blond girls in low-cut jeans and short tops asked me to stop and take their picture, posing themselves with the foothills as a backdrop. A street-person, holding out a cup for donations, told me he was taking up a collection for a down-payment on a cheeseburger. I'd heard the same line from him all spring and summer, but panhandlers don't exactly live high lifestyles, so I gave him a dollar

A few blocks further on, I watched a bunch of little kids play in the random jets of water shooting from a pop-jet fountain, made from 28 stone squares. Kids ran in and out shrieking, dancing between and around the jets—some ran directly into the water, others jumped to avoid it. In one corner of the square, two toddlers—a boy and a girl—faced off over one water spout. She planted her foot over the hole. He pushed her off and put his foot on—but quickly removed it. She jumped in and put her foot over the spout again. The boy picked up her leg with his hands, moved it off the spot, and put his foot there once more. The girl looked at him, grimaced, and ran off in tears to find her mother.

I thought about how the male-female patterns do start early, until a guy next to me said, "Cleo, right? You're Sharon's friend. We met at Wild Oats on Wednesday. I'm Joel."

"Oh, hi," I said, trying for a please-don't-bother-me sort of voice. I was tired and not in the mood to make conversation with Sharon's ex-boyfriend.

I guess my tone was too subtle for him, because he gave me a big smile and said, "Can I buy you a beer at Mountain Sun? Their Java Porter is amazing. And maybe a bean burger or a burrito? I'm guessing you're a vegetarian because I saw you eating at Wild Oats"

I was about to brush him off, when I heard Tyler's voice in my ear—just as if he were standing next to me—saying, "You be Nancy Drew." A quick sideways glance showed me no Tyler, but I had gotten the message.

So I smiled back and said, "Sure, Joel. But I can't stay long."

The Sun is a hippie, tie-dyed sort of place decorated with original art and textiles. The laid-back atmosphere, inexpensive food and great beer attract locals of all ages. After we got a booth and ordered our beers and bean burgers, Joel said, "I want to talk to you about Sharon."

Well, duh, I thought, taking a big gulp of my beer and trying to keep a poker face.

"Do you know if she's seeing anyone since her husband died?"

"You'd have to ask her about that," I said. "But I'm wondering how you found out her husband died when you hadn't been in touch and weren't living here?"

"A friend of mine who lives here heard about it and sent me an email. Actually, it was odd, because I was living in Flagstaff at the time. In fact, I've been a guide for whitewater rafting trips down the Colorado River in the Grand Canyon for the last few years. So it was kind of weird that that's where her husband had that accident and died."

Absolutely weird, I thought. You might even say suspicious. Fortunately, the waiter brought our burgers and fries just then, so I had a few minutes to think before I blurted out what I thought. I decided to skip the synchronicity issue for the time being.

"What do you do during the winter season?" I asked.

"Teach skiing mostly—at the Arizona Snowbowl north of Flagstaff."

"I thought Sharon said you were a behavioral psychologist." I took a bite of my bean burger, and noticed I was hungrier than I had thought. Very tasty.

Joel poured catsup on his fries before he answered. "I was in the doctoral program here back in the early 90s, but academia was a problem for me. So much of it was bogus. In many ways, a university is just another corporation out to control people." He shrugged and gave me a disgusted look. "Only it's more dangerous because it controls people's minds. I couldn't be part of it anymore, so I left."

A somewhat different story than Sharon told, and I yearned to argue. But I decided that was not the best way to detect. "So what did you do besides being a river guide and teaching skiing?" I asked, watching him struggle to take a huge bite of burger, as tomato oozed out of its bun.

He chewed slowly and took a gulp of his beer before he answered. "After I first left, I lived in a behaviorist community in Mexico for a few years. It's an amazing place, modeled on Walden Two. Very egalitarian, non-competitive, non-violent. It's a social experiment really, not mechanistic like people think of behaviorism. It's humanistic, focused on how people's environment can bring out the best in them. For example, people can learn to be more cooperative if they're living in a place that promotes cooperation rather than competition."

Joel was pretty self-involved for a guy who had been part of a community that focuses on cooperation. I wondered whether he had left the place voluntarily or had been gently informed he wasn't a good fit.

We finished our burgers, ordered coffee and talked for another hour. Although Joel had said he wanted to talk about Sharon, I had no trouble keeping the conversation focused on him. I found out that after he left the behaviorist community—according to him it was because he felt he was stagnating—he backpacked around the country, earning money at various jobs that were mostly outdoor stuff. He had also studied Buddhism and gotten into meditation and yoga. The message he wanted me to give Sharon was that he had become a much different person than he was when he left her, and he wanted to be a father to his son.

"I could teach him to ski—if he doesn't already know how—or snowboard, if he wants. And we could go camping, maybe backpack." Joel's face lit up as, in his mind's eye, he saw himself and Nathan outdoors having fun.

I figured it was up to Sharon whether or not she wanted Joel in her life and Nathan's, so I wasn't making any promises to try to persuade her. Joel was an engaging guy, but a bit unreliable and possibly broke, so I could see where she might not want to have anything to do with him. And, in my new Nancy Drew role, I thought it was a little creepy that he had been so close to the Grand Canyon when Adam fell.

14

The next day being Saturday, I went over to Shady Terrace to visit Gramma. I make sure to go at least once on weekends, when they don't have as many activities. I don't want her parked in front of the TV all day. And I wanted to see how the new medications were affecting her. Confirming my worst fears, I found Gramma lying on her bed fully clothed—very unusual for her in the middle of the morning. The TV was on, but she wasn't watching. She didn't move or look up when I walked in.

"Hey Gramma, can I help you up?" I asked, kneeling at her bedside and looking into her eyes. She mumbled something unintelligible and rolled over to face the wall. I put my hand on her shoulder. "No," she wailed. "No, no, no." I yanked my hand back and jumped up.

I knew I should take time to calm down before I vented my anger on any staff, but I don't always follow my own best advice. So, I marched straight down the hall to the nurses' station. Tanya was at the desk, writing in a chart. I didn't wait for her to look up. "Tanya, I can't believe the way Gramma looks," I said. "She won't even let me help her get out of bed. Is this your idea of an improvement?"

"Calm down, Cleo. You know it takes a few days to adjust to medication changes. We only started her on the Ambien on Thursday. Let's give her a chance to adjust." Tanya kept on writing in the chart in front of her.

"No! I want her off this stuff! She's like a zombie. She has enough problems without filling her full of chemicals she doesn't need."

"Cleo, you heard Dr. Ahmed prescribe the Ambien." Tanya finally looked up. "I can't take her off it without an order from him. I think he's in his office over on the Rehab unit, trying to catch up on some paperwork. Why don't you go find him, and talk about it?"

I stormed off to find Dr. Ahmed, determined to get him to take Gramma off the Ambien. As I turned the corner from the main lobby into the Rehab Unit, I heard raised voices coming from Ahmed's office. His door was partially closed, so I couldn't see who was with him, but I could hear their conversation from the hall.

"You need to calm down and be more careful," Ahmed said.

"It's too risky. I'm not going to take all the blame if this comes out," a female voice responded.

"Look, you're doing pretty well here. Are you ready to give up all that extra income?" Ahmed again.

"The money's good, but I think she's suspicious and that makes me nervous," the woman said.

I knew I should leave before they opened the door and saw me in the hall, but I couldn't get my feet in gear. What risk? What blame? What money-making scheme were they discussing?

I heard a chair scrape across the floor, and what sounded like Dr. Ahmed getting to his feet. "Pull yourself together and go back to your unit. I don't want to discuss this any longer right now. Just do what you're supposed to do and everything will be fine."

I scrambled to get around the corner and back into the lobby before anyone came out of the office. Since it obviously wasn't the right moment to approach Dr. Ahmed with my complaints, I went back to the Alzheimer's Unit to see if I could pry Tanya loose from her bureaucratic mindset.

As I walked through the Fireside Lounge, I noticed Flora Gypsum on her usual couch, surrounded by newspapers. She was dressed in a blue and yellow paisley dress, with a bright orange jacket, red shoes, and a red hat with blue and purple feathers. I wondered whether she made her own daily clothing choices, or whether staff had some say. And if so, what they were thinking.

"Hi Flora, what's new?" I said.

She turned a scowling face in my direction. "I'm worried about the Queen of England. She's a friend of mine, you know, but I think she might be sick."

"Well, I'm sure she has plenty of doctors," I said, hoping to reassure her.

"Doctors! What do they know? Around here, we don't even get the right medicine. And no one even cares." Flora's voice took on a strident tone, as she waved her hands around, sending newspaper flying.

At this point, I was inclined to agree with her about doctors—at least Dr. Ahmed. I would have liked to explore her medication comments further, but I knew getting Flora more agitated wasn't a good idea. Not to mention her limitations as a reliable source. So I picked up her newspapers, distracted her with a shoe store ad, and went on to Gramma's room. She was up in her chair, which was progress, but she didn't smile when I came in.

"Why are you here?" she asked.

"Just visiting," I said, "to see how you're doing."

She scowled. "Not today," she said, looking at her hands. "Come some other time."

As Gramma's Alzheimer's disease has progressed, she's become increasingly moody. I've found it's best not to push her when she's like this. So, I said "Okay," trying not to take her rejection personally. At that point, I decided I'd had about enough of Shady Terrace for one day. I no longer felt like tangling with Tanya. I said goodbye to Gramma and left, wondering how I could find out more about whatever risky business and extra income Ahmed and the woman were arguing about.

15

I had a few errands to do, and was in the parking lot at Whole Foods when my cell phone rang. It was Pablo, his voice all apologetic. "Hey Cleo, I'm sorry we ended up in such a bad place the other night. I have tonight off. Do you want to try again?"

I took a minute deciding whether to accept his apology or stay mad. Pablo and I have a long history of breaking up and making up, dating back to when we were madly infatuated with each other during our last two years as art students at the university. Our first breakup was about 15 years ago during the year after we graduated from college. Almost on a whim—or so it seemed to me—Pablo decided he had to move to San Miguel de Allende, a colonial town in Mexico that is filled with artists, art students and art galleries. He said he needed to nourish his creative spirit and take his art to a new level. And he said he needed to do it alone. At the time, I thought we were soulmates destined to be together forever. When he left, I took it very hard. It took me almost a year to get over him.

We both moved on to other partners and years went by. Then, a few years ago, we were both unattached and started spending time together. Since then we've jumped in and out of this relationship like a couple of high school kids. Neither one of us wants a serious commitment, so we're mostly drifting. We have fun together and I think we love each other. But I still have trust issues, and he still has independence issues, and in many ways we drive each other crazy.

But here he was apologizing, so why stay mad? Making up is a lot

more fun than continuing a fight. And to be honest, I really wasn't
sure any more why we'd been fighting. So I accepted his suggestion.
"Tonight sounds good. I'm on my way into the grocery, so how about
I get some stuff and cook tonight? You bring the wine."

"Okay. Does 7:00 work for you? I have to finish up some reports
here before I come."

"Perfect. See you at seven."

In Whole Foods, I picked up fresh shrimp, garlic and lemon for
scampi, organic greens and other salad stuff, a crusty French loaf—and,
as an indulgence and peace offering, chocolate raspberry mousse torte.
I looked forward to what I hoped would be a romantic evening. And
at the same time, I wanted to pick his police-trained brain for some
technical information. If I approached him right, maybe I could get
some answers without pissing him off and ruining the evening.

Driving home, I turned over in my mind what I wanted to ask.
I still needed an answer to my question about how the police decide
whether someone who falls off a cliff to his death was pushed, jumped
or fell accidentally. Or at least some idea of what clues they look for.
And I wanted some information about what Dr. Ahmed might be into.
I thought drug scam, or maybe ripping off Medicare or Medicaid.
But I had no idea how to check out those theories. And there was the
threatening call on Adam's answering machine. Was there any way
to identify the caller from the voice recording?

I spent the rest of the day cleaning house, doing laundry and
watering flowers and bushes. By the time Pablo arrived, I felt a sense
of accomplishment and was ready for some fun. I had set the table
on the back patio, where it was cool in the early evening thanks to
tall trees and the shadow of the foothills. I put candles out for later
when the sun went down, and Norah Jones CDs on the stereo, loud
enough to hear on the patio from the kitchen speakers.

Pablo got there right at seven—which I took as a sign he wanted
to make up, since he's not exactly an on-time type of guy. We drank
some Chardonnay on the patio and talked about art. Pablo's artwork
is mainly contemporary abstract metal sculpture. During his years
doing the starving artist thing in his twenties, he began to realize

art wouldn't support him. When his younger brother got involved in a street gang selling drugs and ended up in jail, Pablo came home and applied to the police department. So now he's a full-time police detective and a part-time artist.

Lately he's focused on what he calls "found object" sculptures, making whimsical birds, dogs, cats, and such from old metal yard tools, bolts, springs, car parts and stuff. It's good work, and he sells a reasonable amount of it at local art fairs. But that's partly by keeping the prices low—plus spending the time to take his work to the shows and sit out there selling it. He doesn't get rich from his art, and it eats up most of his free time—but, like me, he finds the flow of immersing himself in creative work provides an essential balance in his life.

As we sat on the patio, the wine, the art talk, the sensuous ballads, and the lazy summer evening brought a peaceful mellowness. Just as Norah Jones began to sing "Don't Know Why," Pablo leaned over to refill my glass. Our eyes met in a soul-shaking gaze that blotted out any remnants of last week's argument. Without a word, we put down our glasses, stood up, and dashed to the bedroom, tossing clothes as we went. The sex was breathtaking, as it almost always is with him—that is, when we can get along long enough to actually have sex. Afterward, we lay comfortably in each other's arms until Pablo's stomach rumbled, reminding me we had skipped over dinner.

We worked companionably in the kitchen, saying little. He made the salad and sliced the bread, while I shelled the shrimp, sautéed it in olive oil and garlic, added lemon, salt, and a dash of hot pepper. We took the food out to the patio, lit the candles, and dug in—both ravenous by then. It was a sweet evening, at least up to that point.

I made some coffee and brought out the chocolate torte, which was as yummy as it looked. I decided the time was never going to be better for my questions, so I started in. "Pablo, I really need to ask you some police questions. It's important, and I don't know who else to ask."

"Okay. But let's keep it short. When we're having such a great evening together, I don't want to have to think about police work."

I leaned forward in my chair. "Remember I asked you how the

police decide whether someone who falls off a cliff and dies was pushed, jumped or fell accidentally? Well that's my first question."

Pablo sighed. "Well, first of all, the police have to call the county coroner's office to investigate any sudden or unattended deaths. It's the coroner's job to investigate the death, maybe do an autopsy, and eventually make a determination as to the cause of death, the manner of death, and the time of death. Police investigate the scene, talk to witnesses and stuff. If the coroner determines that the death isn't accidental, we do a criminal investigation."

"So, how would the coroner decide whether the death was accidental or not?"

Pablo started gathering the plates and coffee cups from the table. "The coroner could look for signs of a struggle at the top of the cliff the guy fell from. Or look to see if he left a backpack or maybe a note at the top that would point to suicide. Or maybe the autopsy would find drugs in his system that could have led to an accidental fall. Or maybe there were witnesses." He stood up, blew out the candles, and started in toward the kitchen with the dishes.

But I wasn't done yet. I'm a Scorpio. When I have a question, I keep probing until I find what I'm looking for. So I grabbed the candles and the tablecloth and napkins and followed him in, talking as I went. "Do they write this all up? Is it public information? Can I get their reports about someone who died?"

"You can call the Boulder County Coroner's office and get the autopsy report, but only the next-of-kin or the police or the District Attorney can get the part about the cause and manner of death." Pablo loaded the dishwasher as he spoke.

"Oh, he didn't die here. It was at the Grand Canyon," I said, handing him the frying pan and other cooking utensils.

He stopped the cleanup and turned to face me. "Okay, Cleo, this is my last answer. Some states have medical examiners, some have coroners, but the procedure is pretty much the same. So you'd have to find out who to contact there."

"Does your department have some kind of list?"

"I thought I said that was my last answer," Pablo said, reaching under the sink for the dishwasher soap. "Let's go turn on Saturday Night Live."

"Oh, come on, Pablo, I don't want to watch TV. I have a lot of other questions to ask you, and I need the answers tonight."

"Cleo, I'm done with questions for tonight," Pablo said, walking off into the living room. "You have a bad habit of asking too many questions." He flopped onto the couch and reached for the remote.

Pablo's not the only person who's told me I ask too many questions. But I find the comment annoying. I can see that people find questions unnerving, but I don't know why. Is it because they don't know the answers, or is it that they want to keep things to themselves? Or maybe it's that my asking questions puts me in control of what we talk about. Maybe they'd rather choose when and what to tell. In any case, I wasn't willing to accept his ruling. So—stupidly, I admit—I grabbed the remote out of his hand.

He jumped up, reaching toward me for the remote. "Cleo, what's going on? Can't we just relax and enjoy the evening?" He pulled the remote out of my hand and turned on the TV.

I walked over to the TV and hit the off switch. "Pablo, I'm trying to help someone whose husband died under suspicious circumstances. Can't you be a little compassionate?"

"Maybe you should make an appointment and come in to the office with your questions. This is my free time." Pablo sat back down on the couch and pointed the remote at the TV again.

"If you want to watch TV so much, maybe you should just go home and watch," I yelled, completely exasperated as I thought about my long list of unanswered questions.

"Fine. I will." Pablo got up and walked out the front door without so much as a goodbye.

I wandered into the bedroom and sat among the tangled sheets, recalling the earlier sweetness of the evening. How did things escalate so quickly between us? Could we ever get past these flare-ups? I didn't like the answers that came to mind, so I switched gears to think about Sharon's problems, where I didn't have to struggle with how much of it was my fault.

I ran through the various possibilities. Maybe Adam did fall accidentally. But if that was true, why was Tyler pushing me to get involved? Maybe Erik was right that Adam jumped. But again, how to explain Tyler's comments? Also, Adam didn't sound like the suicide type. And why wouldn't he leave a note?

So it looked like someone pushed Adam off the edge. Who wanted to get rid of him? There was a growing list of possible suspects, starting with Joel, maybe Dr. Ahmed—if Adam knew more than he had told Sharon about him. Maybe Natalie—she had tried to kill him once before. And there was the unknown caller who left the threatening phone message. And Erik had a big stake in the suicide theory. Why was he trying so hard to convince me?

"Yo, Cleo." I heard Tyler before I saw him in the dim bedroom light.

"Tyler! You scared me to death! And I'm mad at you! You've gotten me into a mess. Can you at least answer a few questions? Like what really happened to Adam?"

He was perched cross-legged on the stool next to my dressing table, looking right at me. "You're all knotted up, Cleo. Just surf."

"I don't surf. And in case you didn't notice, we don't exactly have an ocean in Colorado."

"Bummer. When you're out there, things make sense."

"Well, I'm not out there, and nothing makes sense right now. So could you please be more specific about what's going on?" I was exasperated.

"You have to ride the waves, not fight them. Let the waves support you," Tyler said as he vanished into thin air.

I figured he was somehow speaking metaphorically, although Tyler didn't seem that sophisticated. Maybe stuff like metaphors comes easier after you're dead, I thought. Then I realized I was actually sitting alone in my bedroom on a Saturday night wondering whether dead people use metaphors. It was clearly time to go to bed and hope for a better day tomorrow.

16

Sunday morning, I got up early to hike the Mount Sanitas trail before the day got hot. In this dry mountain climate, nights can be wonderfully cool even when days are 90 degrees. I needed the exercise, and I wanted to think about my relationship with Pablo. After all, I am a therapist, and I do know a fair bit about human behavior. I don't much like turning that magnifying glass on myself, but sometimes my own behavior strikes me as so inappropriate that I have no choice. This was one of those times.

First I asked myself, "What do I love about Pablo?" That was easy. I love that he's a very sweet guy who cares about family so much that he came home to live near his parents after his brother got into trouble, and that he's such a great uncle to his nieces and nephews. I love that he wants so much to make the world a better place that he went into police work to try to stop other kids from getting into trouble like his brother did. I love that he's an artist, and a good one, and that he still works on his art even though he's so busy. I love his enthusiasm for his art, especially when he gets a new idea. I love that he takes me seriously as an artist.

When he's not doing his bossy 'I'm a police officer, you're an idiot' thing, he can be sweet, sexy, and sensitive. And he's very attractive. Even though I don't always act like it, I do really care about him.

But we bicker a lot—and I don't want to end up like my parents. So I asked myself, "Why do I push Pablo so much? Why do I goad him into so many arguments? What do I want from him?" These

99

were the harder questions. I knew part of it was I wanted him not to be like my father who criticizes me like I'm the weakest link on a third-rate ball team. I wanted Pablo to accept what I say at face value, without cross questioning. But last night wasn't about acceptance, and I was actually the one asking the questions. My approach to getting information from him obviously sucked. I decided I should meditate more so I'd be more centered and less reactive, and work on remembering to back off and take a deep breath when I felt an angry retort bubbling up. Of course Pablo could be more accommodating too, but I was trying to focus on what I could do.

The trailhead on Mapleton is only a few blocks from my house, so while I thought about Pablo, I'd begun climbing the steep, rocky trail to the summit—along with a couple dozen other hikers, runners, and their dogs. You do trade solitude for a convenient location with this hike, but I liked sharing the path. Being part of a group of energetic hikers perked me up. Two young women walking behind me were discussing home remedies. One said, "I make a mix of rose hips and other stuff and mix it with a little brandy. It makes me feel much better." I wondered how much brandy, and at what time of day she usually imbibed, but I had gotten too far ahead of them to hear any more details.

I was pleased to see many responsible pet "guardians." (This word has legally replaced the word pet "owner" in Boulder.) They dutifully scooped up their wards' poop with green plastic bags and brightly colored newspaper covers. Dog poop is a serious issue on the trails here, especially this trail. A local plant ecologist has made it his personal crusade to make sure the police enforce the law requiring poop pickup, even going to the extreme of videotaping offenders, handing the tapes to police and demanding they press charges. Dog guardians nicknamed him the "pooper snooper," and brought harassment charges against him. But the snooper was acquitted after he showed the jury the extent of the problem by displaying a "crap map" he created. He had walked the trail with his GPS device, counted piles of droppings, plugged the GPS into his computer, and generated a map that marked each pile with a green X. Some think he's slightly over the top, but I can sort of understand his obsession and I certainly appreciate poop-free trails.

The steep ascent and the view of the Continental Divide from the top relaxed me. On my way back down the trail, optimism kicked in. I decided I'd call Pablo and apologize for insisting he talk about police work after he'd clearly said he didn't want to. I'd do what I should have done last night and ask him to name a time when he'd be willing to answer my questions. I resolved to try to find ways to build on the good parts of our relationship, and not to bristle so quickly when he pushed my buttons. I was so focused on playing our imaginary conversation in my mind, that I was almost at my house before I noticed someone lounging on my porch reading a newspaper. It turned out to be Erik, reading my Sunday paper.

"Hey," I called out. "This is a surprise," thinking he had an odd way of showing up without notice, which was a little creepy. Why were so many odd things happening lately? Had I somehow become a magnet for weirdness?

Erik looked up from the paper with a big grin. "I woke up yearning to sit out in the sun with coffee, a muffin, and a beautiful woman. So of course I thought of you. Let's walk down to Spruce Confections."

It sounded like he wanted to have me for breakfast. I was just about to tell him to bug off, when he looked wistfully at me and said, "Sunday mornings are hard. I get so lonely without Jenny. Please indulge me."

So I agreed to go, if he was willing to wait while I took a shower. He said he'd keep on reading the paper while I showered, which I assumed meant he'd be outside on the porch. But when I came out of the bedroom, he was in my living room looking around. "Why haven't you planted the seeds?" he asked, pointing at the starter kit he had left for me the previous week.

"Um…I've been busy. And to be perfectly honest, I really don't have time for another project right now."

"Hey—you're hurting my feelings! This isn't just another project. It's a gift from me to you, and it will have a big payoff."

A gift? When he brought the kit, I thought he'd said he would charge me $250. "You're giving it to me? Why?" I asked.

"Because I want you to have it. Plus, you're going to love growing these plants. Everyone does," he said with a winning smile. His eyes met mine in a guileless gaze. "Let's go grab some breakfast, and I'll help you plant the seeds when we get back."

He looked so cute and cuddly, I felt a kind of melty warmth moving through me, loosening my defenses. Certainly Erik had his problems, but I thought maybe I could help him. Still, I was ready to leave before the situation got any more intimate. "Okay, let's get that coffee, and we'll take care of the seeds later," I said shooing him out the front door.

We dawdled along the Pearl Street sidewalk toward Spruce Confections, enjoying the sun, its intensity cut by shade trees and a morning breeze. It was a typical Boulder summer Sunday morning. Runners wearing earphones attached to iPods passed us without looking up. Bicyclers, wearing those tight, stretchy biker shorts, with the multi-colored microfiber jerseys and the flat lattice-type helmets that look like they're ready for outer space, sped by on their way up the canyon. A thirtyish guy wearing faded baggy shorts and flip-flops walked by talking intently on a cell phone about a three-million-dollar deal.

I was feeling relaxed and comfortable until Erik blurted out, "So, I hear Sharon tried to contact Adam, but got her mother. And, she was so excited about talking to her mother that she couldn't keep herself from telling her dad. I guess Waycroft was furious."

"She told her father that? Oh my God! No! What was she thinking?" It was like I'd been kicked in the gut.

"Not thinking, I guess. I'm sure glad I missed him. I went over last night to pick up Sharon and Nathan for pizza and a movie, and he had just left. Sharon was pretty upset. She said her dad had been yelling at her big time in front of Nathan. You know, Cleo, I warned you not to get Sharon into this contact voodoo, but you went ahead anyway, and now you've created major problems for her with her dad."

We were standing outside the bakery by then. In an unusual moment of clarity, I decided to collect my thoughts before I answered. I didn't want to be defending myself or Sharon to Erik, when this whole thing was actually none of his business. So I went on in to stand in the order line without answering him.

Spruce Confections is part of a new mixed-use area of shops and condos on West Pearl. It's a real bakery with a large area behind the counter filled with huge stainless mixing machines, bread slicers and ovens. The front space has a retro diner-like feel, with formica tables, a glass case filled with muffins, scones and coffee cakes, and a counter to order coffee drinks, espresso, tea, chai, and such. A not-so-retro sign above assures customers each espresso drink is made individually from locally roasted, certified organic coffee beans. But the big attraction, and what makes it a Sunday morning favorite, is the spacious flagstone patio outside in front and to the east.

We stood quietly in line, ordered, and took our lattes and coffee cake out to one of the contemporary gray metal tables littered with sections of the Sunday paper. But we didn't read. Erik wasn't going to let me off the hook that easily. He gave me an uneasy look and started in again. "Here's the thing, Cleo. Now that Nathan knows about this contact thing, he wants to reach Adam, too. I think that's an even worse idea than Sharon doing it."

"Don't worry. I've never worked with any children in this project, and I'm not planning to start," I assured him. "Personally, I wouldn't have told Nathan about it, but I guess once Sharon told her dad, she couldn't control that." I briefly flashed on my mother reminding me not to talk with my mouth full, as I washed down a slightly-chewed chunk of blueberry coffee cake.

"Yeah, Waycroft's not much for secrets. Basically a loose cannon when it comes to information. I guess he also told Nathan that his real father is in town and wants to meet him." Looking at his plate, Erik crumbled his coffee cake and said, "Nathan kept bugging Sharon about it last night, until she admitted that Joel is in town, but she didn't think it would be good for Nathan to meet him."

"How did Nathan take that?"

"Not well. But I supported Sharon. After all the guy left before Nathan was born and has never tried to see him all these years."

"True. But most kids want to at least meet their birth parents."

"Well, Nathan may get to meet Joel. He was so insistent that Sharon said she'd think about it some more."

Glancing around, I noticed a woman over at the funky West End Gardener shop setting out their daily display of flowering plants, pots, lawn chairs and decorations. Among them were some of Pablo's metal yard ornament sculptures—rusty birds and cats crafted from yard tools. I felt proud seeing his work displayed so prominently in Boulder's trendy west end. That strengthened my resolve to call him to try to make up from last night. We were done eating by then, so I gathered my dishes and told Erik I needed to get back. He looked a little disappointed, but followed along without objection.

We didn't say much walking back. I was thinking about how to get him to leave so I could call Pablo. But as soon as we got back to my house, Erik said, "Okay Cleo, I'm going to set up this growing system and plant the seeds for you. You're going to love this. I promise. I can see you're a gardener by looking at your well-tended rose bushes and flower beds out front."

I'm a sucker for compliments about my garden, so I wavered. "Can you do it really quickly? I know you're trying to help, but I have a lot to do today, and I need to get started on it."

"That's fine. Go ahead with whatever you need to do. I'll just put this together. Do you have a container I can use for some water?"

I decided it would be quicker to help him and get him out of there than to leave him to his own devices, so I moved the whole operation out to the kitchen, where we could work next to the sink. Unfortunately, just as we were finishing the planting, Pablo stopped by. He walked right in, not realizing anyone was there with me because Erik had parked over in the Settler's Park lot. "Am I interrupting something?" he asked, looking like he'd like to interrupt Erik right out the door.

"Oh, hi, Pablo. This is Erik. He's helping me plant some seeds he gave me. Erik, this is my friend Pablo." Looking back on it, I realize I should have said boyfriend, but instead I heard myself saying friend. Not a good start.

"Why are you planting seeds inside? It's summer," Pablo said.

"These seeds are an investment for Cleo. I gave her the plants to grow, so she can sell the roots later and make $5,000," Erik said in a confident infomercial tone.

"Are you so hard up you need to get involved in work-from-home schemes, Cleo?" Pablo challenged.

Somehow his challenge made the project more interesting. I knew I was being oppositional, but my irritation at his bossy tone overcame my new resolutions not to be so reactive. I slipped back into my old habits, took his bait and pushed back. "Pablo, it's no big deal. Just something to try. Don't get all bent out of shape."

"Whatever, Cleo." His tone was icy cold. Then he turned to Erik. "So who's going to buy these plants at that inflated price?"

"My company buys them back. It's a win-win proposition for everyone," Erik said, handing Pablo a Natural Herbal Remedies Company business card, oblivious to Pablo's frosty tone. "Maybe you'd be interested. It's a small investment for a big payoff."

I knew Erik had gone too far when he tried to recruit Pablo. And sure enough, Pablo shut him down without any further discussion.

"No thanks. I'm not interested in any get-rich-quick schemes. I already have two jobs—and I need to get back to one of them right now." Pablo was on his way out the door as he spoke.

"Pablo, you're over-reacting here. Why don't you sit down for a few minutes until we finish planting the seeds, and then we can talk?" I said, thinking I could have handled this better. Reacting first and thinking later was becoming a pattern in our relationship.

"No, I have to go," Pablo didn't turn back. I felt a jolt of disappointment, but trying to get him to stay seemed hopeless.

"Hey, give me a call if you change your mind about the seeds," Erik yelled after him.

My resolve to improve my relationship with Pablo had disappeared again in the heat of the moment, and I was ready to get rid of Erik as well. So as soon as we finished with the seeds, I reminded him I had work to do, and he needed to leave.

After he left, I noticed a message on my cell phone, which I had forgotten to turn on earlier. It was Elisa. "Hey, Cleo. Honey, you have to come to dinner tonight so we can talk. It's important. How about 6:30? I'll be out all day, so leave a message."

More of a summons than an invitation, but dinner at Elisa's is always tasty, her deck is pleasant on a summer evening, and we enjoy each other's company. I decided to accept.

17

When I got to Elisa's, she was alone on the deck, getting out the grill. "Jack's out of town, so it'll be just us girls—you, me and Maria."

"Has Maria recovered from her traumatic babysitting gig at Sharon's last weekend?" I asked, wondering how much Elisa's daughter had told her about what happened.

"Not to worry, she's fine. She's inside making the salad. Hey, grab some wine, we need to talk. And I'm going to grill some fish." Knowing Elisa, she had an agenda, and it wasn't about fish. Sure enough, about two seconds after I sat down on the deck with a glass of Sauvignon Blanc, she started questioning me about Sharon's progress. "Sharon won't tell me much, but I know she reached her mother. Isn't that strange when her mother's been dead for more than 30 years?" Elisa wheeled the grill out away from the wall, and started the fire.

Elisa knew full well I couldn't tell her about a session with a client. But I played it straight. "Come on, you know I can't talk about what happened with Sharon. As far as how long someone's been dead, I have no idea whether it makes any difference in being able to contact them. But if you think about it, why would the afterlife use our time system anyway? Last month, last year or last century may be all the same to them."

Elisa looked thoughtful. "But wouldn't you think it would be easier to reach someone who had just died, especially when that was the person you were trying to contact? Wait, don't answer that until I bring out some stuff from the kitchen." As she dashed off, I admired the intricate pattern of the gauzy, cobalt blue silk shirt she wore over her stretchy black tank top and crop pants. My beige linen camp shirt and drawstring pants weren't even close on the elegance scale. I told myself that at only 5'4" it's harder for me to look elegant than it is for her at 5"8". But in truth I think I just find it easier to go for the simple natural look.

Just as I got up to go inside to see if I could help, Maria's black puppy scampered out the open kitchen door, yapping and wagging his tail as if he'd been waiting all day to see me. "Gustav, stop! No!" Maria scurried out after him, but he was all over me before she even got close. He was so adorable, I didn't even mind the paw marks on my pants. Big advantage of the not-so-chic outfit.

"Sorry, Cleo. I think he likes you though," Maria picked him up. "Anyway, what do you think about Dr. Waycroft?"

"What do you mean? What about him?" I asked.

"Oh…Didn't Mom tell you? He got so mad, I thought he was going to kill Sharon. Yelling at her, calling her stupid, naïve, an ir-responsible mother—telling her she was going to regret not listening to him. And he said it all in front of Nathan." Gustov jumped out of Maria's arms and ran across the deck barking fiercely at a squirrel scampering up a tree trunk. Maria dashed after him, almost collid-ing with Elisa as she came out of the kitchen carrying a tray loaded with salad and raw fish.

I jumped up to reach for falling dishes, but Elisa managed to keep her balance. "What's Waycroft so upset about?" I asked. "Have you talked to Sharon?"

"I talked to her this morning. The argument just happened yes-terday. But Maria was there for most of it, so she can tell you about it." Elisa smeared olive oil and lemon on some salmon fillets before laying them on the hot grill.

Maria put Gustov back in the house and came over to tell me the story. "Okay, I was bringing Nathan back from soccer camp," she said, "and I guess Dr. Waycroft had stopped by at Sharon's. Nathan and I could hear him yelling at Sharon that she was behaving like an idiot, and he wasn't going to put up with it. And then he went on about how she's keeping Nathan from meeting his real father, and spending all her time trying to talk to a dead man. I tried to get Nathan back in the car and go for ice cream or something until they cooled down, but Nathan just ran right in."

"Poor Nathan," I said, wishing I could undo this for him.

"It got worse," Maria paced around the deck with her head down, a behavior I recognized from those long-ago years when I'd been her nanny. It was usually a sign she was seriously upset. She paced faster as she continued her account. "When I followed Nathan in, I saw Dr. Waycroft's face was beet red and his eyes were all squinty. He looked like he could eat us alive. He said, 'Nathan, your mother has lost her good sense—if she ever had any. I'm going to take you to my house tonight. Get your stuff and let's go.'"

"What did Nathan do?" I asked.

Maria stopped right in front of me and gave me a quizzical look. "This is the weirdest part," she said. "Nathan looked at his mom and then he looked at Dr. Waycroft and said, 'Can I have 200 extra points if I go?' And then Sharon blew up. She started yelling, 'Dad, don't tell me you have him on a point system!' Then she said, 'I had to follow your system of getting rewarded with points when I was growing up, but no way is my son going to live that way.'"

At that point in the story Maria stopped to catch her breath and sat in a chair next to me to continue. "So," she went on, "Dr Waycroft said, 'Nathan, that was supposed to be our secret.' And Nathan started crying. Then Sharon grabbed Nathan, and shouted at Dr. Waycroft to leave or she'd call the police. He shouted back that the police might be on his side. And then he said, 'Joel has legal rights, you know. He could go to court and get visitation rights. And I'll be glad to help him.' And then he left. I was going to stay around to try to help Nathan calm down, but that strange friend of theirs, Erik, showed up, so I left."

I was stunned and not at all pleased that Sharon's conflict with her dad had escalated to this level, but client confidentiality issues kept me from commenting. Instead, I picked up on Maria's comment about Erik. "Why do you think Erik is strange?" I asked,

"He's all about those plants, and weird energy drinks," Maria said wrinkling her nose like she smelled something rotten. "And he freaks out anytime Nathan wants to go out to Adam's office. He's just strange."

"Enough gossip you guys," Elisa yelled at us from the grill. "This salmon is perfect right now, so get your plates over here and get some. Let's eat and relax and forget about that tyrant Donald Waycroft for a while. We ate, talked about Maria's music and my artwork, and made plans to go to a summer concert at Chautauqua the next week.

Then Maria left to meet some friends and I finally heard what was really on Elisa's mind. Waycroft had called her that morning, threatening dire consequences if she didn't keep me away from Sharon. "He said he will personally make sure the tenure committee picks my application apart with a fine-tooth comb. And he's good friends with the committee chair, so I expect it's not an empty threat." Elisa poured us each another glass of wine. "But you heard it here first, baby. Donald doesn't know who he's up against. He may think he's hot stuff, but he'll pay a price if he messes with me. I guarantee it."

I knew Elisa was determined to get tenure. She had worked hard to build her professional reputation. Elisa married young, had Maria a few months later, got whatever jobs she could with her undergraduate degree in psych—mostly working in group homes. But she knew it wasn't what she wanted in the long run. So, when she was 29 and Jack had made a fortune in commercial real estate in Boulder, she went back to school and got her Ph.D. in psychology, specializing in research on memory. She got hired to work on some research grants and wrote a successful grant of her own. Her research kind of took off and she was hired into a tenure-track position in the Psychology Department of the University. Now she's 40, and as she says her career is truly cruising. She's up for tenure this fall, and I was certain she would fight tooth and nail to keep Waycroft from derailing her progress.

"Do you have a plan to stop him?" I asked.

"Honey, I'll find a way to fix his wagon." Elisa smirked at the prospect. Then her face turned serious and she leaned forward and put her hand on my arm. "But it's actually not me I'm worried about," she said. "It's you. Donald said he would expose you as a fraud and make sure your therapy practice is ruined. I know we can fight this, but you're more vulnerable because your Contact Project is—I think we can agree—so far outside the mainstream."

I should have paid more attention to her warning. But somehow I couldn't see Donald Waycroft as a serious threat to my career. So I brushed her off with a flip reply. "Thanks for the heads-up. But Waycroft reminds me of my dad—more bark than bite. You know I've been arguing with Dad all my life. No matter what I do, he tells me why I shouldn't do it or how I could do it a better way. Don't worry about me. I can handle Waycroft's attacks."

Suddenly, the wind picked up and we noticed some flat dark clouds signaling an evening thunderstorm, so we scurried around collecting the dishes and leftover food. We got everything inside just as the storm rumbled in, bringing streaks of lightening and fat raindrops splatting on the deck. I took this as a natural transition and turned the conversation to the topic at the top of my mind as we cleaned up the kitchen.

"I have another problem that I need your help with," I said, as Elisa rinsed the dishes before loading them into the dishwasher. "Gramma's doctor—he's the medical director at Shady Terrace—is way too quick to drug the residents. And I also think he may be involved in something illegal. But I don't know how to find out more or do anything to stop him."

Elisa has spent a lot of time in nursing homes doing her research on memory, so she knows how they operate. I told her what I had overheard from Dr. Ahmed's office, why I wasn't happy about him being in charge of Gramma's care, and what Sharon had told me about all the drugs he prescribes at his pain clinic.

"You can bet it's all about drugs," Elisa said, tossing me a wet sponge to wipe the countertops. "Drug diversion is huge in nursing homes. They have staff stealing prescription narcotics for their own use or to sell on the street. It's tough to catch them at it, but you could call the state health department or the police, tell them what you heard and request an investigation."

"Maybe I'll start with the health department. I know I don't have enough facts for the police to do anything," I said, thinking I didn't want to give Pablo any more grounds for thinking I was flaky. "You know, Sharon told me that Adam did some website development work for Ahmed's clinic, and he had some suspicions that it wasn't all on the up and up. Now I'm wondering whether Ahmed was somehow involved in Adam's death, but Sharon doesn't know what Adam knew or whether he said anything to Ahmed."

Neither of us had any good ideas as to how to investigate that. But on the way home, it occurred to me I might find some information about Ahmed by using an internet search engine.

Maybe his past held some secrets. What had he been doing wherever he worked before he came here?

18

On Monday morning I Googled Dr. Ahmed to see what I could get. Over 12 million hits. When I put Dr. Ahmed in quotes, I still got over 400,000. Lots of Dr. Ahmeds out there on faculties around the world, as well as in government, institutes, and such. Most of what I got were people whose first name was Ahmed. Clearly I needed to know his first name, which turned out to be Fahim according to the Boulder yellow pages. I got 58,000+ hits for Fahim Ahmed, MD, but only two when I put it in quotes—one of which was a listing for his clinic with a link to his website. I clicked on that link and found myself at the We Feel Your Pain clinic site.

Lots of information about the types of pain they treat and how important it is to get your pain treated so you can enjoy life again, but not much about Ahmed himself. Nothing about where he'd practiced before, except that he completed anesthesiology training in Tampa, FL and did a one-year fellowship in Pain Management. No dates for any of that.

I figured Fahim might actually be his middle name or even a pseudonym, so it could be worth following some of the 58,000 hits I got when I searched for Fahim Ahmed or some of the 400,000 I got for Dr. Ahmed. But my first client was due in 20 minutes so I'd have to put that off until later.

I did make a quick call to the state health department to explore making a complaint. They explained the procedure, but said I needed specifics for them to initiate an investigation. I didn't know how to get specifics, but I thought maybe Sharon or Erik would have some ideas. I had a full morning of clients, so I went over to Shady Terrace when I had a break in the early afternoon.

I found Gramma painting in the activity room. A very dark picture of people and pills. "Hi Gramma, are you feeling better?" I asked.

"Pills, pills, pills," she muttered, keeping her eyes on her painting.

"Are the pills making you feel better?"

She looked up sharply. "I need to paint now. Come back later." At least she wasn't groggy—maybe she was adjusting to the meds.

I went over to Sharon's office and found Erik there with her. I was struck by what a fit looking pair they were. Not that trim athletic people are unusual in Boulder where fitness is our creed. But together they exuded energy like runners ready for a race.

They were talking about Joel. Sharon had decided to let Nathan meet him, as long as Waycroft wasn't part of the meeting. Erik thought it was a bad idea.

"Cleo, don't you think it would be confusing for Nathan to meet this guy—especially when he's still grieving over Adam?" Erik sounded truly concerned. "Doesn't he need time to get used to losing the man he thought of as his father before he replaces him with his birth father?"

Sharon gave me a pleading look. "The thing is, Nathan is crazy to meet Joel. It's all he can talk about. Shouldn't that count for something? He says he has a right to meet his father."

I didn't want to take sides. I stared at the floor for a minute, then looked at Sharon. "It's hard to say what effect meeting Joel will have on Nathan right now," I said. "But if they are going to meet, I'd suggest you be with them, Sharon, so you know what happens and can be supportive to Nathan afterwards."

"Maybe I'll invite Joel over to the house," Sharon said. "Then we can…."

"Neither one of you is thinking straight," Erik interrupted impatiently. "This guy is manipulating you, and you can't see it at all."

I decided to change the subject, and get to the issue I came there to discuss. I brought up Dr. Ahmed, what I had overheard on Saturday, what Elisa had said about drug diversion, what I hadn't found on the web, and what the state health department had said they needed to process a complaint.

"I don't know much about Ahmed's background," Sharon said, "I think he's originally from Pakistan, but I don't know where he got his medical degree or where he practiced before this. But I agree that he gives out too many drugs, especially to staff." She turned to Erik, "Didn't he give Jenny some Xanax and other stuff, even though he wasn't actually her doctor?"

"Look, I told you both he's a jerk," Erik sounded annoyed. "But he's a smart one. Doesn't show his hand. The best thing is to forget about him until he hangs himself." With that, Erik got up and walked out.

Sharon looked uncomfortable. "Erik never wants to talk about Jenny," she said. "It's strange. I talk about Adam all the time."

"I know what you mean," I said carefully, not wanting to contradict her, but at the same time not wanting to judge Erik. "It's hard to help someone when they shut down. But people grieve differently. Men are less likely than women to share their feelings."

"There may be more to it. I don't know," Sharon said tentatively. A couple of times Jenny told me about problems she and Erik were having in their marriage. She said he lied to her, criticized her, and blamed her for everything that went wrong. Then she said if she raised her voice or told him she was angry at him for something, he would tell her she was going crazy."

I hadn't seen that side of Erik, but, as always, I was curious. "So what do you think? You've been spending a lot of time with Erik."

"I've never seen that side of him. He's always been helpful and considerate with us. And Jenny also told me she was depressed a lot and sometimes had panic attacks, so I guess I figured her picture of their relationship was distorted."

Someone knocked on Sharon's door. It was a family member there for a meeting, so I left and went back over to the Alzheimer's unit. After I punched in the code that opens the door, I discovered one of the confused residents, Maxwell Kohn, standing right inside it, trying to get out. He looked disheveled, as if he were wearing yesterday's clothes, and his thin gray hair was standing on end. "Let me out. I need to get out," he implored. I managed to squeeze in past him and shut the door before he escaped.

An aide came along to entice Mr. Kohn over to an exercise group meeting in the Fireside Lounge. Noticing me, she said, "Oh, Cleo, Martha has been painting all afternoon. Have you looked at what she's done?"

I checked the activity room, and found Gramma still painting. The dark one—depicting a forlorn woman sitting in a sea of pills—was finished, lying on a table to dry. The one she was working on showed three lumpy old people, each clutching an upside-down pill bottle with white tablets raining down to the ground around them. The eyes were wide multi-colored spinning wheels.

"Interesting, Gramma," I said. "I like the eyes."

"I see everything," she said.

Who knows what she sees, I thought. I wondered if I could take some message from the paintings. I'd been to a workshop the Alzheimer's Association put on promoting art as therapy for dementia patients. They said that art gives Alzheimer artists an additional way of processing feelings when words fail them because of the disease. So even though she was very confused most of the time, I thought she might be trying to give us a signal. After all, medications did seem to be an issue at Shady Terrace.

Just then Tanya came in. "Nice paintings, Martha," she said.

"Do you think she's trying to tell us something?" I asked.

"I doubt it," Tanya said. "She's not that cognitive any more."

"But all those pills must mean something," I protested. "Do you think it's possible that Dr. Ahmed is overmedicating the residents, and they know it?"

"Cleo, you have a bad habit of looking for problems. You're reading too much into Martha's pictures—probably because it's hard for you to accept her limitations."

Thanks for the analysis, I thought, but managed not to say it out loud. It was a good time to leave before I said something I would regret, so I said good-bye to Gramma, who barely looked up when I left.

Back at my office, I finished with a couple of clients, and went to my computer to continue my Google search on Dr. Ahmed. But nothing I found fit him. I stared off into space, trying to think of another approach. All at once I noticed Tyler perched on a table in the corner.

"Tyler!" I almost jumped up, but remembered he might disappear if I made any sudden moves. "What's going on with this Dr. Ahmed? Is he a crook or what?"

"Take it easy, Cleo. When the surf's lousy, chill."

"So are you saying this web search is a waste of time?"

"You can't always stand up the first day."

"Tyler, that means nothing to me. Can't you say something that makes sense?"

"Don't choke, Cleo. You need to watch out for sharks."

"Do you mean Dr. Ahmed is a shark? Or Erik? Or someone else?"

But Tyler faded away without answering. Arggh! He'd given me a warning, but it was as meaningless as one of those Homeland Security orange alerts, or instructions to report any suspicious activity at the airport.

I knew I should be looking in to something. But, what?

19

Wednesday morning, I got a big surprise by registered mail. The Colorado Mental Health Section of the Department of Regulatory Agencies sent me a notice of a complaint filed against me, to which I had 20 days to respond in writing. This is the agency that licenses me as a psychologist, so I took it very seriously. The notice included a copy of the complaint, which had been filed by Dr. Donald Waycroft, alleging I'd engaged in fraudulent and unsafe practice that placed my clients' safety and welfare in danger. He also charged that I was mentally ill, and delusional and should submit to a mental examination to determine whether I was fit to practice as a psychologist. I felt sick and furious at the same time.

I'd been way off on my assessment of the trouble Waycroft could create for me. I wanted to kick him in the butt or wring his beefy neck, but settled on a more achievable approach—giving him a piece of my mind in person. I called the university Psych Department, got Waycroft's office hours, and headed up there for a chat.

Despite the drought, the university grounds were green and fresh, thanks to water from the campus lake that irrigates the extensive lawn areas. But I was too steamed to enjoy walking through campus the way I usually do. My stomach was in knots, and part of me wanted nothing more than to lie on the grass by the lake, watch the ducks paddle, and forget all about Waycroft, Sharon, my project—all of it. But the stronger part of me said there was no way I would let Waycroft get away with calling me mentally ill and delusional. I had worked damn hard to get where I was professionally, and I'd match my training and ethics against his before any professional tribunal.

Waycroft's office was in a sandstone and red-tile-roofed building that looked like an Italian villa from the outside, but fit any definition of an old university building on the inside. The halls were lined with bulletin boards jam-packed with fliers advertising study-abroad opportunities, graduate programs in the social and behavioral sciences, and commercial courses to improve your GRE score. Faculty office doors, mostly closed, were bedecked with clever cartoons, class syllabi, and signs detailing the occupant's current office hours.

The halls were quiet except for the dull hum from the florescent lights above and an occasional comment floating out through the open door of the computer lab. Waycroft's door was mostly closed, but through the crack I could see his broad back facing me as he typed away on his computer.

Propelled by my fury, I didn't bother to knock—just barged right in, anger and righteousness front and center. "I thought you were supposed to be a scientist. You don't even know anything about my work, but yet you feel perfectly free to accuse me of fraudulent and unsafe practice? Where's your evidence?"

Waycroft slowly swiveled his desk chair around to face me. "I see I finally managed to get your attention," he smirked. "Look, I warned you to stay away from Sharon with your witchcraft or ghost-finding scams. So now we'll see how your work holds up to scientific scrutiny."

He spoke calmly, which disarmed me. I'd expected the red-faced, roaring Waycroft. I sat gingerly on the edge of a hard wooden chair next to his cluttered desk. "Sharon's an adult. She can make her own decisions without your approval. I'm licensed to provide services. She chose to take advantage of those services." At first, I matched his calm tone, but couldn't maintain it as my anger rose up again like acid reflux. "You're not involved and it's none of your business. So where do you get off attacking me?"

"Cleo, you're demonstrating your lack of professionalism right now." Waycroft kept his cool—probably a skill he had developed over years of confrontations with surly students disputing grades they thought were lower than they deserved. "I'll tell you what. You could consider that notice a warning. If you back off now, don't give Sharon any more therapy or whatever you call it, quit pretending to hook her up with the dearly departed, I'll withdraw the complaint. You can't say that's not a fair offer." He gave me a self-satisfied look and leaned back in his chair.

Could he really think I'd agree to this? I couldn't even begin to see his perspective on this situation. "Wrong!" I shouted, abandoning any pretense of reasonable discussion. "I absolutely do not think that's a fair offer. You have no right to tell me who I can or can't see as a client. And going against your wishes does not constitute malpractice in this state or any other that I know of."

Waycroft straightened in his chair and gave me a steely look. "I'm offering you a chance to save yourself here, but you are bent on self-destruction. So be it. Your choice will have consequences. You will be exposed as a fake, you will lose the money from whoever is funding that Contact Project, and you will be out of business as a therapist. And your friend Elisa is likely to have some difficulty getting tenure in the Psychology Department here."

I felt tears rising to the surface, but I didn't want to give him the satisfaction of showing my distress. So I attacked again. "Taking this stand could seriously hurt your relationship with Sharon, you know. She's had about enough of being told what to do. And seeing her friends hurt could be the last straw."

"You want to talk about how Sharon and I get along?" Another smirk. "She knows she's on shaky ground with the way she's raising Nathan. It's all wrong—no rules, messy house, no consistent structure. Adam was even worse—encouraged her to be irresponsible and left her in debt. And her involvement in your nutty spiritualism thing clearly raises questions about her ability to take care of Nathan. Plus, she can't legally keep Nathan from seeing his real father. So she may face consequences of her own."

"As a behaviorist, you must know your actions will also have consequences. Threats and retribution can go both ways, so I'd suggest you watch your back." With that, I rose and walked out with as much dignity as I could muster.

20

I walked back across campus to my car in a fog. I couldn't abandon Sharon now, no matter what consequences Waycroft threatened. She needed help and as long as I saw some possibility I could help her, I'd be there. Grampa always used to say, "Trust yourself, Cleo. Never be afraid to stand up for what you believe." And—for a lot of reasons—I believe in Tyler and his messages. I've learned he comes for a reason, and it's important for me to follow his directions. It can be problematic to figure out what he's telling me, but I was pretty clear I was supposed to help Sharon.

I didn't think Sharon or Elisa would be willing to give up trying to find out what happened to Adam, either. But I did think we needed to talk about Waycroft's threats and decide how we wanted to respond. So I grabbed my cell phone out of my purse and gave them each a call to find a time to meet.

After a few messages back and forth, we agreed to meet for dinner at The Rio, a popular Mexican restaurant on the Pearl Street mall, famous for its deliciously strong margaritas. They offer only one type of margarita—no premium, no extra-premium, no very special gold like other places—but the one they make is hands down the best. The drinks are made from a secret recipe its owners reportedly stumbled upon in the nick of time just before they opened their first restaurant. I've never tasted a better margarita anywhere, and after my session with Waycroft, I could hardly wait to decompress with at least one that evening.

It was early enough that we got seated right away in a booth next to a mirrored wall in the main room. Elisa looked sleek in a black silk tank top, white pants and high-heeled sandals. Sharon and I were the casual contrast, both wearing shorts, tee shirts and flip-flops.

The Rio is informal, no tablecloths on the laminated black hand-painted tables, and the traditional tex-mex food made fresh every day makes it one of my favorite places. As soon as the server brought our drinks, chips and salsa, we dove in.

"Whew baby—that's a margarita!" Elisa licked her lips and sighed.

"Always the same, always the best," I agreed, relaxing into the casual party atmosphere. Revived, I recounted the gory details of my meeting with Waycroft.

"Maybe I could have handled it better, but he was so patronizing, I couldn't stay cool," I said. "Well, actually I could have stayed cool, but I didn't feel like having a civilized reasonable conversation with him after he had filed a complaint against me."

"He has that effect on people," Sharon said quickly. "In fact, that's one of his techniques. He shows you that he can stay rational, while you explode."

"He doesn't stay especially rational around you when he's not getting what he wants," I pointed out, gesturing with my salsa-covered chip, which left a trail of red dots across the table.

"I've had a lot of practice pushing his buttons," Sharon said. "Whether you want to or not, you learn about stimulus and response when you live with a behaviorist." She laughed and raised her hands in a what-can-you-do shrug. Then she looked a little melancholy as she said, "It's not that I want to irritate him. I do care about him and I appreciate a lot of what he's done for me. But he's so controlling that I have to push him to the wall before he'll give me any space at all."

The server brought our fajitas—sizzling strips of chargrilled chicken, with grilled onion, peppers, tomato, guacamole, sour cream, pico de gallo sauce, and handmade flour tortillas on the side—accompanied by Spanish rice and black beans. We took a break from the Waycroft bashing to fill our tortillas and enjoy.

"So we need a plan to force him to back off," Elisa said. "We should speak a language he appreciates—consequences. Somehow we have to find a way to convince him that the costs of his attacks on us will outweigh the benefits."

We spent the next hour or so brainstorming possibilities. With the help of another round of margaritas, we arrived at a plan. Elisa agreed to do some searching around in Waycroft's projects at the university to see if she could find an area where he was vulnerable. Sharon decided she would keep Nathan away from Waycroft, since that was the main way she could get to him. I would talk to a woman named Holly with whom Sharon said Waycroft had had an on-again, off-again relationship for years. I knew Holly because she was an artist who had studied with my grandmother years ago. Since then we had kept in touch through our involvement in the art community.

After dinner, we went back to Sharon's for ice cream. Escaping the cluttered living room, we sat around the kitchen table. Nathan was off at a Rockies game in Denver with Erik.

As she sliced strawberries over scoops of vanilla ice cream, Sharon told us a piece of good news. She had invited Joel over to meet Nathan, and he fit in like a missing puzzle piece. Sharon admitted she saw changes in Joel, and that it could be good for Nathan to have him in his life—at least on occasion, and in circumstances she agreed to.

"So I think I'll make a deal with Nathan that he can spend time with Joel if he agrees not to make a fuss about not seeing Dad for a while," Sharon said.

"Do you think Nathan will go for that?" Elisa asked. "Maria says he's tight with Donald."

"They have their issues," Sharon said. "Dad can be strict, which Nathan doesn't like. And now that I've put a stop to the point system Dad had Nathan hooked on, Nathan's not so willing to do things Dad's way. You know, you'd think Dad would learn that the downside of rewarding good behavior with points is that if you ever stop the points, you lose the behavior. I'm a living example."

Sharon stopped talking and looked down at her hands. She frowned, licked her lips and said hesitantly, "There is one thing that concerns me about Nathan seeing Joel. It's that Erik is against it. I'm worried that Erik feels threatened by Joel."

"Does it have to be a competition?" Elisa asked. "Can't you and Nathan have two men involved in your lives?"

Sharon looked up and turned toward Elisa. "The thing is, Erik's been sort of like part of our family since Jenny died," she said. " He doesn't have any family of his own, and Jenny's family blames him for not getting help fast enough to save her. So he's been lonely and depressed. He and Adam were close, so Erik started spending time with us, sharing holidays, stuff like that. Since Adam died he's been amazing and so close to Nathan. I don't want to hurt him."

I decided to move deeper. "Okay, don't answer this if you don't want to—but how do you feel about Erik?"

Sharon frowned. "Well, I…" She stopped. "Sometimes he…" She stopped again. "I guess I'm not sure." She got up, grabbed a glass from a cabinet and filled it with water from a five-gallon dispenser in the corner. "Would you like some water?"

After getting us set with glasses of spring water, Sharon came back to the table. "Okay, here's the best I can do. I don't know what we would have done without Erik. But he can be moody and odd. In a way, I feel guilty because I know he wants more, but I'm not there. It's too soon for me."

"You seem to be taking a lot of responsibility for him," Elisa said. "He's a grownup. Maybe you could…"

We heard the front door open, and Erik and Nathan laughing in the living room. "It was a great game. You should have been there." Erik passed out grins all around as he came into the kitchen.

"Look Mom, Erik got me a Rockies cap." Nathan bounced in sporting a black baseball cap with a gray CR embroidered on the front—or what would have been the front if he hadn't been wearing it backwards.

Sharon gave Nathan a big hug. "Hey, thanks Erik—and for taking him to the game. Nathan, you need to get to bed right away. It's late."

Sharon and Nathan headed off down the hall. Elisa followed them out of the room, saying she needed to get home. I decided to stay, so I could ask Erik about Adam's computer. It turned out he had the emergency boot disk in his truck, so we decided we'd try booting it up as soon as Nathan was settled.

Sharon got Nathan to bed, Erik brought in the disk and we were ready to work on the computer. But after fifteen minutes of looking, Sharon couldn't find the key to Adam's office. "Never mind, I can pick the lock," Erik said. "I've got some tools in my truck."

Sharon and I went out to the office door to watch. Erik stuck a sort of screwdriver-looking tool into the lock and turned it. Then he stuck in a long curvy metal thing and jiggled it around, listening as if for a secret code. And we were in.

We headed toward the desk. "Wait a minute! It's not here!" Sharon pointed at the empty space under Adam's desk where the computer tower had been. I looked around. Everything else in the office looked the same as it had last Friday.

"When was the last time you saw it?" Erik asked.

"I haven't been out here since Friday, when Cleo and I were here," Sharon said, "and neither has anyone else that I know of." She moved around the office opening drawers and cabinets. "It doesn't look like anything else was stolen, but to be honest, I don't exactly know what was where."

"Well, the key is missing and the lock is easy to pick, so who knows who may have been in here," I pointed out. "We need to call the police."

About an hour later, a couple of uniformed Boulder police officers came to the house and took the report, but gave us no reason to believe we'd see that computer again. In fact, they were a tad patronizing when we admitted we didn't know the computer's serial number. Do most people write those things down?

And of course there was no forced entry, so they weren't willing to call it burglary. Like maybe Sharon had somehow misplaced the computer or loaned it to a friend? We played the strange phone message on Adam's machine for them, and they took the tape, but didn't think it would help much.

What interested them most was Erik's lock-picking tools and skill. He maintained he had a habit of forgetting keys and was fed up with paying locksmiths, so he learned to pick locks. The police kept teasing him about whether he picked other locks, and was he a recreational hacker who picks locks for the fun of it, and otherwise why did he carry those tools around. He denied picking any locks except when he or a friend was locked out—and pushed the cops to admit it's not illegal to own the tools. Still, the more I thought about it, the more uncomfortable I felt with the idea that Erik could get into my house in five minutes flat.

21

The next day all hell broke loose. It started with a call from Elisa at 7:00 am. "Have you seen the paper?"

"I just got out of the shower."

"Go get it. I'll wait."

Cell phone in hand, I trotted off to the front porch and picked up the paper. "Okay, 'Six Jewish settlers killed, 30 injured, in West Bank attack.' Not good, but you had to call me about it?"

"Try the local section, page 1C."

The headline hit me right in the gut.

Local Grief Therapist Accused of Fraud

A Boulder psychologist and grief therapist was accused of malpractice Monday in a complaint filed by a faculty member from the university psychology department.

Professor Donald Waycroft, who holds the Lois Van Liere Distinguished Chair in Applied Behavior Analysis, alleged that therapist Cleopatra Sims manipulated his 35-year-old daughter into believing she experienced a false reunion with her deceased mother, according to a complaint filed with the Colorado Mental Health Section of the Department of Regulatory Agencies.

Dr. Waycroft, a prominent behavioral psychologist, has consulted on, researched and taught behavior analysis for over 40 years. The complaint he filed against Sims alleges she has engaged in fraudulent and unsafe practice that placed her clients' safety and welfare in danger. He also charges that Sims is delusional and questions whether she is fit to practice as a psychologist.

According to the complaint, Waycroft's daughter sought treatment from Sims for help in coping with grief over the death of her husband who perished in a fall at the Grand Canyon last April. Waycroft alleges that Sims enrolled his daughter in a program called the Contact Project, which purports to help people work through their grief by contacting dead persons.

Waycroft further alleges that Sims used hypnosis and other techniques to falsely convince his daughter she had contacted and had a conversation with her mother, who died over 30 years ago. "This experience has caused considerable distress for me, my daughter and my grandson," Waycroft said, "and I think we need to protect other people who might become victims of this phony spiritualism project."

Sims is a licensed psychologist in the state of Colorado. She could not be reached for comment Wednesday.

"That asshole! I'll call you back later," I screamed, closing my phone. Half way through re-reading the article I got a call from Bruce, the man who funds my project, saying we needed to meet. My anger made room for fear. Bruce didn't sound terribly upset, but he didn't sound happy either. Kind of unnerving. I worried he'd had some second thoughts about funding the Contact Project, but I resisted the impulse to ask him over the phone. We set a time to meet that afternoon.

As soon as I hung up, a couple of clients called to cancel. By then, I'd had about all the phone calls I could handle without screaming at someone. So I turned off my phone and walked downtown to my office. Somehow, I managed to meet with two clients there—one who hadn't seen the story and one who had—but I'll admit I had a hard time focusing on their concerns.

When I had some free time, I warily started playing my phone messages. To my relief, there were no more cancellations. First was Sharon, very apologetic, then other friends offering support. But two unexpected messages got most of my attention. One was from Joel, and the other from Narmada—the former Natalie, Adam's first wife. Each of them said they needed to talk to me urgently. I returned their calls and arranged times to meet each of them.

Joel offered to pick up some take-out from Wild Oats and bring it by for a quick picnic lunch. He showed up with a southwestern tofu salad made with fresh tomatoes and cilantro, feta cheese, focaccia bread, peaches, strawberries and organic lemonade. We took the feast over to a park next to Boulder Creek, where we found a picnic table near the busy playground area. I was in a fog, kind of staring blankly around at the people around me who were going on with their lives as if this was a perfectly normal day. I watched a woman holding a baby on her hip with one hand push a bigger child on a swing with her other hand, while she kept watch over a toddler marching back and forth with a huge ring of keys like a tiny jailer on his coffee break. The mother looked like she could use a grande caffe latte espresso.

Looking for anything to focus on but my own anxiety, I noticed Joel's face had its usual two-day dark beard growth. I wondered how he maintained it at that level. Did he only shave every few days and I happened to catch him on the off days—or did he have some trick of mowing it to a high level like grass in the heat of summer? But his smile was as engaging as ever, and I could see why Sharon might want to reconnect.

Then he pulled me back to reality, his dark eyes drawing me in as he spoke. "I wanted to tell you how sorry I am about Donald's complaint," he said, "and to encourage you not to give up trying to help Sharon contact Adam. It's important that she find out as much as she can about what happened to him. Otherwise she's never going to be able to move on with her life."

I rose to the challenge. "As far as I'm concerned, it's up to Sharon whether we continue. I'm not going to let Waycroft scare me off, but Sharon may have some limits on how much she wants to cross him."

"I know Donald. I worked with him for years, and I got fed up a lot. He can be bossy and rude, and he believes his methods of shaping behavior are supreme. But underneath he's basically good-hearted. I doubt if he'll really go through with the complaint. He's just trying to scare you off because he doesn't believe in your methods."

This made no sense to me. It was like Joel was talking about someone else. There was no way I could see Waycroft as good-hearted. I couldn't even come up with a response.

I drifted off again, watching a stocky middle-aged man dressed for the board room in dark blue dress pants, a long-sleeved blue shirt and a red tie. He helped a toddler in a pink hat climb up to the top of the slide. He coaxed her and carefully stood by the side of the slide as a safety cushion. She deliberated, then chose to back down the steps to the ground. Invigorated by her accomplishment, the toddler headed back up the steps. The man followed behind, squatting at the top of the slide, holding her, arms extended, slowly releasing her to slide down into the waiting arms of a woman wearing a straw hat. Independence triumphs over fear every day I thought to myself.

Joel drummed his fingers on the table and brought me back to the conversation. "Hey, Cleo. If you like, I could try talking to Donald in your behalf. Basically, Donald likes to get his own way and will fight for that, but he draws the line at hurting anyone,"

This finally snapped me out of my reverie. My anger at Waycroft came flooding back, but I kept it in check as I spoke slowly and resolutely. "You don't think he's trying to hurt me? In fact he's already hurt me with slander and loss of income. Joel, I appreciate your support, but Waycroft's gone over the line and I plan to see that he regrets it. No, don't talk to him for me. Thanks for the offer. I really do appreciate it. But I intend to fight this complaint through channels and I intend to win."

I helped Joel clean up the remains of our lunch and thanked him for the delicious food. He decided to stay at the park for a while, so I left him there and walked back to my office to meet Narmada. On the way I, wondered what she could have to say to me that was so urgent, and whether I could believe anything she did say, given what Sharon had told me about her. She showed up promptly at 2:00, bounding into my waiting room with outstretched arms that enveloped me in an I-know-what-you've-been-though hug. "Cleo, I'm here to support your work against the narrow-minded establishment." She stepped back far enough to gaze intently into my eyes.

No quick response came to mind, but I did take the opportunity to move toward my counseling room, motioning her to follow me. Once we were seated with several feet of space between us, I took a better look at her. Narmada looked to be about 35, medium height and built like a dancer, a combination of muscles and grace. A massive mop of brown curly hair hung below her shoulders and stuck out in every direction around her head. She wore a black tank top with a long slim black skirt splattered with pink roses. And she positively radiated energy.

"I know who that Waycroft guy and his daughter are, and I'm here to tell you they are both bad news, and you should stay away from them. But you probably already know that by now."

"The article only told part of the story," I said. "I think it's mostly a misunderstanding that I can clear up."

Narmada looked at me as though I were speaking a foreign language. Which, given her views, I suppose I was. "Don't be naïve, my dear. This is no misunderstanding. Those academic psychologists salivate at any opportunity to trash us."

I was pretty sure I didn't want to be part of the 'us' Narmada included me in, but I decided that to be fair I should hear more of her story. "So, what sort of practice do you have exactly?" I asked.

She handed me a business card. It read: Narmada—Intuitive Psychic, Massage & Healing, Aura Reader, Past Life Regression, Chakra Balancing, Soul Surgery. Hmm… soul surgery—could that help Waycroft?

"Wow, you must stay busy with all those services. How long have you been doing all this?"

"About ten years. When I was married to that cynical loser, Adam, I thought something was wrong with me. I had premonitions of things that were going to happen to people, but he told me I was crazy. So

I learned not to listen to myself, not to trust my intuitions. I wasn't in touch with my abilities. I didn't know I was psychic. I thought I was imagining things."

"So how did you get in touch with your abilities?"

"My inner self wisely knew I needed to get away from Adam. So I ended up unconsciously doing things that split us up. Then after I got off all the drugs they had me on, I went to India to get clear. I had to learn to listen, to find out who I was, to be open to my dreams, feelings, whatever came to me in a nonlinear way. I had some profound experiences. Like I discovered that the voices I sometimes hear inside my head talking to me are people who have left the physical realm."

Hmm…voices in her head talking to her. Is this how I sound to Pablo? I nodded a couple of times and said, "That does sound profound."

"For sure. And once I knew I had the gift of seeing between the worlds, I went to Sedona and set up a practice at the New Age Center. I've only been back in Boulder a couple of years. I came back because it was made known to me that I should be here. But it hasn't been easy with Adam going around telling people I'm a fake. Confidentially, once I learned to read auras, I could see that he was rotten to the core. I'm pretty sure he was a brutal slave owner in a past life. And he didn't do much to redeem himself in this one."

"So you were upset with Adam in the last couple of years?"

"You got that right! He spread lies about me all over town. Said I had no powers, was just after people's money—that I had used him for money. Sure, I had some negative patterns years ago, but I've moved though those. Some were blocks from past lives that I had to release. I tried to tell Adam about this, but he refused to listen. He made ruining my reputation a personal crusade. Life will be much better for me here with him gone, I can tell you that."

"You may be better off, but Sharon and Nathan miss Adam a lot."

"I can not imagine why Sharon wants to contact him now that he's crossed over, but I can tell you it's not going to work. He's not the type who would cooperate with someone trying to connect with him from this side. He wasn't in tune with himself, no self-awareness, no clue about how his mental attitudes were causing him emotional and physical stress. We know people's beliefs will cause them to create or attract the situations and events they experience. No wonder Adam fell into a big hole."

"So you think Adam caused his own death?"

"For sure. Not in the sense that he physically jumped. But spiritually he was so empty, the canyon just sucked him up."

I was too dumbfound to go on. "Interesting, Narmada. But I actually have an appointment out in Longmont in a bit, so I'm going to need to leave soon."

"Sure. I really came to offer support for your work, to stand up against Waycroft's attack. I'm active in the local psychic community, and we want you to know we'll be there for you. We'd love for you to participate in our Fall Equinox Fair in September. And some of us are planning to organize a rally protesting Waycroft's complaint.

I didn't think her rally would help my reputation much. After all, I was a licensed therapist—at least I was so long as Waycroft didn't get his way—and I try to maintain a respectable image, even though my methods may be a teeny bit unorthodox. So I tried to discourage her without being rude. "That's so thoughtful. I appreciate the support. But I'm hoping I can work through the regulatory board and get the complaint dropped. Maybe you could check back with me in a couple of weeks and see where it stands."

"The thing is, I'm pretty sure that organizing against this attack on you is what I'm meant to do here in Boulder. It may be hard for you to accept the love we're offering, but you need to take it in. If you can't swallow the powerful love that's out there for you and your work, you'll choke."

I could feel myself choking already and I was unquestionably in touch with a powerful need to get Narmada out of my office. "Look, I really have to go," I said, standing and moving toward the door.

"No worries." Narmada jumped up, hugged me, and headed toward the door. "Just do what you have to do and know we're there for you." And she was gone.

I had to rush out to my appointment with Bruce, the donor who funds my Contact Project. I felt nervous about the meeting. Plus, thanks to Narmada, I was a little late. As I sped along the highway between Boulder and Longmont to Bruce's office in a Longmont business park, I noticed a truck that looked a lot like Erik's very close behind me. Even when I slowed down, the truck stayed in back of me. I didn't want him or anyone following me to Bruce's office, so I turned off at Niwot.

Downtown Niwot is a tiny unincorporated village dating back to 1875. Today it's mostly an old-fashioned main street lined with antique stores and art galleries, which has been declared a national historic district. The truck turned off behind me, so I stopped in front of Niwot Antiques on Second Avenue, thinking if someone were following me, it would be hard for them to hide in such a small town. The truck sped on by and turned the corner before I could make out the driver or identify the truck. I waited about ten minutes to see if it would reappear. When it didn't, I went back to the highway and continued on to Longmont.

By then I was definitely late. It's easy to get confused in the winding streets of the office parks out there, which added to my anxiety. After a couple of wrong turns, I was about to get out my cell phone and call Bruce, when I finally spotted the place. I wasn't as cool and composed as I would have liked when I rushed in. I also felt I had somehow let him down, and was worried he would lose trust in me.

When I got to his office, I found Bruce working on one of the four computers in the room. The other three machines plugged away on their own, perhaps testing some high-level formulas. Bruce didn't smile when he saw me, but I didn't take that to mean anything, because he's normally reserved.

As usual, he got straight to the point. His mind works so fast you feel like you're on speed just talking to him. He wanted to know all the facts, but was several steps ahead of me all the way along. Like many techies, Bruce is brilliant, but a bit lacking in the social skills department. He's not much for listening—just slaps the facts into a pattern he can scan, and proposes solutions.

"Okay Cleo, you need to respond through the appropriate channels and process, and see if the complaint will go away."

"I agree. That's exactly what I'm planning to do."

"We need to put a stop to this newspaper hype. Don't give them any comments. In fact, don't talk to them at all."

"That's fine with me."

"Can you get Waycroft's daughter to stay away from the press too? And tell her to keep her Contact Project experiences to herself. We don't want to attract more publicity ."

"I'll talk to her. But I can't make her keep quiet. It's her experience, after all. So it's her choice."

"If she doesn't understand the importance of not sensationalizing this project, maybe she's not right for it."

Whoa—that was unexpected! But I didn't just shoot back. I took a few moments to think about how to respond. I was torn between my loyalty to Sharon and my desire to live up to Bruce's expectations. As my client, Sharon deserved and was entitled to my support. As my benefactor, Bruce could certainly expect his opinions to carry some weight. But bottom line, I couldn't let him dictate who I accepted as my clients.

"I think this will blow over," I said. "How about we give it a week or so and see where we are?" I decided to try to keep it vague so I wasn't locked into any promises.

"Okay, today's Thursday. The complaint was filed Monday. Have you written your response yet?"

"I was planning to work on it this weekend. I have 20 days to respond."

"The sooner, the better, I'd say. Could you email or fax me a copy when you get it done?"

I agreed, mostly to buy myself some time. While I wished he hadn't asked for it, I couldn't think of a good reason not to give him a copy. He's discreet, and I trust him completely not to share the information with anyone. Nevertheless, I felt strangely anxious about agreeing to send it to him.

22

Sharon was scheduled Friday afternoon for another try at contacting Adam. I called her Friday morning to see if it was still a go. While I had no intentions of being bullied out of working with her, I wanted to make sure she hadn't changed her mind. But despite Waycroft's brouhaha, she wanted to keep on.

We skipped looking through Adam's stuff this time. Like before, I had Sharon bring a picture of him as well as his favorite tee shirt from the annual Bolder-Boulder 10K race. Before getting her set in the apparition chamber, we walked over to the creek again to relax, talk about Adam, and explore her motivations for trying to contact him.

"I miss him so much. It's like this huge cloud of sadness that hangs over my head," Sharon said as we strolled along the creek path among joggers, mothers pushing strollers, and dogs pulling their guardians by leashes. "Look—all these people enjoying their lives. But in here inside my cloud everything is dimmer and grayer than out there. I find myself wondering how the world can go on as if nothing had changed—when Adam is gone from it forever."

"Of course you feel that way, Sharon. Most people have that experience after a loss. It's hard to look around and see life moving along when you feel depressed." We came to a bench on the creek bank, sat down and gazed out at the rushing water below.

Sharon sat quietly for several minutes, and then continued softly, almost as if talking sadly to herself. "I know I have a lot to

137

live for—Nathan, my job, good friends. But I don't have Adam. All the thoughts and joys and little jokes I want to share with him go unshared. My daily life has a hollow feeling, a big space that he used to fill. Nothing is the way it was when we were together, and it will never be that way again." She sobbed inconsolably. "I loved him so much, and he loved me. I'll never find anyone else I can love so totally and who loves me that much."

I knew she needed to grieve. There's so much bottled up inside after a loss. "It's true that your life won't be the same," I said, thinking to myself that if Sharon could actually reach Adam, she might feel a lot better. I thought about one of my former clients who couldn't stop blaming herself for not having somehow noticed warning signs of her husband's fatal heart attack. She had nightmares where he was drowning and begged her to save him but she couldn't help him. When she finally contacted him in the apparition chamber, he told her how much he loved her, what a wonderful wife she had been, and that she couldn't have prevented his death. After that, she was able to accept his death and her nightmares stopped.

"Somehow I have to move on, build a new life," Sharon went on. "Sometimes I don't think I can do it. It's just too hard. But I know I have to do it for Nathan. So I try to find things we can do to have fun together. Then sometimes when I do find myself enjoying something, I feel guilty that I'm having fun with Adam gone."

I wanted to normalize her feelings and build on any positive emotions she might have, so I said, "That's a common feeling people have. But you know Adam wouldn't want you to feel miserable all the time. Are there times when you don't feel so sad?"

"Sometimes anger takes over the sadness. I'm angry that I don't know what happened to Adam, that maybe someone pushed him over the edge and I'll never find out. But if I do find out someone pushed him, I'll kill that person for taking Adam away from me."

Blaming someone for a loss is a strategy grievers sometimes use to avoid facing their feelings. This can interfere with their healing. But in Sharon's case, there was a real mystery to be solved—possibly someone who deserved blame. So, I didn't try to redirect her back to her grief.

"Do you have any ideas about anyone you think might have pushed him?"

"Not really. He didn't have enemies." She looked off to the left as if mentally checking a list of suspects. "Well, there is the voice on the answering machine. And of course Natalie—Narmada—whatever. But I don't see how she could have actually pushed him. I think I need to know more about what was going on before he died, what was bothering him so much. So today I'm hoping to reach him and get some information."

We went back to my office, where I set her up in the apparition chamber. While she was in there, I tried another web search on Dr. Ahmed. This time, I followed a bunch of the links that came up. I ignored the ones where Ahmed was the first name, and the ones where the Dr. Ahmed was a Ph.D. rather than an M.D. I found an oncologist in California, a gynecologist in Illinois, and several natural healing specialists, but no one that sounded like he'd been running a drug scam.

After about an hour, Sharon came out looking confused and not nearly as delighted as she had after her last session. I handed her a big glass of water and nudged her into the counseling room.

"How did it go this time?"

"I kept thinking about how you said not to try to make something happen. I was sitting there struggling with wanting so much to reach Adam. I felt like I was trying to force him to show up, and it wasn't working. So finally I decided that today wasn't going to be the day. When I sat back and relaxed, I suddenly got a powerful sense of Jenny—and I heard her voice. I didn't see her clearly, only a shadowy figure in the mirror, but I could feel her right there close to me. She said she knows I'm having a hard time."

Sharon took a break for a long drink of water. I waited quietly.

"I told her that Erik was being a wonderful help to me and Nathan and was like part of our family. She asked me if I remembered her telling me that Erik sometimes tells lies."

"Interesting. What did you say?"

"I told her I did remember her saying that, but that Erik has never lied to me. Then she said I should ask him about Amber and Melissa and about his brother Harry."

"Has he ever talked to you about any of those people?"

"Never. I asked Jenny to tell me more about them, but she didn't answer me. Or if she did, I couldn't hear her. I began to feel her fading away, so I called out, 'Jenny, don't go yet. I need to know about Adam.' Then I felt her presence strongly again, and I heard her clearly. She said 'I didn't come about Adam. It's about you. You have to stop the scam before more people get hurt.' Then, before I could ask her what she meant, she just evaporated. I couldn't feel her presence at all, and I couldn't get her back." Sharon looked despondent.

"What scam do you think she meant?"

"It could be about Dr. Ahmed, something about drugs. I know she sometimes took Xanax and other drugs she got from him. And after what you overheard him saying, it looks like there could be a scam. But I don't have any evidence. How can I stop it?"

"That's a problem. I haven't been able to find out anything more about him either. Maybe I can get my boyfriend to do some checking. He's a detective with the Longmont Police Department. We haven't been getting along all that well lately, but I'll give it a try."

Sharon reached over to get her watch from the table where she put it before she went into the apparition chamber. "I have to go in a few minutes. Nathan's with Maria, but she has to leave at 5:00. I don't know what to do about what Jenny said about Erik. None of it makes sense to me. Erik's never said anything about a brother."

"That's strange. Erik told me he had planned on going to the Grand Canyon with Adam, but he had to visit his brother for some important family thing instead."

"He said he was going with Adam? I never heard anything about that! Adam never said anything about Erik going with him. Erik hasn't ever mentioned it either."

"That is odd."

"I do remember I couldn't reach Erik right after the accident. I was going to ask him if he'd fly down there with me and drive Adam's car back, but it turned out he was away somewhere. I thought he told me later that he had to go to Chicago on business. It was a confusing time, but I think I'd remember if he'd said anything about a brother."

"So how did you get Adam's car back?"

"Oh, my dad arranged to have someone there drive it here. It was no big deal." She glanced at her watch again and jumped up. "Wow, I have to go. Maybe we can talk more this weekend?"

"Sure. Call me," I said as she rushed out the door.

What had I gotten myself into? I started to wonder whether I was helping Sharon or making her life more difficult. I didn't want to back off and give Waycroft the satisfaction of believing he'd scared me off—but I wasn't sure where to go from here. At that moment, I felt a need for comfort, reassurance, or at least some peace and quiet.

I went into the apparition chamber to tidy up, but instead I plopped into the chair and gazed off into the mirror. My head felt heavy, my eyelids drooped, and I had just begun to doze off, when I heard, "Yo, Cleo." Tyler appeared in the mirror—the first time I'd seen him there in a while.

Suddenly I was wide awake and determined to get some answers. I sat up straight and gave him my best no-nonsense look. "Tyler, I need some help if you expect me to play detective. Can you give me some direction here?"

"Check out what Jenny said. She's no airhead. It's all about the 411."

"Ok, the message. So we should ask Erik about Amber and Melissa and his brother Harry? What do they have to do with all this? And what scam was she talking about?"

"These are some major issues. Don't be afraid to get wet."

Metaphor again. If I had to think in watery terms, I'd describe myself as drowning. But I decided to try for some more direct communication. "Tyler! I was confused when I came in here, and you're making it worse! Can't you give me a straight answer for once?"

"Later dude, I'm gone." And sure enough, he was.

23

Saturday morning I got a call from Erik asking me to go for a hike and late breakfast at Chautauqua Park. I had other stuff to do, but I was very curious about his brother and other parts of Jenny's message, so I went.

The park contains several hundred acres of open space at the base of the Flatirons. We met at the Bluebird Mesa trailhead, just off the parking lot west of the ranger cottage. Erik greeted me with one of his irresistible smiles and an extra water bottle in case I had forgotten mine. He set a fast pace as we hiked up the trail that rises steeply through a prairie grass meadow to the top of the mesa. Walking behind him on the narrow trail, I admired his solid leg and shoulder muscles. Even in Boulder where fitness is almost an obsession, Erik stood out.

Pride pushed me to match his speed, leaving me little breath for talking. We stopped a couple of times to drink from our water bottles and enjoy the panoramic view of the Boulder valley below. But we kept our thoughts to ourselves.

As we got to the top of the ridge where we'd take the more level Bluebell Baird trail through a ponderosa pine forest, I thought about how to ask Erik about what Jenny had said. I couldn't tell him that Sharon had contacted Jenny, so I couldn't see any way to bring up Amber and Melissa. But I could ask him about his brother, since he had mentioned him to me before.

I didn't need to find a way to broach the subject. I was still catching my breath and admiring the vista of the meadow and the city below, when Erik turned to me with a nasty scowl. "What business do you have interfering in my life with my dead wife?"

All of a sudden, Erik was livid. He seemed to be able to turn his emotions on and off like a water faucet. I was still contemplating my response when he attacked me again. "Don't you have any respect at all for other people's privacy? I hate people poking around in my life. It makes me damn mad."

I was taken aback. "Wait a minute. What do you think I did?"

"I saw Sharon last night. I know what you did. Now I want you to tell me exactly what Jenny said to her—every single word."

I became more and more nervous, and was about ready to run right back down the trail to my car and leave, but I remembered Tyler telling me not to be afraid to get wet, so I stayed. I tried to calm him down with a reasonable response. I said, "I can't do that. I wasn't in the room with Sharon when she talked with Jenny. All I know is what she told me—which I gather she's already told you as well."

"Look—I'm not saying I believe you can connect living people up with dead people. But let's just pretend it is possible. Don't you think you should at least check with the living person who was closest to someone who died before you go resurrecting that person?"

I didn't even know where to start to answer that. Dead people's rights to talk to whomever they choose? My inability to control who appears to someone in the apparition chamber? Client confidentiality? Finally I said, "I didn't resurrect Jenny. As I'm sure Sharon told you, Jenny appeared when Sharon was trying to contact Adam. And if you want to know what she said, you'll have to ask Sharon."

Our conversation was interrupted briefly as a couple with two young children—a baby in a backpack and a little boy with a walking stick— came toward us along the forested trail from the west. We exchanged hiker greetings and stepped aside to let them pass. I hoped Erik would take that as a natural end to our conversation about Jenny. But no such luck. As soon as they were out of range, he started in again.

"Sharon and I did talk. She thinks Jenny gave her a message about some scam involving Dr. Ahmed. She wanted to know whether Adam talked to me about Ahmed. I told her Adam never mentioned Ahmed to me. We never talked about him at all. And, like I said before, I don't like Ahmed, but I don't think he's a criminal."

"So why is Jenny's message about a scam so upsetting to you?" I asked, thinking his anger was way out of proportion to the situation. I wondered whether Erik was worried that maybe the scam Jenny had warned us about was the herb growing kits his Natural Herbal Remedies Company was selling for $500 a pop. Hmm…something else to have Pablo check into?

"I'm upset because she was my wife, and I don't want her memory dragged though the mud as part of some spiritualism experiment."

I wasn't going to argue with Erik about the legitimacy of my project. And furthermore, he was all over the place about whether he believed Sharon had actually talked to Jenny.

Without warning, Erik's bad mood cleared, like clouds swept away by a brisk wind. An engaging smile lit his face. "Look Cleo, I know you and Sharon are my friends, and you care about me. And maybe you thought you could help me somehow by reaching Jenny. Sharon has been telling me I should try it. I had some bad luck with Jenny, but she and I are over. I've moved on, and I don't want to go back. So how about we agree to forget about Jenny, finish our hike, and get some breakfast." With that, he turned and set off at a good clip along the trail to the west.

I wasn't in much of a mood for breakfast with him at that point, but I followed along behind. The trail is a loop and I had to get back to my car one way or another, so I figured I might as well keep going. We hiked in silence through the pine forest to the Bluebell Shelter. As usual, the forest had a calming effect on me, such that I remembered I hadn't yet gotten answers to any of my questions. So why not have breakfast? How nasty could he get in a restaurant full of people? And anyway, I was starving. So I kept following along down the fire road from the shelter to the auditorium and the historic restaurant just beyond.

The Chautauqua Dining Hall was built in 1898, in the style of resort architecture of the time. It was part of the Chautauqua movement to bring lectures to smaller towns. The large wrap-around covered veranda is its main appeal as a summer dining spot. Tables on this porch seat about a hundred diners, who enjoy views of the extensive lawns that make up Chautauqua park, and a wide view beyond of the city below. Erik charmed the hostess into giving us a porch table, where we ordered large glasses of fresh-squeezed orange juice, Belgian waffles with strawberries and whipped cream, and extra-large cups of dark French roast coffee.

While we waited for our food, Erik talked enthusiastically about his herb and nutritional supplement business, boasting he would get rich while helping people at the same time. He was wildly optimistic about the potential of his business, and I couldn't help but be captivated by his passion for his work. So I listened quietly, enjoying the luscious combination of crisp waffle, smooth cream and ripe berries.

Just as I finished the last bite, Erik leaned toward me and said, "I decided when I was just a little kid that I would get rich. My parents worked hard but got nowhere. They were stupid. They let life use them rather than using life. I made up my mind not to let that happen to me."

This gave me the opening I was looking for. "So what about your brother? Is he rich?"

"What brother? I don't have a brother."

"The brother you told me you had to visit because of some important family thing back in April when Adam was going to the Grand Canyon."

"You must have misunderstood, Cleo. All my family are dead. I don't have anyone."

"Erik, that night we were at the Rhumba, you said you had planned to go to the Grand Canyon with Adam, but then you couldn't go because you had to go visit your brother instead."

"Well you know—I didn't really want to go with Adam, but I had said I would, so I made that up about my brother. I was doing Adam a favor, making it easier for him by not telling him I didn't want to go," Erik said earnestly.

"So you don't have a brother?"

"No, I do. But I usually don't like to talk about him. He's a real jerk. We were both abused by our parents and ended up being raised in foster homes. He never got over that—been a whiner all his life. I never see him or my parents. They're dead to me and that's what I tell people."

My head spun with all his contradictions. But in spite of his confusing stories, I couldn't bring myself to write Erik off, even if he was a little scary. He had such an endearing way about him, plus—I'll admit it—he was hot. And overall, he still seemed mostly sincere and caring. As a therapist, I deal with some very difficult people, and while I see their weaknesses, I generally like them and believe they are basically good people. I did consider asking him about Amber and Melissa and maybe about how Jenny came to forget her inhaler, but I didn't. I guess I wasn't ready to get that wet.

24

Saturday afternoon, Sharon called to invite me to Nathan's soccer game so we'd have a chance to talk. He'd been attending an intense soccer camp for the past two weeks, and this was the final event. The game was at 4:00 at the South Boulder Rec Center, off Gillaspie in the Table Mesa area. When I got there, I found Sharon wearing beige linen shorts that showed off her long legs to their best advantage and a reddish-brown sleeveless shirt that matched her hair perfectly. She was all set up with blankets to sit on, big jugs of water and lemonade, and a platter of watermelon slices. Looked like she expected more guests than just me.

I joined her on a blanket, admiring the outstanding long view of the Flatirons you get from south Boulder. No clouds, so it looked like we'd escape the thunderstorms common to summer afternoons.

"Gorgeous day," Sharon said with a smile. "I had to do a bunch of laundry and stuff this morning, so it's good to finally get out." I think this was the first time I'd seen Sharon looking truly happy. I noticed when she was relaxed she had one of those wide infectious smiles that draws you in to a place where everything is more amusing than you had realized before.

I hesitated to intrude on her good mood, but I thought I should tell her what Erik had said. I tried to put it gently. "I went hiking at Chautauqua with Erik this morning. He was kind of upset about you contacting Jenny yesterday. Somehow, he had the idea we should have asked his permission."

"That's strange. When I told him about Jenny last night, he said the whole thing was way too new-agey for him, and he didn't believe I'd actually talked to Jenny."

"Did you ask him about Amber and Melissa and his brother Harry?"

"I did. He said he had no idea what I was talking about, that he doesn't know anyone named Amber or Melissa and he doesn't have a brother."

I poured myself a glass of lemonade, and took a big gulp to give myself time to decide how to respond. I decided I needed to tell it like I saw it, even though Sharon felt close to Erik. "He told me that, too—but then when I reminded him that he had mentioned visiting his brother, he admitted that he does have a brother. But he said the brother is a jerk, and he never sees him. At this point, I don't know how much of what Erik says is true and how much he makes up. I can see why Jenny would say he sometimes lies."

"It is confusing, I'll admit." Sharon hesitated as if pulling the words from under a rock. "But Erik has been so helpful to us, and I don't have any evidence that he's lied to me, so I have to give him the benefit of the doubt." She gave me a questioning look as if asking my approval for this stance.

I felt conflicted. While I didn't want to trash Erik, I wanted to warn Sharon to be careful. Before I could frame a reply, the game heated up. A penalty was declared on a player from the opposing team who had pushed Nathan with his hand. Nathan got a direct free kick and scored a goal. The other kid stomped around and had what looked to be an intense talk with a coach. When normal play resumed, we watched without talking for a while. Sharon didn't bring up Erik's brother again, so I decided to move on to another topic.

"I did some web searches on Dr. Ahmed," I said. "But I didn't find anything. Did you talk to Erik about what Adam said to him about Ahmed?"

"I asked him, but he said Adam never talked to him about Ahmed. I'll do a little nosing around with staff at Shady Terrace to see what I can find out there without being too obvious," Sharon said. "Oh look, there's Joel. Nathan asked him to come, but I didn't think he'd actually show up."

Given their history, I could see why Sharon wouldn't count on Joel for much of anything. But she looked happy to see him, and made room for him on the blanket next to her. He wore a dark green sport shirt and chinos instead of his usual tee shirt and baggy shorts, and he looked like he had shaved that morning. Could all this be for Sharon?

"I would have been here earlier, but I was talking to some folks about a possible job," Joel said reaching for a chunk of watermelon. So he hadn't dressed up for Sharon. But he was looking for a job in Boulder? Interesting.

Sharon looked a bit taken aback. "You're looking for a job here? What kind of job?"

Joel grinned. "Teaching at a new private high school that focuses on giving students real-world responsibilities and opportunities to give back to the community." His eyes lit up as he continued. "The people who are starting it are committed to the idea that we should teach students that they have a responsibility to use the knowledge they gain for the benefit of others. So citizenship and community building will be a big part of the education." Joel stopped to wipe at the watermelon juice dripping down the front of his shirt.

"Here, I brought some towels," Sharon said handing him a brown striped dish towel. "How did you find out about this job?"

"A friend of mine told them I had lived in Los Amigos—the humanistic cooperative community in Mexico. That interested them because they want to teach kids to continually ask themselves, 'How can I help?' rather than 'What can I get?'"

"That sounds like a great idea, Joel," Sharon said. She looked impressed. "I'd love to have Nathan go to a school like that someday. If I could ever afford a private school. Do you think you have a good chance for the job?"

"Well they like that I've taught skiing and been a river guide because part of the teaching will involve challenging the students to work together in difficult outdoor adventures. And they like that I'm into meditation and yoga, because they also want a contemplative piece. So I think I have a reasonable chance. It doesn't pay very well, but I'm used to living poor."

"So, how do you teach a group of today's high school students to focus more on giving than getting?" I asked. "It can't be easy, especially when most of them will come from well-off families if they can afford private school tuition."

"At Los Amigos, the idea is that if you change the environment so cooperative behavior is reinforced more than competitive behavior, people will change the way they behave. In other words, if people have learned to compete, they can also learn to cooperate—if we set up an atmosphere where cooperation and teamwork are rewarded most."

"That sounds kind of idealistic, don't you think?" We all looked up to see Erik standing behind us. "Cooperation may sound good, but it doesn't pay the bills," he went on.

"Erik!" Sharon jumped up to face him. "This is Joel, Nathan's birth father. He was just telling us about a new school in Boulder where he might get a job. Um, Joel, this is our good friend Erik."

Joel stood to meet Erik, leaving me alone on the blanket looking up at all of them. They seemed a little tense, so I said, "How about you all join me down here, have some watermelon, and watch Nathan play soccer. I'm thinking that's why we're here."

They loosened up a little, sat down, and at least pretended to be interested in the soccer game. Erik grabbed a piece of watermelon, but as soon as he finished it, he started up again. "In my nutrition business, I have to stay one step ahead of the competition if I want the big bucks. And by doing that, I can give a lot of other people the chance to make some money too." He turned toward Joel. "Maybe Nathan has shown you the herb plants I gave him to grow. He'll be able to sell those back to the company for thousands of dollars once the roots get big enough. I think that will help him more than teaching him some naïve ideas about cooperation."

"We can all help Nathan in different ways," Joel said. "I expect he'll learn a few things from growing the herbs."

"I've been here helping Sharon and Nathan ever since Adam

died," Erik said. "What have you ever done for him?"

Sharon looked stunned and more than a little upset at Erik's attack. Fortunately, the game ended just then, and we all went out onto the field to meet the kids. Nathan ran straight to Joel yelling, "Did you see me? Did you see me?" Joel gave him a big hug and whispered something in his ear.

"Hey, Nathan—you're the champ!" Erik easily lifted him over to where he stood and turned on the charm with his engaging smile. "Guess what? I have a big surprise for you, and we need to go pick it up right away."

"Cool!" Nathan said. "What is it?"

"If I told you, it wouldn't be a surprise," Erik said. "Let's get your mom and go pick it up."

"Can we, Mom?" Nathan had lost all interest in Joel who watched silently from the background.

Sharon agreed she and Nathan would go with Erik and pick up her car later. I felt kind of bad for Joel, but couldn't really say anything. Maybe to save face, Joel said he had to meet someone. I needed to be somewhere as well. We all went off to our cars a little awkwardly and headed off in different directions.

I went north on Broadway over to Canyon to stop at Liquor Mart for a bottle of wine. I had arranged to get together with Holly that evening, ostensibly to look at her latest work. She had volunteered to fix a spicy Asian shrimp and noodle salad if I would bring some wine. As I drove, I thought it wasn't too surprising Erik and Joel did not hit it off, since they both seemed to have designs on Sharon. And I could see Sharon was conflicted about her relationships with these guys. I had concerns about both of them, but I figured after all her years of dealing with her father, Sharon could manage whatever those two came up with.

25

Holly lives in the foothills off Mountain Pines Road on Sugarloaf, so from Liquor Mart I drove straight west up Boulder Canyon. Her house is only about fifteen miles from town, and she has two acres with groves of evergreens and a great deck with a hot tub. I think the house is the main asset she ended up with after her divorce back in the late 1970s. She was in her thirties then, running a boutique dress shop in Boulder while raising three kids. She didn't have time to take her artwork seriously until the mid-1980s when she started studying painting with Gramma. That's when I met her.

The two-lane road up the narrow mountain canyon was crowded. Gorgeous mountain scenery with fir trees, massive granite outcroppings, and a rushing stream beside the road attracts summer tourists looking for picnic spots, as well as hikers and climbers. Much of the traffic that day was likely headed farther up to Boulder Falls, where melted mountain snow provides icy cold water that drops 66 feet into the creek.

About five miles up the canyon, I turned off onto Sugarloaf Road and wound my way up to Holly's place. Her house is one of the older mountain homes, mostly dark wood and stone, with vaulted ceilings in the large main room, which serves as both living and dining room. After her kids were grown, she combined two of the house's three bedrooms into a large studio, where she spends most of her time. That's where we went as soon as I got there.

I'm always taken aback by the size and vivid colors of Holly's paintings. Most of her works are large, some as big as four feet by six feet—while Holly herself is tiny, barely five feet tall and maybe 90 pounds. She paints in oils with an amazing use of color and shape. Her work is all abstracts, using geometric shapes in various brilliant colors like turquoise, scarlet, ochre, and lime green, offset with basic black, white and dark brown. You'd never match her with her work if you didn't know it was hers. Looking at her, you'd be more likely to expect small watercolors of English gardens.

She had some terrific new pieces since I'd last been up to see her, and we spent an hour or so talking about art, problems with local galleries, and exciting news about a new internet site that brought her customers from places she'd never even exhibited. Then she said, "Enough about the art business. Let's take some of that wine you brought out to the hot tub and relax."

Holly's place is secluded enough to hot tub in the buff, so we shed our clothes, grabbed some towels, the wine bottle and glasses, and headed out to the deck. The sun sank swiftly behind the mountains, and the hot water felt wonderful in the cool conifer-scented evening air. We relaxed in the mountain stillness and sipped our wine.

"How is Martha doing? Is she still painting?" Holly asked. I ran through the latest on Gramma, trying to put as much of a positive slant on it as possible, but Holly could sense my uneasiness. "It sounds like you're worried that her doctor isn't giving her good care."

"I guess that's true," I said. "But it's worse than that. I'm afraid he's doing something illegal there, and I don't know what to do about it. Maybe I should move Gramma somewhere else. But Grampa picked out Shady Terrace for her because he thought it was the best place. And the staff know her there, and they let her paint. I don't know where she'd do better."

"Ah, Cleo. Martha's had a good life. It's too bad she doesn't know who she is or where she is right now, but you can't do anything about that. Now this doctor and whatever crooked swindles he's up to is another matter. Have you considered talking to the police?"

I told her some about Pablo and our relationship and why I was hesitant to involve the police without more hard evidence. "He already thinks I'm flaky, and I don't want to make it worse," I said. "And with my reputation right now, they'd never take me seriously. Did you know Donald Waycroft filed a complaint against me with the Colorado Mental Health Regulatory Board? You know him, don't you?"

"Oh yes, I know Donald real well," she said with a laugh. "He likes to push people around some. I hadn't heard about the complaint, but I wouldn't take him too seriously if I were you. Actually I haven't seen Donald for a while. We're in one of our standoff phases right now."

I wanted to ask why she'd ever actually choose to spend time with him, but that was too pushy even for me. So I said, "His daughter is a client of mine, and he's taken offense at the work we're doing, so he filed this complaint saying that I'm mentally ill and delusional, and engaging in fraudulent practice."

"Well, that sounds like Donald. He never does anything half way. I'm starving. Let's dry off and go in and eat, and I'll tell you all about him."

While we were getting dressed and getting out the food, I told her more about the Contact Project and Waycroft's complaint against me. She was so excited about the project that she kept me talking about it all through dinner. But when we settled in the living room with coffee and a plate of chocolate dipped strawberries, I finally steered the conversation back to Waycroft.

"The truth of it is, he's good in bed, but a little hard to take the rest of the time," she said with a chuckle. "Actually, I've learned to ignore a lot of his bluster. He's all bark, you know. He's so sure he's a realist who makes sensible choices and lives his life exactly as he wants to live it—but he has feelings just like everyone else."

Holly put her feet up, leaned back, and continued. "Donald's such an ideologue. He believes that rewarding good behavior and punishing bad is the only way to save the world. He tries out those theories on everyone, but it hasn't worked too well on me. It came to a head one time when we were fighting about something and he told me he wasn't going to reward my bad behavior by going along with what I wanted. Well that didn't sit too well with me, so I kicked his ass out of my bed and my house and told him to find someone else to use his behavior shaping techniques on. He's so stuck in his reinforcement theories that I figured he'd be punishing me with his absence for a really long time."

She sat up, took a gulp of coffee, and gave me a broad grin. "But here's a surprise. He showed up the next morning with flowers, croissants and coffee, and the sweetest apology I've ever gotten from a man. Now I'm no psychologist, but I'd say he was reinforcing my so-called bad behavior big time. We didn't talk about it and he's never mentioned the incident since."

She shrugged and took on a more thoughtful look. "But some-times I get tired of his insistence that most people are lazy, sloppy, and illogical. And that everyone needs more structure. Then we take a break until we miss each other."

"So, when you miss him, it's mostly the sex?"

She picked up a strawberry and bit in "That's about it. At my age, there aren't that many good male bodies around to hook up with. And with him, the sex is really good. In the beginning, I thought we could have more of an intimate relationship, but I gave up on that once I really accepted that Donald believes introspection is bogus."

My mind wandered briefly to my relationship with Pablo. Was I just using him for sex? And, maybe as a source of police department information? Was he just using me for sex? And maybe as someone to talk about art with? No question we do have sensational sex together. And if we were each getting what we wanted, would that be a bad thing? Maybe I should ask Holly's opinion.

As if she had read my mind, she said, "I think Donald and I have both accepted that what we have works for us as long as neither of us wants more. And that's fine with me. He fills a niche in my life, I guess you could say," she said with a big laugh.

I got back to the purpose of my visit, nosed around some more, and found out Waycroft's pet peeve was the university's institutional review board. The board's members review research projects involving human subjects to ensure people aren't placed at undue risk. They also require that people who serve as research subjects give un-coerced, informed consent to their participation. Waycroft saw these requirements as a lot of stupid rules created by bureaucrats to get in the way of his research. Holly said he'd had some proposed projects rejected, and he'd been having more and more trouble getting the go-ahead to continue his ongoing projects when they were reviewed each year. He thought the board members were harassing him out of spite, and he was pretty bitter about it.

I also learned he was involved in several large research projects, one of which involved travel to Mexico. Holly didn't know anything about the actual projects, except that Waycroft said there was more freedom in Mexico to do the research he needed to do.

All in all, I didn't get anything obvious I could use against Waycroft, but I figured I could get Elisa to explore his problems with getting his research projects approved by the university. Maybe there was a reason the review board members didn't like his work. And—as always—it was fun catching up with Holly

On the way home, I got to thinking about whether Waycroft's Mexico project could have anything to do with Joel. After all, Joel had studied with Waycroft as a graduate student, and after he left Boulder he lived in Mexico for a while. Of course Joel also told Sharon he hadn't talked to Waycroft in years. But I had no way to know whether or not he was telling the truth about that.

26

On Sunday, I spent some time at my office writing a response to Waycroft's complaint. I found it tough to explain what I do in the Contact Project in a way that made it clear I adhere to high professional standards. To make matters worse, my father called. Wouldn't you know, someone had sent him the newspaper article. He was so disgusted that my work had led to charges being brought against me by a distinguished professor that he tried to convince me I should give up the Contact Project. This was nothing new. My father is, to say the least, not pleased with the direction my life has taken. In general, I want to get along with my father—or at least I think I do. Every time I go back to Kansas to visit, I promise myself I'll be the person he wants me to be so we can enjoy being together. But somehow I always slip up. Like last summer, when he kept making cracks about my "special ties with the supernatural." I just couldn't let it go by. So we were at it again.

Today he started right in. "Cleo, you could do some significant work, make a name for yourself. You're wasting your life on this ridiculous contacting dead people nonsense."

Giving up, I snapped back. "People are willing to pay me for this ridiculous nonsense."

"People pay for all kinds of things—pornography, junk food, illegal drugs. That doesn't justify the activity."

"What difference does it make to you anyway—it's my life," I replied somewhat petulantly. "Are you going to give me a prize for

157

doing it your way?"

"I already gave you a quality education. So why are you wasting that expensive education on this silliness?"

Over time, I have learned to stop when we get to this point. My father doesn't care how much we fight. In fact, I think he argues just to keep me going. My mother sometimes says Dad would call a dog a cat to get an argument going and by the time he was done you'd trade that dog in for a cat just to shut him up. At least my mother can sometimes laugh about it. I never did enjoy my dad's bickering. So I told him I had to go and hung up.

I sat there for a bit, staring off into space and feeling sorry for myself that Grampa, who had really understood me, was gone, while my father and Waycroft were very much here and making my life more difficult. When I looked up, I saw Tyler leaning on the edge of my desk.

"Yo Cleo. You feel like you been totally axed?"

"Well, you could say not a lot is going my way, Tyler. I'm feeling like I'm in over my head here. Maybe drowning? Am I speaking your language enough that you can get a clue and give me some help?"

"Don't get all bent. It's a little choppy, but you can't bail now."

"You have a big stake in my staying with this, but I'm the one getting all the flack from people. You're dead. You don't have to deal with them!"

"Cleo, this isn't about you. But you're on to something gnarly. Some dudes need serious help from you. They're going under fast, so you need to line up. Find your take-off point. Then make the wave. Don't get pounded. And remember to watch for sharks."

"TYLER! I need some specific advice. Who are the sharks? What should I do about Dr. Ahmed? And what about Erik?" But I didn't get an answer, because Tyler had vanished. Arrrgh!

I glared at the corner of my desk where Tyler had been, as if I could conjure him up—but of course nothing happened. Except I noticed Erik's business card lying there, where I had dropped it almost two weeks ago. I realized I had never gone to his website, so I decided to check it out.

The home page for Vaughn's Holistic Healing featured a lush mountain meadow dotted with colorful wildflowers and surrounded by an aspen grove. A fit young woman in a purple leotard sat in a yoga pose beside a meandering mountain stream. New-age harp music played softly in the background. A floating banner read, "Your life, your choice. Surprise yourself! Exceed your personal best!"

Links on the left side of the page took visitors to a company mission statement, staff biographies, descriptions of innovative and affordable products for the journey to optimal wellness, testimonials, and ordering instructions. Vaughn's mission statement was "To offer the very best natural alternatives in weight-control, life-enhancement, and health promotion so everyone can feel great about themselves." In his biographical statement, Erik described himself as a sports nutritionist who had two science degrees and was widely recognized as an expert in nutrition and human performance.

His products professed to help people reduce stress, enhance energy production, maintain a positive outlook, improve memory and focus, lose weight, improve immune system functioning, protect against cell damage, and more. The various capsules, tablets and tonics contained an assortment of herbs, natural extracts and compounds, food concentrates, caffeine, green tea, and other natural substances. One weight-loss supplement claimed to be the most significant advancement in over a decade. A medicinal mushroom extract was said to have been used successfully for over fifteen years in hospitals worldwide to improve immune system functioning. All the products were backed by testimonials listing the dramatic benefits people experienced while taking them. Most were touted as scientific breakthroughs. And most ran $100 or so for a month's supply.

In addition to offering the products for retail sale, Erik gave people the opportunity to become associates who could order products at a discount for resale. By "partnering" with him, associates could not only make money, they could also "bring the benefits of natural good health to others." Overall, it looked like a major money-maker. No wonder he was so optimistic.

I called Elisa to tell her about Erik's website so she could check it out, and to tell her what Holly had said about Waycroft and see what she had uncovered. I began with Holly's information.

"Right on," she whooped. "It turns out our boy Donald got in some trouble for misrepresenting a project to the university's institutional review board. From what I heard, he's obsessed with proving that behavioral principles work, but he can't get approval to do the studies he wants to do because they violate ethical guidelines. So he lied in his application. He said he was going to explore at what ages babies can learn to recognize different animal puppets and pick out the ones they like. But what he really planned to do was show that he could control the babies' behavior by conditioning them with either cute or scary puppets. When the board found out what his research was really about, they withdrew approval and he was in big trouble. My source says it was all hushed up at the university, but I'm thinking we could threaten to expose it and maybe get Donald to back off."

"Good idea, but we need to do it soon. I need his complaint to go away before I lose any more business, or maybe even my funding for the Contact Project."

"I agree. I want him to back off well before I put in my tenure application in the fall. Let me think about the best way to put pressure on him in the department, and we can talk about it in a few days."

"Great. And if you have a few extra minutes, check out Erik Vaughn's website. I'm curious to see what you think of it. I'm starting to wonder if he's really a nutrition expert or if he's mostly a salesman. And there's something about him personally that I can't quite figure out. I never know whether to believe what he says. Sharon agrees he can be moody and odd, but she still wants to keep him close."

"I hardly know him, but I'll look at the website," Elisa said. "Oh, and by the way, have you found out any more about that doctor at Shady Terrace?"

I filled her in on my fruitless web searches, and told her about Sharon's contact with Jenny and the comment Jenny made to Sharon about a scam. "I guess I am going to have to talk to Pablo about him even though he'll probably think it's another of my wacky issues," I said. "I can't take the chance that a lot of people may get hurt just because I don't want my boyfriend to laugh at me."

"Good thinking, Cleo. Anyway, who knows—the last laugh may be yours."

27

When I hung up with Elisa, it was mid-afternoon. I decided to call Pablo. Sometimes when he gets angry, he needs some cooling off time, so I usually don't run right after him and try to make up. But it had been a week since his disastrous encounter with Erik at my house. I was ready to try to make peace and I figured he was too.

I reached him on his cell phone. It turned out he was at a family picnic at Eben Fine Park, which is only about a block from where I live. He invited me to join them. I told him I thought we needed to talk first, to try to get some stuff figured out between us. He said let's eat first and talk after. I love his parents and the rest of his family—plus, they always have terrific food—so I agreed.

Like most summer Sundays, Eben Fine Park was jam-packed with family picnickers—mostly Latino. It was a hot afternoon, and people of all ages were wading in the creek just past the bridge in a somewhat level shallow area—sort of Colorado's version of the beach. Kids and teenagers climbed on rocks in a deeper area and jumped off into the knee-deep water below, shrieking and splashing each other. Others floated in inner tubes or rubber boats over the shallow falls. Dogs chased tennis balls thrown into the creek, then climbed out soaking wet and shook water onto everyone nearby.

The grassy park area beside the creek overflowed with barbeque grills, coolers, playpens, strollers, kids and dogs. Multigenerational families sat on the picnic table benches and lawn chairs—eating, chatting and watching kids play. One family had even put up a small tent. It was almost as if the population of a small south-of-the-border town had emigrated here for the day.

Smoke billowing from grills mixed with strong smells of roasting meat. Picnic tables were loaded with jars of mayonnaise, mustard, catsup and pickles, bowls of salad, bags of chips, paper plates and cups, cakes, cookies, and jugs of sun tea and lemonade. Coolers below the tables held beer and soda. People were here for the duration—to kick back, eat and play.

Pablo and his family had pulled two picnic tables together near the bank of the creek. They were grilling chicken breasts to cut into strips and roll up in the warm foil-wrapped tortillas waiting beside the grill. Pablo's mom, Juanita, fixed one for me with shredded lettuce, diced tomatoes, onions, grated jack cheese and homemade salsa. A little bit of heaven! I bit in, and forgot all my problems.

Pablo was in a laid-back mood, trying to teach one of his young nephews to hula hoop. First he demonstrated the technique. Then he carefully put the hoop over the toddler's head, and showed him how to put his hands in the air and shake his body to rotate the hoop. The hoop hit the ground, the kid laughed, jumped out of the middle of the hoop, and handed it back to Pablo. They went on like that for a while, until a young woman came along pushing a cart selling mangos on a stick. Pablo handed her some money, she picked up a mango, stuck a stick in one end, then deftly peeled off the green outside with a paring knife, exposing the bright yellow fruit. After making cuts in the fruit every inch or so, she handed it to Pablo, who sat the little boy down on the grass and gave him the treat.

"Hey, Cleo, come sit over here with us," Pablo called. "I need to stay with Miguel so he doesn't walk around with this stick in his mouth."

I grabbed a soda out of the cooler, and a piece of chocolate cake and joined them on the grass. I switched into holiday mode, letting myself relax into the leisurely atmosphere. I absently watched a young woman on a nearby blanket strewn with clothes and food spread mayonnaise from a gallon jar onto split buns. She slapped meat, cheese, lettuce, and tomato onto each bun, topped it with pickled jalapeños from a half-opened gallon can, put mayonnaise on the bun top, set the sandwich on a paper napkin from a package of about a thousand napkins, and went on to make another. I wondered whether she had stopped at Sam's Club on her way to the park or whether these huge jars of condiments were her everyday supplies.

It was a relief to just sit quietly, listen to the laughing, talking and shouting around me, and enjoy some people-watching. A tiny dark-haired boy, dressed only in baggy brown shorts that hung down to his ankles, slurped ice cream from a styrofoam dish as he chased a slightly older girl in a bright pink and yellow swim suit. A heavy man in long pink and blue shorts, topped with a purple shirt too small to fit over his fat belly, strolled hand-in-hand with a large woman in red shorts and a yellow tank top stretched tight over massive breasts. A fleshy dark-haired young woman walking a Chihuahua came by wearing a wet white tee shirt that said "My Big Fat Greek 5K." Close behind her came a boy who looked to be about ten, wearing a backwards baseball cap and speaking rapid Spanish into a cell phone as he checked his man-sized wristwatch.

My eyes wandered to the creek. A teenage girl in a skimpy two-piece blue swimsuit and a guy with dreadlocks floated along in a large inner tube. They stopped in a shallow area, and stood encircled in the tube for a long kiss. Nearby, I noticed a young couple sitting on a large rock in the middle of the creek holding hands and talking intently, as their feet dangled in the rushing water. Just as I started thinking about how much fun it can be to share a summer Sunday with someone you love, Pablo suggested we go over to my place for a while to talk.

It was about 6:00 by then, Miguel had finished his mango and gone off to the playground, and the family had started to pack up. We said goodbye and followed the pedestrian path along the bridge over Boulder Creek, through the tunnel under Canyon Boulevard, and across another bridge over the Farmers Ditch back to my house.

I had a new Merlot I'd been wanting to try, so we took the bottle and a couple of glasses out to the patio. I told Pablo I needed to tell him about what had been going on with Sharon's situation and with my involvement. I made it clear he didn't have to believe in Tyler or any of Sharon's contact experiences, but that I needed to tell him the whole story. He took a big drink of wine, and agreed to listen.

I went through it all, trying not to leave anything out—even the parts that could make me look flaky. Pablo was much more concerned about what was going on with Dr. Ahmed, and about Erik's plant-growing business than he was about what might have happened to Adam. Strangely, he didn't know about the complaint Waycroft had made about me. Of course, Pablo lives in Longmont, doesn't get the Boulder paper—actually he's usually too busy to read any paper. Still, you'd think someone would have told him about it. But maybe they thought it was too much of a ticklish situation.

After he heard all I had to say, Pablo was full of warnings. "Cleo, you're in way over your head with this Dr. Ahmed situation," he said, using his overbearing police-detective voice. "You have no idea how dangerous he may be. You should steer clear of him and anyone connected to him."

I tried to keep it light. "That could be a little hard to do. He is Gramma's doctor after all."

"Come on, Cleo. You know what I mean. It's one thing to talk to him about Martha's care, but you'd be better off not prying into his other activities. And that guy Erik is beginning to sound more and more like some kind of con artist after whatever money he can get from anyone."

No surprise there. Pablo had disliked Erik from the get-go. I tried to get him to rethink that reaction. "I know you don't like Erik, Pablo. But I'm wondering how much of the way you feel about him has to do with his spending time with me."

"Mostly, I just don't see why you would want to get involved with someone who's out to rip people off with sleazy business deals."

"I haven't invested any money in his business. He gave me the plants as a gift."

"Whatever, Cleo. I guess he's not as important to you as this situation you've gotten into with Sharon. You should let that go. You're not a detective. If the police think there's anything to investigate, they'll do it. But your involvement is creating trouble for you and for Sharon. Now you've got this complaint against you, and who knows what else her father may come up with if you keep on."

I knew everything he said came from a place of concern for me. I didn't like hearing it, but I listened to what he had to say. I didn't agree I should back off of helping Sharon, but I decided not to get into it with him about that. I simply said, "You're right that the whole thing has turned out to be more complicated than I expected." Most likely he thought I would take his advice, but of course I had no intention of doing that.

All in all, Pablo wasn't a lot of help. He did say he'd see what he could find out about Adam's stolen computer and the strange phone message on Adam's machine.

I figured that was pretty much all he was going to offer, so I decided to move on. My mind's eye flashed back to the young couples kissing in the creek that afternoon. I wanted that tenderness and intimacy with Pablo, but we weren't going to get there with the discussion we were having. So I said, "Thanks for listening, Pablo. And I appreciate your suggestions. But I don't think there's much more to say about it right now."

I asked him about a few friends we'd known back in college when we were all art majors and we talked lazily for a while about who'd gotten their art into shows and how they were doing. Pablo told me how excited he was about a conference on marketing for artists he was going to in Oregon the next week, and we fantasized about finding ways to make good money from our art. Then I got up, walked over to his chair, leaned down, and gave him a soft kiss. He pulled me on to his lap for more kisses. When tenderness gave way to passion, we made our way to the bedroom. For a minute I had the strange feeling Tyler was watching us, but I quickly got caught up in our lovemaking and forgot about it.

Before Pablo left in the morning, he re-issued his warnings. I smiled sweetly and ignored the lot.

28

On Monday I had a busy morning with clients. By noon voice messages were piled up on my phone. One was from Sharon, asking me to drop by her office if I came over to Shady Terrace to visit Gramma. I was already feeling guilty about not visiting Gramma over the weekend and had planned to go over after my 1:00 client.

When I got there, I noticed a police car in the parking lot. I went by Sharon's office to see what was up. Her door was closed, but looking through the glass side panels, I saw a policeman and two men in suits talking with her. I decided to go on to visit Gramma and stop by to see Sharon after. But she noticed me walking by, and came out and got me. The men in suits turned out to be drug enforcement agents investigating Dr. Ahmed. Sharon wanted me to tell them what I had overheard in the hall outside Dr. Ahmed's office a week ago Saturday. They had a bunch of questions, but I didn't know anything other than what I'd heard in the conversation between Ahmed and the unidentified woman in his office, so they didn't keep me long.

Over on the Alzheimer's unit, staff were whispering to each other in corners. Tanya pretty much ignored me. The residents were agitated, as if picking up the bad vibes somehow. I found Gramma in her room. As soon as she saw me, she asked, "When will James be here? I need to see James." Her eyes darted around the room and she fidgeted with the buttons on her blouse.

"He's not going to be able to come today, Gramma. Maybe I

can help you."

"No, I need James. Tell him it's important." Her eyes pleaded with me.

Gramma, I'm here now. Is there something I can do to help?"

"No, I need to talk to James." Gramma grabbed my arm and pulled me closer. "I need James."

We went on like that for a few more minutes, getting nowhere. I would have liked to ask her what bothered her, but I knew she wouldn't be able to tell me and talking about it would have only frustrated her more. So I sat with her, held her hand and calmed her down by playing one of her favorite CDs until I had to leave to get back to my office for a late client.

I was on my way out of the parking lot when Pablo called. "Cleo, you need to stay away from that Dr. Ahmed, and don't be talking about him either," he said in his police voice.

"Actually, I'm at Shady Terrace. The police are here, and they've already asked me about him. So what's the big deal?"

"It's a big undercover drug trafficking bust. I can't tell you any more, but you should check tomorrow morning's paper."

"So, do they have Ahmed in custody now?" I asked, momentarily forgetting that Pablo had just told me to stay away from Ahmed.

"I told you I can't talk about it, Cleo. I just wanted to tell you to stay out of it—okay?"

"Fine. Thanks for the heads up. I'll talk to you tomorrow." I had to hurry to get back to my office, and I figured Pablo wasn't going to tell me any more anyway.

That evening, I called Sharon to see if she could fill me in. She said Ahmed wasn't at Shady Terrace that day, but everyone was talking about him and a couple of the nurses. No one really knew what was happening, except it had something to do with drugs. All the resident charts were being audited. I told her what Pablo had said about tomorrow's paper.

"So things should be popping tomorrow over at Shady Terrace," I said.

"Actually, we're going camping tomorrow up in Rocky Mountain

National Park—with Erik," Sharon said. "The surprise Erik had for Nathan on Saturday was a tent! Nathan was so excited, he could hardly wait to go camping. It turned out that Erik had already reserved a camping site for this week, hoping we could go. I decided a break would be good for me and Nathan, so we're going tomorrow."

"Wow, I'm surprised you could get time off from work on such short notice."

"I had already been planning to take most of this week off to spend some time hanging out with Nathan, once soccer camp ended. Actually, Erik knew that—so that's why he made the reservation for this week."

That didn't surprise me. Erik seemed to be good at knowing everything about everyone. I began to think we were all part of some master plan of his.

"So, tomorrow is Tuesday," I said. "When will you be back?"

"Don't worry. We'll be back in time for my Contact session Friday afternoon. I have a strong feeling that I'm going to reach Adam this time."

First thing the next morning, I got the paper off my porch. Sure enough. There it was on the front page.

Local Physician Accused of Drug Trafficking

(DENVER) – Colorado U.S Attorney Morris Maxwell today announced the arrest of pain clinic owner Dr. Fahim Ahmed and pharmacy owners Todd and Samantha Hadden, all of Boulder County, on 12 counts of trafficking in Oxy-Contin and other controlled substances, and other charges involving improper narcotic drug prescriptions that resulted in more than $1 million in Medicaid fraud.

The felony criminal charges allege that the Boulder physician and pharmacy operators provided the controlled narcotic oxycodone to patients unnecessarily and in potentially lethal doses at high cost to taxpayers.

"We have shut down a medical practice and pharmacy kickback scheme that our investigators found was fraudulently billing the state Medicaid program over a million dollars," Maxwell said. "We are prosecuting a sophisticated drug-dealing operation. By taking this action, we are shutting down suppliers of a highly addictive drug that has been improperly distributed."

The lawsuit charges Ahmed with prescribing Schedule II and Schedule III controlled drugs without providing good faith medical examinations and without need or medical justification. Drug Enforcement Administration and Colorado Bureau of Investigation investigators found the physician to be running a patient mill with patient examinations typically being cursory at best and lasting no more than a few minutes. After these exams, he routinely prescribed a mix of Lortab, Oxycontin, Soma and Xanax that local pharmacists dubbed the "Ahmed cocktail."

The DEA and the CBI estimated that Ahmed's prescription pads were used to deliver more than 10,000 illegal doses of OxyContin, sometimes for resale on the streets. As police were taking him into custody, Ahmed said he only prescribed pain killers to people who genuinely needed them.

But undercover agents said that when they went into Ahmed's We Feel Your Pain Clinic, they were able to get out quickly with a potent painkiller. "They would go in with old MRIs or old x-rays. Most of the time he didn't even look at the x-rays, and he would write them a script for OxyContin or methadone," explains Lt. Gary Absher.

Some of Ahmed's patients have also been arrested in this investigation. Police say they were cashing in on the painkillers by selling them on the streets.

The felony complaint also alleges that the physician pursued an illegal kickback and referral scheme that directed business for drugs prescribed for residents of Shady Terrace Health Care Center to Todd's Pharmacy, owned and operated by the Hadens. The scheme facilitated improper drug billings to the state Medicaid program totaling more than

$1 million.

Shady Terrace employee, Penny Easterbrook, LPN, was arrested yesterday on a warrant while leaving Todd's Pharmacy. She had with her owe sheets—a list of people to whom she had fronted drugs, who still owed her money.

Also involved in the investigation were the Colorado department of Health and Environment, the Boulder County Drug Task Force, the Boulder Police Department, the Longmont Police Department, and the Boulder District Attorney's Office.

Ahmed's Colorado physician's license was suspended under an emergency order. Administrators at Shady Terrace Health Care Center, where Ahmed is the medical director, refused to comment for publication.

I had almost finished reading the article for the second time, when Sharon called. "Can you believe it? This must be what Jenny was talking about. Remember I told you that when Adam was working on that website for Ahmed, he was kind of suspicious about all the drugs? I'll bet he confronted him and Ahmed realized he knew too much and had him killed!"

"You could be right," I said. Do you think he would have known that Adam was going to the Grand Canyon.?"

"Absolutely! Adam talked about the trip to anyone who would listen before he went. After he died, I can't tell you how many people told me how much he'd been looking forward to being at the canyon. Everyone knew. And he did that work for Ahmed not long before he went."

"I wonder how we can find out how much Adam knew about him. If you can actually reach Adam, maybe he can tell us. Of course we'd still need proof. No one is going to accept a dead man's word."

"I'm going to talk to the police this morning before we go camping," Sharon said. "I want to be sure they question Ahmed about what happened to Adam."

29

At about 10:00 that morning, Sharon called again. The harsh reality of police department procedure had crushed her earlier excitement. She sounded as frustrated as a rat running circles in a maze.

"They refuse to question Ahmed about Adam's death because they say they have no evidence of murder or any foul play. I told them over and over that Adam would never be so careless that he'd slip off a trail like that, but they just said, 'Ma'am, his death was ruled accidental by the county medical examiner in Arizona. We can't question someone about a death we have no reason to believe he was involved in, especially when the death was ruled an accident.' It's so frustrating! How are they ever going to get any evidence if they won't question anyone?"

"I agree that's disappointing, but I'm not surprised. Maybe when they're questioning Ahmed about the drug trafficking, he'll let something slip that will make them suspicious about Adam. Or maybe we'll find out something if you contact Adam. Maybe we should wait a few days and talk to them again. If Ahmed had Adam killed or did it himself, he's going to have a hard time covering it up now that he's in so much trouble."

"Couldn't you talk to your boyfriend? Isn't he a policeman? Maybe he could convince them."

"The thing is, Pablo doesn't actually believe that Adam was murdered either. He says the same thing about no evidence. I can bring it up with him, but I don't think he'll be much help."

"Please try. I don't want to let Ahmed get away with this." She was silent for a few seconds, then sighed, "I'm not really in the mood for a camping trip, but I promised Nathan, and I don't want to disappoint him, so we're going. I guess I'll talk to you on Friday."

I met with a couple of clients, and had just finished some charting while lunching on yogurt and fruit at my desk when I got a call from Narmada.

"Cleo, I need to bring you something. Are you going to be at your office this afternoon?"

Great, just what I needed—another visit from Narmada. "I'll be here, but I have clients. What is it that you need to bring me? Can you put it in the mail?"

"Not exactly. It's a computer."

"Why are you bringing me a computer?"

"It's actually Adam's computer. I want to get it back to Sharon, but being around her unbalances my energy connections and messes with my intuitive sense. I thought I could bring it to you, and you could get it back to her."

"Wow! You have Adam's stolen computer?"

"Look, I didn't steal it. But I have it now, and having stolen property is bad karma. I need to get it back to Sharon. So, can I bring it to you?"

I had some questions, but I told her to bring it by at 4:30, when I'd be done with my clients.

She showed up right on time. I had moved my car so she could park in back of the office, and went out to help her bring the computer in. She wore a tight white cropped top that showed off her flat bare midriff above a long pink and white gypsy-style skirt. No question all that yoga gets results.

This business of her bringing me the computer felt strange. I was curious and a little skeptical. "How can I tell if this is Adam's computer?" I asked as she opened the back of her SUV.

She stopped dead and turned to face me with a troubled look. "Lack of trust can be toxic, Cleo. You should know that. You need to accept what the universe offers you." Well, she had me there. How did she know trust is one of my issues?

"It's not that I don't believe you. I'd just like a few more details about how you ended up with Adam's computer, and how you know it's his."

"I have a very high level of trust, and I am also attuned to people's emotional frequencies, so when the person who gave me this computer said it was Adam's, I knew it was true."

I still wanted answers. "So who was this person who stole the computer, why did they take it, and why did they give it to you?"

Narmada shook her wild mop of dark hair vigorously in my direction. "None of that is important to you. You don't need to know, and I don't want to pass that negative energy on to you."

"Oh, go ahead and tell me. I think I can handle some negative energy."

"Look, Cleo, I'm returning the computer. Isn't that enough? Whatever—it will have to be, because I'm not going to talk about it anymore."

I figured I could mention the police, or even call them, since Sharon had reported the theft, but I decided getting the computer back was the main priority right now. If I involved the police, they'd probably impound the computer as evidence or something and we'd never be able to look at what Adam had on there. So I kept quiet as we took the computer inside.

"I have to tell you, no one was able to boot up this computer anyway," Narmada said, as we set the computer down on a table. So it's not as if Adam's privacy was invaded or anything."

"I don't know whether that will make Sharon feel any better about someone stealing it, but I guess it's good that no one messed with Adam's files."

"Cleo, you might not want to keep this computer around here too long. I have a strong sense that it contains some evil material.

I'm glad to be getting rid of it. By the way, how are you coming with Donald Waycroft's attack?"

"I'm still working on my written response to the regulatory board," I said, thinking the less discussion I had with Narmada about this, the better.

"Don't forget you have waves of positive energy supporting you." The woman actually waved her arms through the air as she said it. "I hope you can feel that. We're getting a protest rally together soon. Well, I've got to run. Have faith!"

And with that, she bounded out the back door to her SUV and took off.

30

I sat there for a while staring at the computer. Sharon wouldn't be back until Thursday or possibly Friday morning. And Erik, who supposedly had a disk that would boot it up, was gone too. So just to see for myself, I took it over to my desk, connected it to my monitor and keyboard, and turned it on. Sure enough, it asked for a user name and password. I made a couple of guesses, but got the error message *"The system could not log you on. Make sure your user name and domain are correct, then type your password again. Letters in passwords must be typed using the correct case. Make sure that Caps Lock is not on."* So I unhooked the computer and put it in a closet to keep it safe until Sharon got back.

It was 6:00 by then and I was ready to go home, grab a quick bite to eat, and get some painting done. With all that had been going on, I'd been totally neglecting my art.

I was in the kitchen microwaving some frozen chicken tandoori with spinach and rice, when Pablo called.

"So did you read the article? What did you think?"

"Interesting, for sure. Sharon thinks Adam found out some of this stuff when he worked on Ahmed's website, and maybe confronted Ahmed and maybe Ahmed had him killed. She talked to the Boulder police about it this morning, but they wouldn't take her seriously."

"Of course not. From what you said, there's no evidence that her husband was murdered. And didn't you say it was ruled an accidental death in Arizona?"

"Well, yes. But that doesn't mean they were right. And if they refuse to ever consider any other possibilities, how can they be sure they were right?"

"Okay Cleo, we're way past anything I have any jurisdiction over. You were right about Ahmed giving out too many drugs and being involved in some illegal activity, but that doesn't mean he's a murderer."

"But he might be."

"True, but anyone might be. We need evidence, not just supposition. Anyway, I have something else to tell you. I did some checking into Erik Vaughn—which, by the way isn't his real name."

"What is his name?"

"He's used quite a few aliases. But his real name is Horace Honigman."

"Well, I can see why he'd want to use a different name," I said, thinking I couldn't really picture Erik as a Horace.

"It may not be a great name, but I don't think that's his reason." Pablo sounded exasperated with me, which I thought was unwarranted.

"I guess there's no way we'll know what his reasons are unless he tells us.."

"As a matter of fact, I was able to track down his brother in Minneapolis. He said Horace has changed his name a lot because of some shady business deals."

"You found Erik's brother?" I refused to call him Horace. "Is his name Harry?" I asked, remembering that Jenny had told Sharon to ask Erik about his brother Harry.

"Yes, Harry Honigman. He runs a seafood restaurant there—called Harry's Grill—very upscale and popular. He didn't want to talk much about Horace. Said he's no good and don't lend him any money."

"How did you find out all this?"

"A few people owed me some favors. But that's not the point. The issue is this guy isn't who he says he is, and his business may not be legitimate. I'm still looking into that. But I wanted to let you know you should stay away from him."

"Thanks for the advice. Maybe he is dangerous. But I am a therapist and I deal with quite a few strange people. I can handle Erik if I need to."

"Hey Cleo, you could be a little more appreciative. This guy could be big trouble for you."

"Well you could give me a little more credit for being a professional who knows what I'm doing. And anyway, I asked you to help me find out what happened to Adam, not to snoop around about Erik." I knew I should be grateful he watched out for me, but I was feeling irritated and kind of smothered by his superior attitude.

"Since when is police work called snooping? And you're the one who told me all the stuff about his slippery business deals."

"And you were jealous that this good looking guy paid some attention to me, so you jumped on the chance to bring him down." I knew I was exaggerating and also being contrary, which wasn't quite fair, since I had questions about Erik, but I hated Pablo telling me who I should stay away from.

"Look, Cleo, if you want to take your chances with him, so be it. But don't say I didn't warn you."

And before I could come back with a quick retort, he hung up.

31

After I finished eating, I went out to my studio to paint. But I couldn't keep my mind off Erik, or Horace or whoever he was. I thought about getting the phone number for Harry's Grill in Minneapolis and calling his brother to try to get some information. But I was afraid the brother would just hang up on me, since he'd told Pablo he didn't want to talk about Erik.

In spite of my assumed nonchalance with Pablo, I did have concerns about Erik and I did want to know more about him. I thought about Tyler telling me on Sunday that I needed to line up, that people were going under fast and needed serious help from me. Of course, those people could be the ones being scammed by Dr. Ahmed, and now that would be stopped. But I wasn't involved in investigating Ahmed, so why would Tyler push me to do something about him? It was more likely he meant I should stop Erik from scamming people with his herbs and nutrition business.

I wished Minneapolis were closer so I could drop in on Harry. But wait—Minneapolis is less than a two-hour plane flight. Why not just do it? I had a bunch of frequent flyer miles with Frontier, so I gave them a call. No problem. I booked myself a flight leaving Denver at 7:00 am the next day. Even with the one-hour time change, I'd be there at 10:00 am, giving me plenty of time to track down Harry before my return flight left Minneapolis at 7:30 that evening. I spent about an hour on the phone canceling my Wednesday appointments, and went to bed to get some sleep before my early-morning flight.

The flight was uneventful and on time. On the plane, I sat next to a young woman from Minneapolis who was on her way home from visiting her parents in Boulder. I asked her about Harry's Grill. She knew it—said it was a casual but expensive art-deco seafood restaurant in downtown Minneapolis on the Nicollet Mall.

While following the airport signs to ground transportation, I debated whether to take a bus or a taxi downtown. Since I didn't know exactly how to get to Harry's Grill, I decided to spring for the taxi. There were lots of them lined up, so I was soon on my way, enjoying my first view of Minneapolis—a tall city skyline where gleaming modern high-rises seemed to have pushed their way up between substantial brick buildings that looked like they had withstood many a frigid winter.

That July day was anything but frigid. A wave of hot, humid air hit me when I stepped out of the air-conditioned Minneapolis-St. Paul airport. It was sunny and, according to the pilot's report before we landed, about 80 degrees. But it felt much warmer to me because of the stickiness, which we don't get in Colorado. The muggy air enveloped me again as I got out of the cab at Nicollet Mall.

I found myself on a festive pedestrian mall with a narrow driving lane for busses and taxis. Stores and restaurants lined each side of the street, which was bordered by wide sidewalks with trees, flowers and outdoor restaurant seating. Harry's Grill was in an elegant brick building with dark green awnings and a black wrought iron door. I took a deep breath and walked in.

Inside was quite a contrast to the outside. The air was cool and the décor accentuated that feeling—mostly shiny black with peach accents. An enormous mirrored wall behind a long rounded bar was lined with liquor bottles. Seating was in curved booths with chrome accents.

It was about 11:30 by then, so Harry's was serving lunch. I asked the hostess if I could see Harry Honigman.

"Harry's in the kitchen right now. Was he supposed to meet you?"

"No. But I'm here from Colorado just this one day, and I really need to talk to him."

"If you wait until I seat these people, I can call him," she said, motioning a party of six to follow her to a booth. She got them set and returned to her hostess desk. "What did you say your name was again?" she asked, picking up the phone.

"It's Cleo, but he doesn't know me. Tell him it's about his brother, and it's very important."

The hostess spoke to someone on the phone, who relayed the information to Harry. "Can you come back at 2:30?" she asked me.

"Sure. That will work. Thanks for taking time to call him."

I headed back out to Nicollet Mall to find something to do for a few hours. The food smells in Harry's had brought on some hunger pangs, so I decided to look for a place to eat. At a nearby bakery café, I filled up quickly on a huge spinach salad, a generous slice of cheese and mushroom focaccia bread, and an enormous iced tea. I suspected that large portions might be a Minnesota tradition to help locals stoke up for the long winters.

After lunch, I wandered through Marshall Field's, Neiman Marcus, and Saks Fifth Avenue. Big city shopping is a novelty for me, as Boulder doesn't have these department stores in town, and I don't often go to Denver or its suburbs to shop. The hours passed quickly, and it was soon time to walk back to Harry's Grill.

The hostess recognized me when I walked in. "Harry's over at the bar," she said pointing to a dark-haired man wearing chinos and a white shirt, seated on a barstool and talking intently with the bartender. I walked over and stood next to him until he finished his conversation, turned his head in my direction and looked at me. He looked amazingly like Erik, except nowhere near as fit. He was medium height like Erik, but stockier, without the muscles. He had Erik's dark eyes and curly brown hair, but his face was marred by a two-inch scar on his left cheek.

"Are you Harry Honigman?"

"That's right. Are you Cleo from Colorado?" He was still seated facing the bar, looking sideways at me.

"Yes. Could you spare a few minutes to talk about your brother?

I guess his name is Horace, but I know him as Erik."

Harry looked bored, his eyes half-lidded. "I've spent way too much time in my life talking about my brother. What do you want to know?"

I decided I needed to get his attention quickly, or at least get an answer to one of my questions, so I said, "Who are Amber and Melissa?"

Harry spun his bar stool around to face me. His eyes were wide open now, boring into me. "He told you about Amber and Melissa?"

"No, Jenny said we should ask him about them."

"Jenny's been dead for over a year. Why are you here now?" He sounded like I was trying to sell him a used car, but I ignored his suspicious tone and answered in my calm-therapist voice.

"It's a long story. Could we talk somewhere a little more private?"

He motioned me over to a booth. "Would you like something to drink while we talk?"

"Water would be great," I said, scooting into the middle of the booth.

As Harry joined me in the booth, the bartender brought over a couple of bottles of Evian, two ice-filled glasses and a tiny dish of lime wedges. As I poured some water into a glass, I speculated as to what it would be like to have your own bartender.

"Jenny was a sweet lady," Harry's face had softened. "How did you know her?"

"My grandmother lives at the nursing home where she worked. Jenny was Gramma's favorite nurse."

"So what did Jenny tell you about Amber and Melissa? And have you talked to Horace about them?"

"It's complicated. I've only known Erik—or Horace—for about a month and he insists he's never heard of Amber or Melissa. In fact, half the time he denies having a brother, says he has no family at all. Are Amber and Melissa your sisters?"

Harry sighed. "No, they were Horace's first two wives."

"So he's divorced from both of them?"

He stared off into the distance as if trying to recollect long-forgotten details, then looked back at me. "Not exactly. It's a long story, but I need to hear more about your involvement with Horace before I tell it."

I told him about Adam's death, Erik's friendship with Adam and with Sharon and Nathan, Erik's nutrition and herb-growing business, what Erik had told me about his belief that Adam's death was suicide, and how he told conflicting stories about his background. When I got to the Contact Project part, and described Sharon's contact with Jenny, he looked skeptical, but kept listening. I finished by saying, "So after I found out that you really do exist, I decided I needed to meet you to find out if you have any idea what Jenny was trying to tell us."

Harry sighed again, but this time he gave me a tiny half-smile. "Okay, I'll tell you what I know. But you may need something stronger than water to hear this story. We're famous for our martinis. Or maybe you'd like some single malt scotch?" He jumped up and started toward the bar, looking back to check on my order.

I was tempted but I decided I needed to keep all my faculties sharp. "Thanks, but I'll stay with the water for now."

He got himself a drink of something on the rocks, came back to the booth, settled in, and began his story. "Well, first of all, we lived with our parents, who did not abuse us, when we were growing up in L.A. Dad was a construction worker, Mom was a waitress. We weren't poor, but certainly not rich—just comfortable. I'm six years older than Horace, and we got along fine when he was really little. He looked up to me, and I enjoyed teaching him stuff. But, by the time he was six and I was twelve, that changed. His true character was coming out. He made a game of getting me to let him use my stuff, even when he didn't really even want the stuff. And sometimes he'd break or damage my things on purpose, just for the heck of it. Like the time he dropped some of my best baseball cards in a mud puddle in front of the house."

Harry stopped and looked down pensively, as though he could

still see those precious cards floating in the muddy water. He took a long sip of his drink and went on. "Sometimes I'd go after him and fight with him. He was vicious—that's how I got the scar on my face. But usually when I got mad, Horace would cry and pretend to be really sorry, and I would let him get away with it. I kept thinking I could get him to change."

I began to see why Harry didn't like to talk about his brother. "Didn't your parents do anything to stop him?"

"My parents tried, but Horace was immune to punishment. He lied and stole like a pro and nothing worked to change his behavior. It was like he knew the difference between right and wrong, but he didn't care because he was special. He saw no reason to feel sorry about the pain and destruction he caused. Sometimes he'd pretend to feel remorse but they knew he was faking. So they pretty much gave up."

I began to feel kind of stupid for ever finding Erik attractive or feeling sympathy for him. Maybe Pablo's take on him was more accurate than mine. But Erik had managed to convince three women to marry him, and Sharon liked him. "He has a way of attracting women," I said.

"Oh man, does he ever!" Harry rolled his eyes. "I was always amazed that as a teenager, Horace could have his pick of girls, even though he was really bossy with them. Like one girl in high school who liked pleasing him, and the harder he made it the more she liked it. Sometimes Horace would make demands just to see how far he could push her. Then, after he had her totally under his thumb, he dropped her with no warning. She kept calling him begging him to tell her what she had done, but he refused to talk to her at all."

"Did that happen a lot?" I wondered how Jenny had done with that.

Harry swirled the ice around in his drink and shook his head. "Actually, I wasn't around much while he was in high school. I know most of that from what my mom told me. I moved up to San Francisco to study at the California Culinary Academy and then I apprenticed at some restaurants up there to get experience. So during that time I was mostly only seeing Horace at vacations. But in 1988, I got a great job offer at a restaurant in L.A., so I moved back there. Horace was involved in some multilevel marketing scam where they got people to buy supplies to assemble holiday decorations at home that they could supposedly sell back to the company. But the supplies were crummy and the directions were worse and when the people tried to get paid, the company told them the products were no good and refused to pay. So Horace and his partner were making money selling supplies but no one else got anything."

"Hmm…that sounds a lot like the herb growing kits he's selling right now," I said.

"I'm not surprised. Horace just keeps on using people. He told me once that most people lead such silly little lives, it's stupid not to take advantage of them. He said it's like they are some sort of wind-up toys set on a path to chug along. They just go until they run out of steam and then stop, dead in their tracks. And all the time they are going along, they don't even see what is going on around them."

I was stunned. Was this actually Erik's philosophy of life? He sounded like a sociopath. I needed to hear more. "That's amazing," I said. "He gives the impression that he genuinely cares about people. Or about Sharon and Nathan at least. So what was the story with Amber and Melissa?"

Harry drained his drink, set his glass to one side, and said, "Okay, here's the story. Amber was Horace's first wife. He married her in 1990, when he was 24. She was one of those clumsy fat girls who thought she'd never get a man, much less a good-looking guy like Horace. But her father, Jim, was a widower who had tons of money. Amber was an only child, and he doted on her. A perfect setup for Horace. The father was suspicious at first, but Horace turned on the charm, and in no time he convinced Jim that he was earnest, sincere, hard-working—whatever Jim wanted to believe. When Horace and Amber got married, Jim gave them a house and a bunch of stock. And he took Horace into his construction business as a full partner. A few years later, Jim died from a bad fall from the top of a building they were working on. Horace took over the business. Amber was never the same after her dad died. She got more and more depressed until she overdosed on pills and booze. Most people thought Horace was heartbroken, but from my view all was going according to Horace's plan. He was only 28—took his inheritance and moved on."

The story shocked me, but I didn't react because I didn't want to distract him from the telling. "So, how long ago was that?" I asked.

"About ten years ago, and it was the last time he lived anywhere near me," Harry said. "I had met Loretta by then, and we were getting married. She didn't want to stay in L.A.—thought it was too plastic. And her family lived here in Minneapolis. I was lucky enough to find a good chef position here, so we moved. We decided to stay, I opened Harry's Grill, and we've been here ever since. I haven't had much to do with Horace except when he's showed up here—always to ask for money—or as he puts it, to let me in on an incredible investment opportunity. I never bite, so I don't know why he keeps trying."

I felt more and more alarmed about what Erik might have in mind for Sharon, but I kept a poker face and made no comment. I was after information—which I was getting—and I didn't want to interrupt the flow.

Harry looked increasingly disgusted as he continued his summary. "Horace has lived all over, had all kinds of businesses. I couldn't tell you much about them. I do know he married again in 1994. Her name was Melissa. I don't know much about that marriage, except that Melissa left him a couple of years later and disappeared. I don't know whether or not they ever got divorced. I hope they were divorced before he married Jenny. I guess you know they were only married two years before she died." He stopped and looked at me inquiringly.

"Yes," I said, "that was so tragic—her forgetting her inhaler and having that asthma attack when they were backpacking. She was only 34. When did you meet her? I'm guessing Erik—or Horace—didn't bring her here to meet you, since he didn't want her to know anything about him or even his real name."

Harry nodded. "You're right. Horace never brought her here. I only met Jenny once. It wasn't long before she died. She came up here alone to see me, without telling Horace. It was …" A crash of glasses from the bar behind us interrupted Harry in mid-sentence. As Harry jumped up, I heard a woman yelling obscenities from the other end of the restaurant.

I sat where I was, trying to revise my impression of Erik in a way that incorporated this new information—and hoping Harry would come back and finish the story.

32

fter twenty minutes went by, I started to worry about the time. My flight back to Denver was at 7:30, so I figured I needed to leave for the airport by 5:30 to allow for traffic delays, airport security and all. It was already 4:30, and there was more I needed to find out from Harry.

Just then he showed up carrying a tray with a bottle of chardonnay, two wine glasses, and a plate of crab-stuffed mushrooms. "I can't let you leave without tasting anything," he said with a grin. "And a little alcohol usually helps anyone who is talking about Horace."

I couldn't refuse, and I was so glad I didn't. The fruity wine was the perfect complement to the spicy cheese-topped crab filling nestled in the hot mushrooms. I savored the flavors and relaxed into the moment.

After I'd devoured two mushrooms and half a glass of wine, I decided to get back to business. "So you said Jenny came to see you before she died?"

"Right. She had some concerns about Horace and she nosed around in his stuff until she ran across a letter I'd written him about some money we inherited after Dad died. My address was still the same so she was able to find me right away. She had begun to realize there was a lot she didn't know about him, so she came up here to get some information."

"What kind of concerns did she have?"

Harry shrugged in a what-can-you-expect sort of way. "No big surprise. She had inherited some money from her grandfather that she had in an account of her own, and Horace had forged her name and withdrawn most of it. When she found out and confronted him, he blew up—denied that he'd done it, accused her of being crazy, told her if she didn't trust him, he didn't want to have anything to do with her. I guess that was kind of the last straw for her, given some other stuff he'd done—like lying to her, writing bad checks on their joint account, and running up huge credit card debts that he couldn't or wouldn't pay."

"What did you tell her?"

"Pretty much what I've told you today. It was mostly a surprise to her, although she had once found some papers with Amber's name and asked Horace about her. He got mad, refused to answer any questions, told her to stay out of his business. She had clearly begun to suspect that Horace had lied to her about himself, but she didn't have any facts to back up her doubts." Harry made a sour face. I wouldn't have told her all this if she hadn't asked, but she did, and I didn't want to see her end up like Amber."

"But she did end up like Amber," I said. "Well, not exactly the same, but they both died young." The parallels were hitting me smack in the face by then. So I took the risk and asked the nasty question. "Are you saying that you think Erik is responsible for both of their deaths?"

Harry flinched, but only slightly. "In different ways, yes. As far as Amber goes, he just set the wheels in motion. But with Jenny, I'd say there's a strong possibility that Horace made sure that inhaler wasn't available. She knew too much about him, and she was tired of putting up with his shit."

Clearly Harry had given Jenny's death some serious thought. Why hadn't he gone to the police with his suspicions? It was sticky, but I had to ask. "If you think that, why didn't you report it to the police when Jenny died?"

He stared down at the table for a moment and shook his head. "No point. No one will ever prove it. Horace is too slick."

I decided to go for the gold. "What about Sharon's husband,

Adam? Do you think Horace killed him too?"

Harry shrugged. "He could have if he wanted the guy dead. You said it was a few months ago?"

"April."

"I know he needed money then, because he came up here to try to convince me to invest in his latest project. A bunch of nutritional products. What a laugh! Horace knows about as much about nutrition as a pig knows about philosophy."

"So I'm guessing you passed on the investment opportunity?"

"As usual. But come to think of it, it was April when he was here. We were having a big celebration for our fifth anniversary of the restaurant. I'm not sure why, but I sent him an invitation. Every now and then, my brain goes soft or something, and I start thinking of Horace as the cute little brother I loved years ago. Anyway, he showed up, and then we couldn't get rid of him. Loretta's never liked him, wasn't happy having him at the house. But he didn't want to leave without getting me to invest in his business."

"Do you know the exact dates of when he was here?"

"Well, the celebration was on the anniversary of our opening, April 17th. That was a Thursday. Horace actually showed up before it started—surprised the hell out of me. I never thought he'd come. He even brought a gift. Now that's so like him. When he was a kid, he'd often give me something when he wanted something. Of course what he wanted was always much bigger than what he gave. But he's smart that way—knows how to soften people up."

I surreptitiously glanced at my watch. It was after 5:00. I didn't want to be rude, but I needed to get out of there, and I needed to find out exactly when Erik was in Minneapolis last April. Just as I was about to interrupt Harry by repeating my question, the hostess came over with a complicated question about some reservations for that evening.

Harry excused himself, got up and walked over to the hostess desk with her. They examined the reservation book, discussing the problem at length. Harry came back over to the table, but didn't sit down. "I have to get back to work now to get ready for the dinner crowd. Feel free to sit there and finish the wine if you want."

"Thanks, but I have to get to the airport. But it would help a lot if I knew exactly when Erik was here in April."

"Okay, let's see. I know he stayed a week, because Loretta kept telling me that seven days was as long as she'd put up with having him. And I finally had to kick him out after a week. He blew up, swore at me, accused me of being a selfish egotistical asshole who wouldn't even help his own brother when he was down." Harry laughed. "More like he was describing himself. I was glad to see the back of him. Anyway, the day I threw him out was a Wednesday. I remember because I come in early on Wednesdays to do inventory, just like I did today. So if he'd been here a week by Wednesday, he must have come on the 16th and left the 23rd."

"Thanks, Harry, for taking time and telling me all this. And thanks for the wine and mushrooms—delish! If I ever get back here, I'll be sure to come for a whole meal." I grabbed my purse and slid out of the booth.

"I'd just as soon you don't mention this trip to Horace," Harry said, following along behind me toward the front door. "He wouldn't like me telling you about his past, and I don't need any more of his retaliation."

"Sure, no problem. And thanks again."

In the taxi on the way to the airport, I thought about the gifts Erik had given Nathan. Did that mean he wanted something from Sharon? And if so, what? And come to think of it, he'd given me a gift as well. Interesting.

I felt sad for Jenny. I could understand how she could have been easily seduced by Erik's looks, charm, and persistence. He wanted her, he got her, and then he tossed her away—apparently without even minor pangs of conscience.

Now Erik was a prime candidate on my list of suspects for pushing Adam over the edge. Elisa had said she remembered that Adam died on April 15, because she was taking her taxes to the post office when she heard. If Erik followed Adam to the Grand Canyon and pushed him off the edge, he could have easily made it to Minneapolis by the next day, and used the visiting-his-brother story as a cover if he needed to explain why he was out of town.

On my return flight to Denver I mulled over the list of people who might have had reasons to get rid of Adam and who could have been at the Grand Canyon on April 15. I didn't know of a specific reason why Erik would want to kill Adam, but with all I'd just found out about him, I figured there were plenty of possibilities. Maybe Adam had found out some of Erik's secrets, like his real identity and his shady business dealings. Maybe Erik had said something that led Adam to suspect Jenny's death wasn't an accident. If Adam had confronted Erik with any of this, he was doomed for sure. And Erik could have surprised him on that trail that day.

Then there was Joel. He seemed like a nice enough guy to me, but my radar wasn't working that well lately, so I couldn't trust my gut. Joel was jealous of Adam raising Nathan, and he wanted Sharon back. In April he was living in Flagstaff about 80 miles from the Grand Canyon, and he'd been a guide for whitewater rafting trips down the Colorado River in the canyon.

And Sharon's father, Donald Waycroft was in Las Vegas, which is farther—nearly 300 miles from the canyon's South Rim—but doable, especially for a clever, disciplined fellow like him. It was no secret he didn't like Adam, but it was a stretch to see that as a reason to murder his daughter's husband.

To me, Dr. Ahmed seemed to have the most likely motive. If Adam was onto his fraudulent business, he would have surely wanted him gone. I had no way of knowing where he'd been on April 15. Could have been at the canyon. Or, he might well have connections with hit men who could have handled it for him. But how to get the police to look into this possibility when they were so convinced Adam's death was an accident?

Less likely, but still possible was Narmada, who hated Adam, even though hate is a toxic emotion that surely had a negative effect on her energy connections. She'd called Adam an asshole and said he spread lies about her all over town. And what had she been doing with Adam's computer? Of course I had no idea where she'd been on April 15th and no obvious way to find out. Maybe I could come up with some acceptable reason to ask her some questions about her schedule last spring.

Leaving aside my grim musings, my flight was uneventful. But the Colorado weather on arrival matched my ominous mood. By the time I got to my car the entire Denver-Boulder area was under a severe thunderstorm warning, with a possibility of hail and strong winds. I made it almost to Boulder before the storm hit—sheets of driving rain mixed with hail battering my car. I could barely see, but couldn't stop in the traffic, so I gritted my teeth and kept going. No good options in these severe storms.

In town, traffic was slow as cars forged through the deep water. At Arapahoe and 28th, a long line was stopped at the light. I didn't want to sit in the swirling stream. So I stayed back—then gunned the motor and charged through when the line started to move again ahead.

I was exhausted by the time I pulled into my driveway at about 9:30 p.m. To top it off, I got soaked running just the few feet from my car into the house. In the kitchen, the ceiling was leaking, so I had to mop the floor. By the time I had stripped off my wet clothes, put on a robe and fixed myself a peanut butter and jelly sandwich, it was almost 11:00.

I sat at my kitchen table in a daze contemplating the power a hail storm unleashes. It's too much, too fast, too forceful—can do a lot of damage in a short time. Hmmm…nature could be a lot like Erik—pleasant, seductive, then suddenly violent, stopping for nothing until it's ready to stop.

"Yo, Cleo. You're full on this case. But if it gets wild, you need to kick out so you don't get sucked into the falls."

"Tyler!" He was perched on my kitchen counter. "Did Erik take Jenny's inhaler out when they went camping so she would die if she had an asthma attack?"

"Chill, Cleo. Stay in the zone. It's about Sharon, not Jenny. Erik thinks he's all that, but he's a chickenhead."

"So I'm supposed to just let Erik get away with killing his wife and running who knows how many scams?"

"Watch where you are. When a wave crashes over your head, it can seem like you're in deep water, but it may be only two feet."

"Whatever, Tyler. I'm too tired to make sense of this. Either tell me something straight or go."

And he went. I dragged myself off to bed and slept until my alarm jolted me awake at 7:00 a.m.

33

As soon as I was awake enough to think, it hit me that Sharon and Nathan were camping with Erik. His camping record wasn't so good, and with all I'd heard from Harry, I was terrified for them. But I didn't know exactly where they were or how to find them. Rocky Mountain National Park is huge, with five large campgrounds, some many miles away from others. Cell phones rarely work there, and there are no land phones other than at the ranger stations.

I had just jumped into the shower when I realized Sharon might have told Joel what campground they were going to. I hustled myself out and ran dripping wet to the bedroom to grab my cell where Joel's number was programmed in from the time he'd left me a message after the horrible newspaper story. He answered on the first ring, but he didn't know any more than I did. He did want to know why I wanted to find Sharon.

"I forgot to ask her when she's coming back, and I need to know when we can meet tomorrow," I said in an admittedly feeble attempt to explain.

"So you were going to drive an hour up to Rocky Mountain National Park and look for them at a campground just to find out when they were coming home?" Joel asked incredulously. "Come on, Cleo. What's up?"

I didn't want to tell him about Harry, but I knew I had to say something convincing enough to get him off the phone so I could try something else. "Okay, here's the thing. My boyfriend's a detective with the Longmont Police. He did some checking and found out a few things about Erik that got me a little worried about Sharon and Nathan being out there alone with him."

"Like what?" Joel sounded so upset I began to regret calling him.

"Look Joel, I just want to find them. You don't know any more about where they are than I do, so just forget about it—okay?"

"No way! I'm going up there right now to find them. Do you want to come or not?"

I felt like I had unleashed a tornado. "Wait a minute, Joel. Let's see if we can find out where they are first. Sharon told me Erik had reserved a camping space, so someone must have a record of it. I need to get to my office, because I have clients I really can't cancel. Can you meet me there in twenty minutes and we'll decide what to do?"

After a little more convincing, he agreed. With the bad publicity I'd had lately, I didn't dare cancel any more clients. I didn't have anyone scheduled until 11:00 and I hoped we could somehow get this handled by then.

By the time Joel got to my office at 8:00, I was livid. I had called the National Park Service number for Rocky Mountain National Park, but the man who answered said he couldn't give out any information about camp reservations or campers—that there was a pay phone campers could use to contact me. I struggled to stay calm while I explained that these campers didn't know they needed to contact me. He repeated his script about being unable to give out information, this time calling me "ma'am" in an exasperated tone. I tried every way I could think of to convince him this was an emergency that warranted suspending the rules, but bureaucracy won out.

"Good grief!" I screamed when Joel walked in. "Those idiots at Rocky Mountain National Park care more about preserving privacy than they do about human life."

"Cleo, think about it," Joel said. "For all they know, you could be trying to find someone to hurt them. They can't be giving out names."

"You're probably right. It's just so frustrating! I can't see how we can find them without some information."

"Didn't you say your boyfriend is a police detective? Why don't you call him? He could find something out."

There was no way I wanted to call Pablo about Erik, after having been so snippy with him on the phone when he told me Erik might be trouble. Plus, Pablo didn't know about my little Minneapolis jaunt yesterday, and I preferred to keep it that way. "Finding people isn't exactly his thing," I said, "unless they're selling drugs."

Joel grabbed my shoulders gently but firmly. "Cleo, if you think Sharon and Nathan could be in danger, you have to do whatever you can."

"You're right. I'll call him." But I got voice mail at Pablo's office and on his cell. I left messages for him to call me right away.

"I don't know what else we can do," I said to Joel. He looked dejected. "If you want to go search for them, go ahead. But I have to stay here and meet my clients. I'd cancel them if I thought we had half a chance of finding Sharon and Nathan, but I can't see how driving up to Estes and cruising around the park is going to help."

Joel said he had the time, so why not give it a try. Right after he left, Pablo called.

"I decided you were right about Erik—or Horace, whatever you want to call him," I said, "and now I'm worried about Sharon and Nathan because they're camping with him. The park service won't give me any information about where they are and I have no way to reach them. Could you find them and get them away from him, maybe arrest him?" I heard myself getting shrill.

"Whoa, Cleo. What brought on this sudden concern? Less than two days ago, you were accusing me of being jealous and snooping into this guy's business, and now you want him arrested?"

"I talked to his brother. He told me a lot of shocking details, but I promised I wouldn't tell Erik that he's told me. So if I tell you what he said, you can't tell where you got the information."

"Never mind, Cleo. We can't arrest someone because of what his brother said anyway. But I will see if I can locate them and find out whether they're okay. If we don't find them today, I won't be able to do much, though. Don't forget I'm leaving tonight for that artists' conference in Oregon. I'll be back Sunday afternoon. You can reach me on my cell, but if you need some quick help in the next few days, you'll need to call 911."

As soon as he said it, I remembered how much he was looking forward to this conference on marketing for art show artists—hoping to get some new ideas on selling his work, and also to enjoy a gorgeous Oregon resort. It's not easy for him to get time off for an artist thing, and I didn't want to bog him down with my problems, so I told him not to worry. I promised if we didn't find Sharon and Nathan by this evening, I'd call the sheriff or police.

I went back to my work, met with several clients and returned some calls, but I had a hard time concentrating. I kept imagining grisly scenarios in which Sharon and Nathan were victims of a horrible accident. My stomach twisted and lurched as energy surged through my body in nauseating jolts. As I debated taking a break and going to the gym to work out as a way to burn off some of the tension, my phone rang. I jumped and grabbed it on the first ring. It was Sharon.

"Sharon! Are you and Nathan okay?"

"We're fine. A little tired, but we had a great trip."

"I'm so relieved to hear from you."

"Why, is something wrong?"

Oops. Now I needed to give her a reason for being anxious to hear from her. I didn't want to get into the whole Erik thing over the phone. Given her feelings about Erik, it would be a tricky conversation. I preferred to have it in person. Then I remembered the computer, so I said, "I have Adam's computer at my office."

"The police found it?"

"No—believe it or not, Natalie brought it to me."

"What? I can't believe it! She stole Adam's computer? Do you know why?"

"She said she didn't steal it, that someone else took it and then gave it to her later. She wouldn't give me any details—just a lot of nonsense about negative energy connected to it."

"You can't believe anything she says," Sharon said in an exasperated tone. "I told you she's a total liar. I bet you anything she stole it herself."

"But then why would she give it back? And she said no one was able to boot it up, so they didn't do anything to it."

"Did you tell the police? I'd love to see Natalie arrested."

"No, because I figured they'd take the computer, and we might not get it back for who knows how long."

"Good point. But I have a mountain of laundry and stuff to do tonight, so I really can't come get it now. Anyway, we can't get into it without Erik, and he's going to Denver to meet with some people who might invest in his business. So how about I get it tomorrow when I come for my contact session?"

I was relieved to hear Erik would be otherwise occupied. I wanted to keep him away from Sharon and Nathan, and from Adam's computer—but I hadn't yet decided what I would tell Sharon about him. I needed some time to think without distractions. So I took her suggestion with enthusiasm. "Tomorrow is good for me. But let's look at the computer after your contact session, so it's not a distraction."

"Okay. I'm dropping Nathan off at a friend's at 1:00, so I'll be there by 1:30 with no problem."

"Great. Don't forget to bring Adam's shirt and a picture."

34

I called Pablo to let him know Sharon and Nathan were safely home. Got his voice mail and left a message. I couldn't reach Joel either, so I left a message on his cell. I finished at my office, had a good workout at the gym, and picked up a grilled chicken burrito at Illegal Pete's to enjoy on my patio with a cold beer. Sitting out there, where Grampa and I had had so many deep discussions, I tried to access some of his wisdom. How could I best warn Sharon away from Erik, without telling things I promised Harry I wouldn't tell? And how dangerous was Erik? When Pablo got back should I tell him everything Harry told me, and let him decide what to do, or was information from a family member useless as he had implied?

"Hey Cleo, do you have any more of that beer?" I almost fell out of my chair. It was Erik. My heart thumped. Where had he come from? The sun had sunk behind the mountain while I ruminated, so I didn't notice him until he was right in front of me. Come to think of it, I hadn't heard a car either, so he must not have parked in my driveway.

"Erik! What are you doing here?" My voice sounded shrill. I knew I needed to stay calm so he didn't pick up my fear and exploit it. So I took a couple of slow deep breaths before I went on. "I thought you were in Denver talking to investors."

"Can I grab myself a beer out of the refrigerator?" Erik flashed his usual winsome smile, but after my meeting with Harry, I was forewarned.

I tried to take control of the conversation, speaking in an even no-nonsense voice. "No, Erik, you can't. I'm not in the mood for guests tonight, and I don't appreciate you showing up uninvited like this."

He scowled. "You're in a nasty mood, Cleo. What's going on?"

I was so exhausted and overwhelmed and so fed up with Erik that I lost my cool. My emotions bubbled up—my anger at his manipulative behavior, my anxiety for Sharon and Nathan, my outrage about Jenny's death. Almost as if my voice came from outside my body I heard myself blurt out, "I think I'm the one who should be asking what's going on, Erik. Or should I say Horace?"

Erik stared at me sharply, amazed I had uncovered his lies. "Why have you been spying on me? You have no right to pry into my business." His face contorted in anger. "You'd better not be telling Sharon a bunch of lies about me, or I promise you, you'll regret it." I could feel waves of rage rolling off him in my direction.

I jumped up and hastily backed away to put a little distance between us. "Don't threaten me, Erik. I'm not as easy to get rid of as Jenny was." At least I hoped I wasn't.

Erik went limp and sank into a chair. He hung his head as if in defeat. "Okay, Cleo, let's talk. Come on. Sit down."

More of his fake quick-change behavior? I didn't want him to think he could manipulate me at will, but I did want some answers. Like Harry said, the police can never pin anything on Erik. But I wanted him to have to pay for at least some of his evil deeds. I thought I at least had a chance to get some incriminating details out of him, so I decided to let him go on a little longer. I sat in a chair facing him, but about five feet away. I kept my hand on my cell phone in my pocket. "Okay, you have the floor."

He leaned forward in my direction. "Cleo, you don't know anything about my relationship with Jenny. You hardly even knew her. Don't make judgments about a situation when you don't know the facts."

"Okay, I'm listening." Calm voice again. "What are the facts?"

"Jenny had problems. She took a lot of drugs that she got from Dr. Ahmed. I knew she shouldn't have been taking all that stuff, but it helped her in some ways, so I didn't complain. She was pretty crazy, so I figured, whatever worked. Even with the drugs, she was a bitch to live with."

Now I was shocked as well as angry. No longer cool, I lashed out like a three-year-old. "So you stood by while she died from her asthma attack on that camping trip?"

"Jumping to conclusions again, Cleo. And even if you were right, you could never prove it. Your reputation around town isn't so favorable that people will be likely to believe your accusations. You're just a small-time therapist who figured out a way to trick people into believing you can contact dead people. Anyway, what business is it of yours?"

Those words stung! He knew exactly how to zing in to my most vulnerable spot. Even so, if I'd been thinking straight, I would have dropped it right there. Knowing what I knew about Erik, why push him, especially when we were alone in a fairly secluded area. But like my namesake, Cleopatra VII, I don't take kindly to being put down, and I will stand up for what I believe even when the personal consequences may be dire. So I plunged ahead. "It's my business what happens to Sharon, and I don't think she's safe with you. I'm thinking Adam had discovered your lies, which was what had him so worried. Did he know, or guess too much? Did you find a way to eliminate him like you did Jenny? Is that why you're so against Sharon contacting Adam?" I stopped for a breath.

Erik seemed strangely calm. Or maybe he was getting ready to smash me. I couldn't tell. He sat there saying nothing, just staring at me for maybe two minutes. As a therapist, I've learned to wait for people to speak, and I had vented most of my pent-up emotions by then, so I sat quietly.

Finally Erik said, "It wasn't me Adam was worried about. It was Sharon's dad, Donald Waycroft."

Wow—yet another story? "I thought you said Adam was stressed out from losing money on internet gambling."

Erik shrugged. "I said that to shut you up. I didn't want to upset Sharon by bringing up problems involving her dad."

"Oh come on, Erik. Do you expect me to believe you now, after you've lied about everything including your name?"

"Look, you wanted to know the truth. I'm telling you the truth. If you don't want to believe me, that's your problem."

"No, Erik, it's your problem. Because I'm not going to give up until we contact Adam, and find out what really happened."

"Who exactly do you think will believe the testimony of a dead man that you supposedly contacted? Think about it, Cleo. You already have a reputation as a flake. You even have a complaint filed against you as a fraud. How far do you want to push this?"

Who was calling who a fraud? I couldn't let that go by. It came over me like road rage. "You're the expert fraud artist, from what I've heard—Horace. What about all this nutrition nonsense? You're no nutritionist." I heard myself shouting this out, at the same time I thought I needed to back off before things got any more ugly.

Erik jumped up from his chair, heading in my direction. In my rush to get up before he got any closer, I turned over my chair. But he walked right by me toward the side of the house.

"Don't panic, Cleo. In spite of what you think, I'm not a killer. You're safe with me, and so is Sharon." With that Erik disappeared into the dusk, leaving me trembling like Aspen leaves in the wind.

I pulled myself together, took my dishes inside, locked the doors and sat down to figure out my next move. The wind picked up outside and clouds rolled in heralding an early-evening thunderstorm. I was jumpy, startling at every little sound. What if Erik decided to come back? Pablo was on a plane to Oregon by now. I thought about calling the Boulder police, but what could I tell them that would get them to do anything about Erik? I had no proof he'd hurt anyone and he hadn't even threatened me.

I considered going out, just to be around other people, but I was worn out from my trip the day before, plus all the emotional energy I had expended worrying about Sharon and confronting Erik. Finally I took a bath and went to bed early. I slept fitfully dreaming about someone chasing me down a long dark trail.

35

On Friday, I was still stewing about Erik when Sharon arrived for her session at 1:30. But I didn't want to distract her by talking about anything other than Adam, so I didn't mention Erik or the camping trip.

It was sunny and a bit breezy as we took our soothing stroll along Boulder Creek to help Sharon clear her mind and focus on Adam. I tuned in to the sounds of the rushing water, trying to clear my own mind, hoping to get some fresh insights. I found myself thinking about Adam's computer, which I wanted to get into without Erik's help. But I had no idea how to do that.

We got back to my office about 2:30. After I got Sharon settled in the apparition chamber, I sat down at my desk to finish my letter to the Colorado Mental Health Department of Regulatory Agencies in response to the complaint Waycroft had filed against me. Ten of the twenty days they had given me to reply had already gone by and I'd promised Bruce I'd respond in a timely way, so I wanted to get my letter into the mail.

I thought about the criticisms of spiritualists like John Edward and Rosemary Altea, who supposedly use their psychic abilities to bring messages to the living from the spirit realm. Investigators say these psychic mediums only pretend to get information from spirits, but in fact cleverly collect material from their subjects and offer it up as a mystical revelation. I was sure Waycroft saw me as just one more charlatan who pretended to be in contact with someone's dead loved one, but was actually feeding back information obtained from the living.

I am quite prepared for people to doubt me and the contact process. Which is why I'm so selective about who I take into the project, why I don't promote it or publicize it, and why I don't participate in events like Narmada's psychic fair. In fact, I mainly offer the contact opportunity to people whose grief is complicated or severe, and who I think will benefit from handling their grief in a more direct way. Sometimes they can make peace with the dead person, tie up loose ends or get answers to questions—all of which promotes healing.

I was so completely immersed in making these points in my letter, that I didn't notice how much time had gone by until the chamber door opened. It was nearly 4:00. Sharon stood in the hall, tears streaming down her face, but smiling at the same time—like a rainbow in a summer afternoon storm.

"Adam," she sobbed. "I saw him. We talked. It was amazing."

I led her slowly to the sofa in the counseling room, handed her a box of tissues, put a tall glass of water on the table next to her, and sat down in the armchair. Sharon sat wide-eyed staring off into space for several minutes, then turned to face me. "He was just like he always was," she said in astonishment. "It was like he'd never left."

"I'm so happy for you, Sharon," I said softly.

"He walked out of the mirror and was right there in the room with me. We talked. He said he's sorry to have left me and Nathan, and wishes it could be easier for us, but he's okay where he is. He put his arms around me and hugged me. It felt so soft and loving. It was wonderful—I needed that so much!"

"What about your questions? Did he say anything about how he died?"

"He said he was walking on the trail and someone pushed him from behind. He didn't see who it was."

"Did he say who he thinks it might have been?"

Sharon took a long drink of water and sighed. "No. He wanted to talk about other times, times we had together, times with Nathan. The question of who pushed him didn't seem to matter to him at all."

"Did he tell you what he was so worried about?"

"Not really. I asked him if it was Erik he was worried about, and he said, 'Get the money from Erik. You need the money.' I tried to get him to explain that but he didn't. Then he said not to trust my dad with Nathan. I told him I'd already stopped the point-system thing Dad was doing. I have no idea how he knew about that."

"Did you ask him about his computer?"

"I did, but I forgot to ask until he began fading away. Then, when I asked about it, he said, 'Don't trust customers to pay on time.' I told him that we need the password to get into the computer, but he just kept saying, 'Don't trust customers to pay on time.' He seems mostly worried that Nathan and I won't have enough money. Maybe there are some invoices on his computer from customers who owe him money."

I decided to take the plunge. "Sharon, I'm thinking we should find a way to get into that computer without Erik's help. After what Adam said about getting the money from Erik, I'm wondering whether there might be something on the computer about that. And, I have to tell you, Erik isn't exactly who he seems to be."

I had been focusing intently on how to phrase this because of my worry that any criticism of Erik would not sit well with Sharon. When she didn't respond at all, I was afraid I had gone too far. But I noticed she had fallen asleep right there on the couch. She looked so relaxed and peaceful, I decided not to wake her. I hoped she was dreaming of Adam, maybe reliving their reunion.

About fifteen minutes later, Sharon woke with a start. "Wait! Now I've got it! That's the password. Don't trust customers to pay on time—that's the password. Give me a pen and a piece of paper."

I handed her the pen and paper. She grabbed it and wrote "Dtc2Pot." Then she jumped up and said, "Where's my watch? What time is it? I'm supposed to be home for Nathan to be dropped off at 5:00."

"It's 4:30," I said, handing Sharon her watch. "Maybe you could go ahead, and I'll put Adam's computer in my car and bring it over. We can try the password at your house."

"Great! Thanks, Cleo. I'll see you in a few minutes." Sharon picked up her purse and dashed out.

36

I loaded up Adam's computer, locked my office, and took Broad-way across town to Sharon's house on Ash. When I turned into her driveway, I noticed smoke coming from Adam's office in the back. I dashed around the house to see what was going on. Sharon, Nathan and another boy who looked to be about his age were standing on the stone patio between the house and the office. As I ran over to them, I could see Nathan's face was streaked with soot and tears. Both he and his friend were filthy and dripping wet. Sharon talked intently to them.

As I walked up, she paused, looking to the boys for a response. "But Mom, I need to talk to Dad as much as you do," Nathan sobbed. "You wouldn't let me go with you to Cleo's, so how was I supposed to reach him?"

Sharon turned to me. "Nathan and Brad snuck over here this afternoon when Brad's mom thought they were at Martin Park near Brad's house. They tried to hold a séance to reach Adam—used a bunch of candles and managed to set Adam's office on fire. They got a hose to put out the fire, soaked themselves, the office and everything in it." Sharon sounded beyond exasperated.

"How did you learn about séances anyway, Nathan?" she went on.

"Brad and me watched a movie on TV about ghosts, where this woman had people sit around a table and light candles. They closed their eyes, and the ghosts came and talked to them. I thought we could do it to talk to Dad."

"I know how much you miss Dad, Nathan. We need to talk more about that," Sharon said, giving him a hug. "But you and Brad could have gotten hurt doing this. Right now, I'm going inside to call Brad's mother. I want you two to stay right here with Cleo until I get back." She walked over to the door into the kitchen and went inside.

"Cleo, my dad didn't come," Nathan said sadly. "Why didn't he? We had the séance in his office because that's where he mostly hung out. We turned out the lights and used a lot of candles just like in the movie, but he never came. We even tipped the table and banged on it like in the movie. That's when the fire started. Some candles fell off onto a bunch of papers. Then we had to stop and put out the fire. Do you think Dad didn't want to talk to me?"

"No, Nathan, I don't think it was because he didn't want to talk to you," I said, as I scrambled to think of a way to discuss this with a eight-year-old. "Um…the thing is, Nathan, spirits or ghosts or whatever can't just show up whenever someone calls them—even if they want to. It's really hard for them to talk to us, I think. It's like they're really far away and there's no phone and no easy way for them to get here."

Before Nathan could respond, Sharon came back out. "I talked to your mom, Brad, and she agreed that you and Nathan need to help clean up the mess you made. So let's go work on that. She'll be here in about an hour to pick you up."

Brad mumbled something as both boys followed Sharon into the office. I tagged along behind. Inside, the office was a smoky, soggy mess. Once they started the fire, the boys had wanted to be sure they used enough water to put it out. So they had doused everything thoroughly.

We began carrying things out from the office to the patio. Lots of wet books, folders, stacks of papers, and a couple of soaked area rugs. We had to bring out the furniture as well, because water had pooled around it. The boys worked hard, said little. Sharon got them brooms to sweep the water out the open sliding glass doors. By the time Brad's mother came to pick him up, he looked grateful to be getting out of there, even though he was probably worried about what his mother would have to say about this escapade.

After they drove off, Sharon told Nathan to go inside and take a shower. "I need to finish taking care of this mess," she told him. "So we'll talk more about this later. After your shower, stay in your room. I'll bring you some supper in a while." Nathan nodded, put down his broom and went inside.

As soon as he was gone, Sharon darted over to a pile of stuff at one side of the patio and came back carrying what looked like a locked steel cash box, about 8 inches by 12 inches and maybe 4 inches deep. It looked like it could hold a good-sized stack of money. "I found this hidden behind some books," she said. "I didn't want the boys to see it, since I have no idea what's inside. I'm hoping one of Adam's keys will open it. Let's take it inside and see."

We took the box into the kitchen. Sharon moved a stack of dirty dishes, jars of peanut butter and jam, a loaf of bread and some banana peels off the table, and put the metal box there. She fished around in a drawer, pulled out a key ring, and began checking for keys that might fit the lock. Just as she was about to try one that looked likely, Nathan appeared in the doorway.

"I'm starving, Mom. You said you were bringing me some food." Then he noticed the box. "Hey, what's that?"

"Nathan, I asked you to stay in your room. This is just a box I found in Dad's office."

"Is there money in it? Maybe Dad left us a bunch of money. Let's open it."

"I am going to open it. You can watch if you're quiet." Sharon stuck a key in the lock and turned it. The box popped open. Inside was a thin manila envelope. If it held money of any significant amount, it would have to be big bills. But all she found inside were some papers.

Nathan's face fell. "No money? He didn't leave any money in there for us? Hey, maybe it's a map to lead us to the money."

"Enough about money, Nathan." Sharon sounded exasperated.

"It's not a map, just some business papers. Now go back to your room and I'll bring you something to eat."

37

Sharon got out some bread and cheese, fixed a sandwich for Nathan, and took it to him with some watermelon and a glass of milk. She offered me a snack, but both she and I were more interested in getting a look at the papers in the envelope, than we were in eating. Sharon spread out the papers on the table, and we sat down to look through them.

The papers were all printouts of pages from a website called Creating An Ideal World. It started with this mission statement:

> This project is designed to demonstrate that it is possible to create an ideal society by sacrificing individual freedoms. People are not born the way they are, they learn to behave in certain ways by their interactions with the total environment in which they live. The philosophy of Creating An Ideal World is radical behaviorism. Behaviorism offers the possibility for change, for improving the human condition by rewarding desired behavior and punishing behavior that is not desired. The principles of behaviorism work equally well for everyone, regardless of race, ethnicity, or socioeconomic status. This project will show that by shaping children's behavior from infancy, we can create an ideal world.

"Wow! This is some strange stuff," Sharon said, reading on down the page. "I can't imagine why Adam had this in a locked box. It's not the kind of thing he'd usually keep. It sounds more like my dad's kind of thing than Adam's."

"It sounds a little scary," I said. "Shaping children's behavior from infancy? How do they get parents to agree to that?"

"Oh look at this." Sharon pointed to a page in front of her. "This project is in Mexico! I wish I knew why Adam had this stuff."

"It looks like this was printed out last March," I said. "See, here's the web address and the date on the bottom of each page."

"So I guess Adam printed it out from that website. But why? And why lock it up?"

We read through more pages that went on and on about how we can become better people and build a superior society by applying behaviorist principles. I found a couple of pages that had data tables with information about individual children. "Look at this, Sharon. This project has about thirty children, all age three or younger. It looks like they were all in it since they were born."

"So these kids' parents all agree to raise them by behaviorist principles? I feel sorry for them. I know I never liked being trained that way as a kid. Whenever I'd complain to my dad about him doing things to shape my behavior, he'd tell me the story of baby Albert. Back in the 1920s a psychologist named Watson taught a baby named Albert to be afraid of a white rat by loudly banging on metal with a hammer every time the baby touched the rat. Little Albert associated the rat with the noise and before long he would cry whenever he saw the rat, or even when he saw any white furry thing like a toy or a fur coat. Dad would remind me that he could have used methods like that, but he didn't. I guess I was better off than little Albert, but I always felt manipulated—all those charts, tokens and point systems."

"Yeah, I guess being the child of a prominent behaviorist can have its downside," I sympathized. "Reminds me of the baby box that B.F. Skinner invented for his daughter back in the 1930s. It was an incubator-like thing, sort of a combination crib and playpen with glass sides and a temperature-controlled environment. Most people thought it was terrible because the baby didn't get enough human contact or affection. People compared it to keeping animals in cages.

But Skinner raised his daughter in it until she was two and a half."

Suddenly I found a page that really hit me. "Oh my God! This project is buying babies from Mexican mothers for this experiment."

"What? Are you sure? How could they get away with buying babies? Let me see that."

I showed Sharon the section I had been reading. "Look, it says right here that they are not only conducting a unique experiment that will change the world, they are providing babies born into poverty with the opportunity for an exceptional life. And, then they say they are compensating the babies' parents significantly so they can lift their entire family out of poverty."

"So who is running this? Is my dad involved in this? Is that why Adam had this stuff?"

It took us a long time to find the names of the project directors, but when we did—sure enough—one of them was Waycroft. "You know, I remember now—Holly said your dad had some project in Mexico."

"Paying for babies to use in research has to be illegal, even in Mexico," Sharon said. "How can Dad be doing this?"

"You know, maybe we should call Elisa and see if she can come look at this stuff. She knows a lot more about psychology research than we do."

We gave Elisa enough information to get her to agree to come down right away. But we knew it would take her at least forty minutes to get to Sharon's. In the turmoil of the past few hours, we'd almost forgotten we had Adam's computer back. Once we remembered, we decided we should boot it up and try going to the website. We got the computer from my car, put it on the dining room table, entered the password Sharon had written down after she contacted Adam, and the computer booted right up. We went to the web browser, typed in the URL that was on the printed pages from Waycroft's project, but all we got was a blank page with the notice: *The page cannot be found. The page you are looking for might have been removed, had its name changed, or is temporarily unavailable.*

We looked in Adam's "Favorites" list for a link to the site, and found one, but when we clicked on it, we got the same blank page with the same frustrating message. We tried a Google search on "Creating an Ideal World." It came up with about 125 links when we put the phrase in quotes—stuff about utopian visions, ecology, religion, progressive political groups, and so on—but nothing that connected us to Waycroft's project.

We were pretty frustrated by the time Elisa got there. We gave her the papers to read, while Sharon went to get Nathan to bed, and I continued the fruitless computer search. By the time Elisa had read all the stuff and Nathan was down for the night, it was 9:30. Sharon and I realized we were starving, so we made some grilled cheese sandwiches and got out the watermelon to snack on while we talked with Elisa.

"This is some serious shit," Elisa said, handing the papers back to Sharon. "I told you Donald is obsessed with proving behavioral principles work. But I never thought he'd go to this extreme to prove his theories."

"And didn't you find out that the university's institutional review board wouldn't let him do some of the research he wanted to do?" I asked.

"Well, there's sure no way they'd let him take babies and raise them in a controlled environment to test behavioral principles," Elisa said. "I'd think Donald knows better than to even ask permission for that."

"So you think he just decided to run this illicit project in Mexico?" Sharon asked. "But who are these other people? And where do they get the money to pay the families and run the project? And how did Adam know about it?"

"It looks like Adam found the website somehow, and printed out these pages," Elisa said. "He clearly thought this material was important, or he wouldn't have locked it in this box. But he must have been worried about how you'd react. I assume that's why he didn't tell you. Maybe that's what he was so worried about before he died."

I remembered Erik had told me the night before that Adam had been worried about Waycroft, but I didn't want to bring up Erik and explain why I hadn't believed him. So I just asked, "Did Adam ever say anything that gave you the idea he had concerns about your dad?"

"It's hard to say. Adam and my dad never got along—which was mostly Dad's fault. Adam didn't have too many good things to say about Dad, but I can understand why he wouldn't have wanted to tell me about this. I'm sure he was freaked out about it."

"I would say Donald has some explaining to do," Elisa said. "And with this information we shouldn't have any trouble getting him to back off and quit harassing the three of us."

"But shouldn't we report this somewhere?" I asked. "We can't just use it to get him to leave us alone."

"I don't think we have enough information to report it," Elisa said. "You can't even find the website now. And who would we report it to? The project isn't even in this country. I think we need to talk to Donald. Maybe we can find out more."

"Okay, let's go to his lab tomorrow morning while Nathan is at soccer practice," Sharon said. "Dad's always at his lab on Saturday morning. That way we can find him without having to tell him in advance that we're coming."

We agreed to meet at my office at 9:30 the next morning, so we could go together to confront Waycroft.

38

Waycroft's lab was part of a cluster of research buildings on the East Campus, off 30th and Arapahoe. We drove over together in Elisa's car. Not surprising on a summer Saturday morning, the property was mostly empty.

The building that housed his lab was one of those so-called "temporary" buildings that have been around university campuses for generations. This one was the typical prefabricated flat rectangle with gray plastic-coated steel walls. We parked behind and walked around to the front door, which was unlocked—so we walked in.

Banks of stainless steel rat cages lined one wall. A long shelf on another wall held about fifteen desktop computers, each connected to a white rectangular box on a shelf above it. Waycroft sat with his back to us typing on a computer at a built-in desk. Ceiling-high shelves crammed with electronic equipment surrounded his desk on both sides.

He swiveled his desk chair around to face us as we came in. "To what do I owe this unexpected visit?" he asked with a scowl. "I thought none of you were speaking to me."

"We want to talk about your ideal world project in Mexico," Sharon said.

Waycroft looked momentarily startled, but quickly regained control. "I have no idea what you're talking about," he said.

"Dad, we know about the project. Adam printed out stuff from the website and left it in a locked box. I found it last night."

"Sharon, I don't know what you think you found, since I haven't seen it. Why don't you tell me about it?" Waycroft appeared calm and cool.

"You can drop the act, Donald," Elisa stepped closer to him. "We have detailed printouts of your Creating An Ideal World project, including the part about paying poor families to give you their babies to use for your research. You know as well as I do that research like that is immoral, unethical and illegal. Did you really think you could keep a project like this a secret?"

Donald remained calm. "Look, I've finally gotten this project going with some great scientific minds involved," he said. "We're not hurting those kids. In fact, we're helping them. Their lives would be nothing without us. But the project's not politically correct. We'd be wiped out if people knew. Obviously we have to keep it secret."

Elisa took that as an opening. "Okay, we're here to offer you a deal. You stop this project now, and return those children to their parents. You drop your complaint against Cleo, quit interfering with the way Sharon is raising Nathan, and stay out of my tenure process. If you agree to all that, we won't tell anyone your secret. But if you don't agree, I'm going to give all this material to the university administration."

While Elisa issued her ultimatum, Waycroft swiveled his chair around so he faced his desk again. As she finished, he opened the desk drawer in front of him, took out a gun, jumped up and pointed it at us. I froze. My legs were rooted to the floor. I don't think I could have moved if the building had been on fire.

"Dad! What are you doing?" Sharon gasped.

"Shut up, Sharon! None of you has any idea what you're doing. This project is the culmination of my life's work. I have no intention of dismantling it. It's taken me years to find investors and put together this international research group. I'm not going to let anyone destroy this project. It's too important, too valuable. I'll do whatever I have to do to keep it going."

"So where did you find the members of this so-called research group?" Elisa said, not intimidated by Waycroft's gun. I admired her guts, but I couldn't see what good could come from continuing to confront him.

"None of your business. But we're already seeing amazing results, even though we've only had the project up and running for three years. Children raised in our controlled environment will show the world what can happen if we take control and design a society that is totally consistent in rewarding good behavior and extinguishing bad behavior. Someday this project—my project—will change the world. And all those bureaucrats who tried to hold me back will find out how wrong they were."

Could he be serious? I didn't feel anywhere near as confident as Elisa sounded. I was scared. This was the first time anyone had ever pointed a gun at me, and I took it very seriously. I stood rigidly in my spot slightly behind Sharon and Elisa, moving only my eyes around and around the room in search of an escape. Eventually I began to regain feeling in my legs, like I could move if I had to. But I couldn't see any good moves to make. While I figured there was no way he could shoot all three of us if we ran in different directions, it seemed likely he'd get one or maybe even two of us. Not good enough odds. Nor did I think we could overpower him and get the gun, even if we could find a way to jump him all at once. We were all in good shape, but Waycroft was stocky and solid with the broad well-muscled shoulders of a former football player who worked out daily.

"Is this project worth killing for?" Sharon challenged. A look of horror came over her face. "Wait a minute—have you already killed for it? Did you know Adam found out about the project? Did you push him off the trail? You were right there in the area when it happened."

"Yes, I knew Adam had gotten on the website." Waycroft somehow maintained his cool in the face of Sharon's allegations. "It was a password protected site for internal use only, but somehow Adam found it and got on. He used my password—that was my mistake, using Nathan's birthday for my password. Adam didn't have to work too hard to figure it out. As soon as he told me, we took the site down, but he already knew too much."

"What do you mean, he knew too much?" Sharon screamed, her face contorted in anger. "You mean he might have told people you were buying babies?"

"I thought I had him convinced not to tell anyone about the project. I was going to make it worth his while. But right before he took the Grand Canyon trip, he told me he was going there to think about what to do and he'd tell me what he'd decided when he got back. He had begun to lose his nerve. He was a liability. He was going to destroy my greatest accomplishment. I couldn't take the chance."

"My God, Dad! You killed Adam! You killed my husband. How could you do that to me and Nathan?" Ignoring the gun, Sharon ran at Waycroft as if to choke him.

I held my breath, waiting for the shot. But Waycroft only reached out with his left arm and pushed her away from him. She staggered, but didn't fall.

"Back off, Sharon," Waycroft said, sounding irritated, but still in control. "Adam wasn't Nathan's father. And he was a bad influence. He encouraged you to raise Nathan in a sloppy home with no structure to his life. You'll both be better off without him."

"So will Nathan be better off without me too?" Sharon asked icily.

"He'll have me," Waycroft said, "and I'll make sure he gets a good education. Too bad Adam didn't tell me he'd printed out pages from the website. I could have found them and destroyed them, and we wouldn't be in this situation."

I finally got a grip and spoke up. "You can be a complete jackass, but I can't believe you'd kill your own daughter just to save a piece of research," I said.

"Believe it," Sharon said giving Waycroft a look of pure hatred. "In his eyes, I'm mostly just a piece of research gone wrong. I never behaved according to the learning theories he used on me, never followed the script he set out for me, never lived the life he had planned for me. He'll be glad to see the last of me and have Nathan all to himself."

"I know where I went wrong with you, Sharon," Waycroft replied.

"I can do much better with Nathan, especially if you're not around to get in the way."

Elisa had surreptitiously reached into her purse and started fishing around. Waycroft noticed her movements and grabbed the purse out of her hands. "Give me your cell phones and drop your purses on the floor in front of you," he barked. "Now!"

We gave him the phones, still too stunned to resist. Any hope of calling for help had vanished.

"Donald, you don't seriously think you can get away with killing all three of us, and simply continue your work?" Elisa asked incredulously.

"Of course I know it's not that simple," Waycroft said in a mocking tone. "But accidents happen." He pointed to a door on his left, marked "Lab." "In here! Now! All of you! You first, Sharon, then Elisa, then Cleo. Now move."

We were moving slowly in the direction of the lab room when we heard noisy chanting from outside the building. "Enlighten, empower, expand. Seek to believe, not understand. Enlighten, empower, expand. Seek to believe, not understand."

Waycroft turned toward the window. I realized in a flash that if any of us were going to get out of there alive, now was the time. I couldn't meekly walk into that room and let Waycroft kill us all. I bolted, ran past Waycroft toward the front door, and pulled it open. I heard a shot ring out, but didn't realize it had hit me until I got outside and saw blood running down my arm.

"Cleo, what's happening? Is someone shooting at you?" It was Narmada with a bunch of women carrying cardboard signs with painted slogans like "My spirit group rejects Waycroft!" "There's more to life than Waycroft knows!" and "We foresee disaster for Waycroft!" I realized this must be her protest rally supporting my cause.

"Do you have a cell phone? Call the police!" I yelled. "He's got Sharon and Elisa in there, and he's got a gun."

"You're bleeding! Are you okay? Do you need an ambulance?" There was a group gathered around me now.

"Call the police! Hurry! We have to get Sharon and Elisa out!" I felt panicky, desperate to somehow save them from Waycroft.

"I called the police," someone yelled. "Do you need an ambulance?"

I felt around my left shoulder where it was bleeding. The bullet had grazed my shoulder. It seemed to be a superficial wound. "I'm okay. But we need to save my friends."

"So let me get this straight," Narmada said. "Donald Waycroft shot you, and he's holding his own daughter and someone else at gunpoint? We knew he was an asshole, but this is over the top even for him. What's going on?"

"I can't explain it all now," I said frantically. "But he's extremely dangerous. He'll kill them if we don't stop him." I realized now that I was out, Waycroft's secret was moot. He couldn't come after me with so many people out here. So he must be considering some strategy for getting away.

Sure enough, before the police had time to show up, Waycroft appeared at his lab door pushing Elisa in front of him, his gun in her back. "Don't come anywhere near us, or I'll shoot her," Waycroft threatened, moving Elisa in the direction of his Red Jeep Cherokee.

"Where's Sharon?" I yelled at him. "You know you can't keep your secret now, so why not let Elisa go?"

He ignored me, pushed Elisa into the passenger side of the Jeep, kept the gun trained on her as he walked around to the driver's side, got in, and drove off. I memorized his license plate number, then ran inside to find Sharon.

She lay on the floor in the small lab room. One side of her face was bruised and bleeding. She looked to be unconscious. "Now we need that ambulance," I shouted to the women who had followed me inside.

"Let me check her. I used to be a nurse," said a young blond-haired woman wearing a black tee-shirt dress. She knelt beside Sharon on the floor. "She's breathing, and her pulse is good," she said, after checking Sharon for a minute.

"Hey, Cleo," Narmada called from the doorway, "The police are here. You need to tell them what happened."

"Tell them to go after Donald Waycroft," I shouted back. "Red Jeep Cherokee, license number J57163."

"I told them he's armed and has a hostage," she called in a minute later. "They need to talk to you for more details about her."

I jumped up, ran out, and gave them identifying information about Elisa as well as Waycroft. The ambulance arrived and loaded Sharon up. She was still unconscious, so I had to give them information about her. As I did that, I remembered Nathan was at soccer practice and would need to be picked up. I rescued my cell phone from Waycroft's desk where he'd left it, and called Joel. "I can't give you the details now," I said, "but can you pick up Nathan at the soccer field at 11:30?

"Where's Sharon? Has something happened to her?" he asked anxiously.

"She's okay," I reassured him. "But I think she hit her head, and she's unconscious. She's on her way to the hospital in an ambulance now. Could you take Nathan out for lunch or something, keep him occupied for a while. There's a lot going on here right now and I need to go. I'll call you as soon as I can."

"A lot going on where? Where are you calling from, Cleo?"

"Joel, I have to go. Can you just trust me and pick up Nathan?"

After he agreed, I hung up and went over to talk to the police to find out what had happened with Waycroft and Elisa. There were quite a group of them there by then, examining Waycroft's lab, taking pictures and notes. They said they had broadcast a statewide wanted person bulletin for Waycroft with information about his vehicle and cautions about Elisa. They wanted me to go to the police station to make a statement about what had happened. I agreed.

We had come in Elisa's car, and she had the keys, so one of the police officers offered to drive me to my office to get my car. I must have been running on pure adrenaline up until then, but suddenly I couldn't stop shaking. When we got to my office, the police officers made me some tea and helped me wash the blood off my shoulder and put some ointment on it. Suddenly I realized Elisa's husband

and daughter didn't know anything about what had happened. The officers said they would locate them, fill them in on the situation, and have them call me on my cell.

After I finished the tea, I felt much better and convinced the officers I was able to drive. They left and I followed them over to the police station to make a statement about what had happened. After that I went to the hospital to see how Sharon was doing. She was still in the ER—awake, a little groggy from some pain medication, bruised, but basically fine and ready to go home. She had been worrying about Nathan and was relieved to hear Joel had picked him up.

While they got the papers ready to release her, I brought my car around to the door. As soon as I got her in the car, I could see that emotionally she was still reeling from the morning's events. I drove out onto the street, found a parking space, and stopped so we could talk a bit before I took her home.

"How are you doing with all this?" I asked.

"It's hard to believe Dad killed Adam. He didn't like him, didn't want me to marry him, didn't want him to adopt Nathan—but I never thought he'd murder him."

"It must be overwhelming. I can't imagine."

"And that Mexico project. Who would have guessed? Maybe I should have paid more attention to what Dad was doing in the last few years. I knew he was fanatical about proving that behaviorism can save the world, but I never would have thought he would go that far. I wish Adam had told me. Maybe none of this would have happened."

"What happened in the lab after I ran out? What did he do to you?"

"After he shot at you, I jumped at him, tried to grab the gun. He hit me—I guess with the gun—and that's all I remember." She suddenly clicked in on the whole thing. "Oh my God, where is he? Did he get away? What happened to Elisa? Is she okay?"

"He brought Elisa out at gunpoint as a hostage, put her in his car and drove off. The police are trying to find them."

"Oh, my God! I feel responsible for getting you two into this. I had no idea he was so dangerous. He can be a self-focused jerk who makes trouble for people who won't do what he wants, but I never thought he'd kidnap or kill anyone."

My cell phone rang. We both jumped. I grabbed it, hoping for good news about Elisa. But it was Joel, wanting an update.

"I just picked up Sharon at the hospital. She's fine and we'll be at her house in a few minutes," I said. "How's Nathan doing?"

"He's fine. I told him something came up, and Sharon couldn't pick him up. We got some pizza and came back to my place, since I didn't know how we'd get into Sharon's. Nathan doesn't have a key with him. So we'll meet you over there."

I closed the phone, pulled out and headed toward Broadway. "We need to get back," I said to Sharon. "Joel is bringing Nathan over to your house now." I realized Sharon would have some explaining to do when we got there. Just looking at her, Nathan would know something had happened.

"Have you thought about what to tell Nathan?" I asked.

"I'm thinking about it. But I don't have any good ideas. I don't want to lie to him. But I don't want to tell him his grandfather killed Adam and threatened to kill me."

I wished I could help her, but some suffering can't be soothed by others at the moment of impact. I could help her with grief therapy in the coming months, but right then it was her family, her sadness, her tragedy to face however she could. We drove on in silence, thinking about the horror we had seen and the pain that waited for us.

39

As I pulled into Sharon's driveway, Elisa's husband Jack called on my cell phone. He was so distraught he could barely choke out the words. "Cleo, what happened? Why did Donald Waycroft kidnap Elisa?"

"Jack, let me come talk to you in person about it. Are you at home?"

He was. I thought Jack and Maria needed my support more than Sharon did at that point. Plus, I thought she and Nathan could talk better without me. So I left her with Joel and Nathan, and drove to Elisa and Jack's house in the foothills.

A police car was parked in their driveway when I got there. Elisa's daughter Maria answered my knock wearing baggy shorts and a tank top. Her hair hung over her face as usual, but I could see her eyes were red and swollen.

"Cleo, tell me exactly what happened. I need to know exactly. The police are so not clear on the details." Her voice was shrill, her words tumbled over each other. I could feel her panic and my heart ached for her.

I put my arms around her and hugged her long and hard, patting her back to calm her like I used to do when she was little. "I'll tell you what I can, Maria. Let's just go where your dad can hear it, too."

We moved into the living room. Jack sat in a chair next to the fireplace, talking to two police officers seated on the couch across from him. Jack is a lanky, sandy-haired man, generally easy-going and sociable. But that morning he had a tense, tightly coiled look to him, a aura of hyper-vigilance. "Cleo!" He jumped up, darted toward me, and threw his long arms around me in a big hug. "I'm so glad you're not hurt." Then he stepped back. "I need to know everything you can tell me about Elisa and Donald Waycroft. Do you have any idea where he might have taken her?"

I sat on the other couch, pulling Maria down next to me, and began the Waycroft story from the beginning—much of which Maria knew, but I wasn't sure about Jack. I talked about how he'd threatened Elisa, Sharon and me, how we'd found out about his horrible project and confronted him—but I left out the part about him pushing Adam over the cliff. I didn't think that part was my story to tell. At least not until I'd talked with Sharon.

The police officers sat quietly, listening without comment. Just as I finished recounting the details of the confrontation and shootout at the lab that morning, one of the officers' cell phone rang. He got up and walked toward the front door as he answered. We listened, drawing what conclusions we could from the side of the conversation we heard.

"Mathews. Right. When? Where was it? How long? So what do we …. Okay." He walked back to where Jack sat. "They found Waycroft's Jeep. He drove up the canyon to some friend's house off Sugarloaf, locked his friend in the closet, stole her car and left his there. When the friend missed a lunch appointment with her daughter, the daughter drove up there to check on her. She found her mother in the closet, and they called the sheriff's office. It looks like Waycroft took your wife with him in the friend's car. They have a bulletin out for it now."

"Holly," I said.

"What?" Jack turned in my direction.

"Holly. Dr. Waycroft's friend. She's an artist who used to study with my grandmother. She and Waycroft have had a sort-of on-and-off relationship for years. Her place is kind of hidden away on Mountain Pines Road, so I guess Waycroft figured his car wouldn't be found there right away."

"So, do they have any leads on Holly's car?" Jack asked the officer.

"Not yet."

"What do we do now?" Jack knew the answer, but he had to ask. I know I felt like I should be doing something to find Elisa, even though I had no idea what.

"The highway patrol will be actively looking for the car. They'll find it. Don't worry. For now, we wait," the officer said. "We'll stay here in case Waycroft calls with demands or has your wife call."

It was 4:30 by then. I thought about calling Sharon to update her on what we knew about Waycroft and Elisa, but decided against it. She had plenty going on, there wasn't anything she could do, and she had my cell number if she wanted to talk. So we waited, speculated, fixed some food that only the cops ate, paced the floor, checked the phone to make sure it was working, and waited some more.

Sharon called me on my cell at 9:30. She had waited until Nathan had gone to sleep. Joel was still there with them. "I did my best to explain to Nathan what had happened without giving him a lot of details. I told him that his grandfather had gone crazy and tried to hurt people. Joel was great at explaining how people can sometimes lose touch and do things that cause a lot of pain to people they love. I didn't tell Nathan anything about Adam—just about what happened to us today."

Sharon already knew about Waycroft ditching his car at Holly's. The police had called to see if she had any ideas about where Waycroft might go from there. She didn't. Sharon sounded exhausted. I tried to convince her to get some sleep, but she said she couldn't sleep while Elisa was in danger. We agreed to keep in touch during the night.

40

It was 11:00 pm when the call finally came. Holly's car had been found crashed off highway 119 near Central City. Waycroft was dead. Elisa was in serious condition at Boulder Community Hospital. We all jumped in our cars and headed into town to the hospital.

I called Sharon, but of course the police had already notified her. She had arrangements to make about Waycroft. Fortunately Joel had insisted on staying, so she wasn't alone.

It was a long night at the hospital. Elisa had multiple injuries, and had lost a lot of blood. For a while it looked grim. They took her to surgery. We waited. Finally, at 3:00 a.m., good news. She was stable. We wouldn't be able to talk to her for a long time, so at 4:00 a.m. I decided to go home and get some sleep. I was pretty groggy by then. I managed to make it home, but was having trouble getting my key in the lock on my front door, when I heard a voice from the shadows of my porch.

"Need some help with that key?"

I screamed, jumped about a foot, and ran back toward my car. But he was quicker than I, and grabbed me before I could reach the car.

"Erik! What are you doing here?"

"We have some stuff to talk about, Cleo."

"Look, Erik. This is one of the worst days of my life. I can't talk. Now go away or I'll call the police."

"No you won't." He grabbed my purse, before I could pull out my cell phone. "Now sit down. We're going to talk." He pushed me down hard onto a wooden porch chair.

I was too exhausted to resist. So I sat there waiting to see what he would do next.

He sat in a chair across from me. "You have me all wrong," he said. "Everything I do is to help people. My products help people feel better, my herb business helps people make money. I help the old feeble people at Shady Terrace get stronger. But you make trouble for me everywhere. You snoop around, accuse me of killing my wife and of pushing Adam over a cliff. Why are you trying to destroy me?"

"Erik, don't try to sell yourself as altruistic. I know about your shady deals, your stolen assets, your self-serving life. Okay. I was wrong about Adam. I know you didn't push him. But the other stuff I don't take back." I should have tried to placate him, rather than confront him. But it had been a long day, and I was too tired to be tactful.

He leaned forward to look me in the eye. "Cleo, I'm disappointed in you. We could have had something together—with our mutual interests in creating opportunities, making the world a better place. But now a lot of people will be hurt, and it's all your fault. Thanks to you and your policeman boyfriend prying and spreading lies about me, I've had to take down my web pages and my companies are history."

I figured Pablo must have been digging around last week and found out more about Erik's businesses. Maybe even had police officers questioning him. It felt good to think Pablo did take me seriously even though he didn't say he was. I felt a brief smile form within me at the thought of him.

I guessed Erik was scared his past had caught up with him. "If your businesses are legitimate, why do you have to disband them?"

"I don't need all this hassle. I've run a lot of businesses in my day, and I can go somewhere else where people appreciate the opportunities I'm offering them. But because I'll be leaving here before I planned to, all the people growing the herbs will get nothing—and that includes Nathan. Sharon will lose, too. She would have gotten big returns on the money Adam invested in my nutrition business.

But now it will all be lost."

So that's where Adam's money went! "I'm pretty sure Sharon doesn't know Adam had invested in your business. If this was such a great investment, why didn't you tell her? Why? Because it was all bogus! Pyramid schemes and other scams that you planned to milk for what you could get and then skip town?"

"I guess you'll never know, will you?" Erik sneered. I don't have to tell you anything. I'm on my way out of town right now. I will disappear! No one will find me. I've done it before."

"Whatever, Erik. I'm tired. If you're leaving, go ahead and do it." I pushed my chair back and tried to stand up.

But Erik quickly stood up and pushed me back down in the chair. "I'm not finished with you yet, Cleo. You deserve to suffer, to pay for the suffering you have caused."

"What about the suffering you've caused? You ripped off Adam so Sharon and Nathan ended up poor. You've cheated who knows how many people out of $500 or more. Don't you owe these people something?"

"That's not your concern, Cleo. We're talking about you here."

"Erik, you know Pablo knows about you. If anything happens to me, he'll know who to look for."

"I'm not going to kill you, Cleo. That would be too easy. But you will suffer. Because you will know I'm out there, watching you. Don't think I'll forget you or what you've done! I know how to find you. You'll never know when I'll show up on your porch, in your house, or in your studio. You'll live in fear that someday when you least expect it, I'll come along and make you pay for what you've done. I'm one ghost that will definitely come back to haunt you. Here's your phone. Call anyone you want. It won't do you any good." With that, he stood up and disappeared into the shadows.

I got up, unlocked the door, went in and locked it again from the inside—knowing, of course, that Erik could pick the lock if he wanted to. I checked all the windows, then staggered into the bedroom, pushed a chair against the door, pulled off my clothes and sank into bed, too exhausted to take any more precautions.

41

The next day—Sunday—I woke up about noon. In contrast to the cheerful sunshine streaming through my windows, I felt groggy and out of sorts. After a shower, I went out to the garden to pick some tomatoes, chives, parsley and strawberries. Out in the yard, I halfway expected to smell some nasty stink of Erik still hanging there. But it was clean and sparkly almost as if Natalie had come over and cleansed its aura while I slept. The scent of my roses and phlox, blooming as though it were a summer day like any other, improved my mood.

I had eaten next to nothing in the past twenty-four hours, so I was starved. I fixed myself a huge breakfast of scrambled eggs with tomatoes and herbs, strawberries, toast and coffee. While I ate, I checked for phone messages.

Pablo had called from Oregon about 11:00. Someone from the Longmont PD had called him and he was up-to-date on what had happened to Sharon, Elisa and Donald. And he knew I had been with them at the lab.

I dreaded the conversation I knew we would have, but I called him back anyway. He had the basics that the police knew, but he had a lot of questions.

"Cleo, what happened? What were you three doing at Waycroft's lab yesterday morning that set him off?" Pablo sounded worked-up. Not that he didn't have reason to be upset, but as a cop he's learned to at least sound calm under almost any circumstances.

"What did we do to set him off? You make it sound like it was all our fault. He's the one who shot at me, knocked Sharon out, and kidnapped Elisa," I said indignantly.

"Whoa, Cleo, relax. I just want to know what happened there at the lab." His tone was steady now.

It hit me that only Sharon, Elisa and I—and possibly by now, Joel—knew what we had found out about Waycroft's project, and, more importantly, knew Waycroft had killed Adam. Much as I would have liked to vindicate my claim that Adam was murdered, I thought it should be Sharon's call as to what would be told about Adam, now that Waycroft was dead. So I told Pablo only what we had discovered about Waycroft's research and how we went to his lab to use the evidence to get him to back off and quit harassing us.

"And then he pulled a gun out of his desk drawer, pointed it at us, and said he would find a way to kill us and make it look like an accident."

"Why did you run when he had a gun on you?" He sounded incredulous.

"There was a demonstration outside that distracted him for a minute, and I thought that was my only chance."

"You were very lucky, Cleo. You could have been killed."

"I know, I know. But I got away with just a scratch. Elisa's the one who was really hurt—actually almost died. And I need to get back over to the hospital to see how she is."

"I don't know, Cleo. I want to hug you because you're safe, but I also want to shake you for taking those chances. We need to talk more about this. How about tomorrow night? I won't be back until 4:00 today and then I have to work late tonight to make up for being gone."

It was a talk I wasn't looking forward to, but I knew we'd have it eventually. And I was curious about what pressures he had brought to bear on Erik that led him to leave town. We agreed on dinner the next night.

When I got over to the hospital, I found Elisa much improved. They had moved her from intensive care to a regular patient room.

She looked battered, with two black eyes, scratches and bruises on her face, a bandage on her head where some of her hair had been shaved off, and a cast on her right arm. Not her usual put-together look. But she was alert and eager to talk to me about what had happened.

"Right after he hit Sharon and knocked her out, he tied me to a chair and gave me some kind of injection that he said would put me under in about ten minutes. Then he untied me and took me out to his jeep. I was asleep before we got to Arapahoe and Folsom. The next thing I remember was being in a different car driving up Boulder Canyon to Nederland. I think I came to just before Boulder Falls."

"So you don't remember anything about being at Holly's, leaving Donald's car, and taking hers?"

"No, not a thing."

"I assume he switched cars to buy himself some time," I said, "because the police were looking for the jeep. But why was he going up the canyon after that? And why was he on highway 119?"

"When I first woke up, I heard him talking on his cell phone arranging for a limousine to pick him up at Central City to drive him to an airport in Pueblo. He didn't know I was awake, and I didn't let on. Then I heard him make a call to someone to arrange a charter flight for him from Pueblo to somewhere in Mexico. I kept on acting like I was still unconscious and I guess he was too busy making all those calls to take a careful look at me. My face was turned away from him toward the window on my side of the car, so I was able to open my eyes and look out without him knowing."

"So how come he crashed the car? Was it because he was on the phone?"

"No. It was because I surprised him, grabbed the wheel, and steered the car off the road when we were on a narrow turn next to a steep ravine. I'd been sitting there thinking about how I could get away. I could tell from the phone calls that he planned to take me with him to Mexico as a hostage, in case he needed a bargaining chip. I figured once I was in Mexico and he didn't need me anymore, he'd arrange for me to disappear or die in some accident. So I decided I'd rather take my chances on an accident here, where at least I had some chance of surviving."

"Wow! That was gutsy. I don't think I would have had the nerve to cause a car crash in the mountains."

"Well, you know me—I've always loved a challenge. Maybe it was crazy, but I'm a risk taker by nature. No question this was more of a gamble than I usually take, but I was desperate to get away from him. And I couldn't just sit there and let that ass have everything his way. Could you hand me that water glass?"

I put the glass in her left hand, waited while she took a long drink and then put it back on the table. "I guess you know Donald died in the crash."

"Yes, Jack told me. Maybe I should feel something, but I don't. Donald was a brilliant man, but he had turned into a monster."

"Have you told anyone that he killed Adam?"

"No. I only told them about the Mexico research project where he's buying babies. I figured the rest is up to Sharon. She has Nathan to think about. It's not like it makes any difference whether the truth comes out about how Adam died, now that Donald is dead. And they'd only have our word as proof anyway."

"Exactly. Losing Donald is going to be hard enough for Nathan as it is. And he's going to have another disappointment as well. Erik Vaughn turns out to be a fraud, scamming people with those herb growing kits. I'll fill you in on the details later, but the gist of it is that he's left town and there won't be any money for the herb growers."

Jack and Maria showed up then, and I could see Elisa had wilted a bit, so I left, gave Sharon a call, and went over to spend a little time with her. When I got there, she was working on Adam's computer, which was still on the dining room table where we had set it up the other night. Joel had taken Nathan tubing in Boulder Creek.

"I haven't found anything about Dad's research project yet, but Adam does have a whole computer folder of financial stuff relating to his business," she said. "I'm trying to figure out who owes him money."

I hated to give her more bad news, but I knew I couldn't hold off any longer telling her about Erik. I began hesitantly. "Um…I saw Erik yesterday…well actually it was early this morning…about 4:00 a.m. He was on my porch when I got home from the hospital."

"Waiting on your porch at 4:00 a.m.? Why?"

"He had some things to say to me. It's kind of a long story—which I'll tell you later. But the main thing is, Erik told me that Adam had invested a lot of money in his business. So that's why Adam's company was in debt when he died."

"That's a relief. Now Erik can pay back the money, and we'll be fine." She stopped and thought for a minute. "But that doesn't make any sense. Why didn't Erik tell me about Adam's investment? He knew I was worried about where the money went."

"Exactly, Sharon. Here's the thing. Erik isn't who he seems to be, and any money invested with him isn't likely to be returned." I went on to tell her the whole story including Pablo's investigation, my trip to Minneapolis, all I had learned from Harry, my confrontations with Erik, and his announcement that he would shut down his businesses and leave town. "So I'm afraid he won't be paying back Adam's investment or making good on Nathan's herb plants. You can try to get your money back by reporting him to consumer fraud or something, but from what Harry said, pretty much no one ever catches Erik—Horace—or whatever he decides to call himself the next place he goes."

Sharon wept on my shoulder. I felt mean for telling her all of this after what she'd been through in the last few days, but I'd been holding it back from her too long already. My trip to Minneapolis had been Wednesday, and it was already Sunday by then.

She grabbed a tissue, blew her nose and wiped her eyes. "I can't believe I felt so close to him, that I let Nathan get close to him, that we went camping with him."

"From what Harry told me, and from what I've seen from Erik lately, I'd say he's an excellent actor, has an amazing ability to charm and seduce others. Basically a sociopathic personality. But his 'dark side' is hard to spot. We're not alone—so many people have been taken in. He's wonderful at making promises and coming across as a great guy but rarely makes good on anything. Maybe some of the time he even intended to do what he said he would do, but mostly he just told people what they wanted to hear so he could get what he wanted. He usually got what he set out to get, and when he didn't, he moved on."

"You're right, but I still feel stupid not seeing him for what he was. Do you think he killed Jenny?"

"Maybe. But there's no way we'll ever know. For her sake, to avenge her death, I wish we could pin it on him. But I can't see how we could do it."

"That's so sad. But you're right. Okay, let's see if we can find anything on the computer about Adam investing in Erik's scams."

Using the computer's search feature, we entered "Vaughn's Holistic Healing." It didn't take long to find the documents. Adam had invested about $80,000 over the past year, for which he had a one-third interest in the business. We tried going to Erik's website several times, but each time we got only the white page with the message: *The page cannot be found. The page you are looking for might have been removed, had its name changed, or is temporarily unavailable.* So it looked like taking down the website was one promise Erik had actually kept.

"Great! I own a third of a non-existent business," Sharon said. "I sure wish I'd known about this before Erik left town. Maybe that's why he never got around to doing what he said he would do to boot up this computer. Hmmm....I wonder whether he was actually the one who stole it."

"But why would he give it to Narmada? In fact why would he give it back at all?"

"Good point. I wonder if she stole it herself and just said it was someone she knew?"

"Wouldn't stealing be bad karma for her?" I asked. "You know what? Not telling us who took it is bad karma too. I'm going to call her right now and give her the chance to redeem herself."

"Good luck with that," Sharon said.

I took out my cell, which had Narmada's number in memory from the times she'd called me. I expected to get voice mail, so when she actually answered, I wasn't prepared.

"Natalie…um, I mean Narmada, it's Cleo. But you probably know that from your caller ID, and anyway you're psychic." Good grief, could I be any more clumsy? All at once I realized I owed her big time for showing up at Waycroft's lab when she did. "I want to thank you for the demonstration. It truly saved my life—and Sharon's and Elisa's too—and we're all very grateful. I don't know what we would have done if you and your friends hadn't shown up when you did."

"Cleo, I told you I was meant to organize this demonstration, and now we know why. I felt it there when you were in danger. The soul bond we have is very strong."

"Soul bond?" I had no idea what she meant, but I was curious.

"Yes, I feel we're sharing a vibration, that we have a cosmic connection. I'm sure we've shared experiences in other times and dimensions. Now we need to transform our negative relationship patterns. Everything needs to be completely clear between us. So I'm going to tell you the whole truth. It was me. I took Adam's computer. I had to do it to see what toxic stuff he had on there about me. The negative energy he spread about me had to be removed. But it didn't work. I couldn't log on. So I knew it wasn't meant to be. And I could feel it dragging me down, just having it in my space."

"So that's why you gave it to me? To get it out of your space?"

"Yes. I knew I had to get it back to Sharon, but I couldn't deal with her. She would have called the police and created negativity. I knew you'd get it back to her."

"So why tell me now?"

"I told you." She sounded slightly exasperated, as if explaining to a backward child. "We have a soul bond. Our connection must be kept clear."

"Oh, right. I understand." Not really, but I didn't want to go any further with the soul bond thing. "Anyway, Sharon has the computer back, and she's able to log on, so no harm done, I guess."

"Exactly!" Narmada said with enthusiasm. "Here's how I see it. I helped you and Sharon and your friend out at Waycroft's lab. Now you and Sharon can help me out by dropping the issue of the computer. I didn't hurt anyone and you have the computer back."

Given all that had happened in the past few days, the stolen computer was a minor blip. And Narmada was right. We owed her big time. So I agreed with her and said I'd talk to Sharon about it.

Sharon had been listening and was eager for the details. When I told her what Narmada had said, she laughed. "Sounds like her karma's pretty shot after all this. No need for me to try to get her in more trouble. And her timing for that demonstration was terrific. So let's forget about the computer theft."

It was good to see her smiling again. It felt like a good opportunity to bring up the issue of what she wanted to say about her dad and Adam. So I jumped in.

"I agree." I said. "And now that we've tied up that loose end, there's something else we should think about. Elisa and I talked about your dad, and we both agreed it should be up to you to decide what we tell people about him and Adam. Now that your dad is dead, there may be more harm than good to be done by revealing he admitted he pushed Adam. The police might not believe us. We don't have any proof. But mostly I'm worried about Nathan. He's already lost Adam, and now his grandfather and Erik. I don't want to make it worse for him. So we haven't said anything about it and we won't unless you want us to."

Sharon sat silently for a minute, gazing off into space. Then she turned to face me. "Thanks, Cleo. I think you're right. It's hard enough for me to accept that my father killed my husband. Why burden Nathan with that? It's not as though it will change anything if we tell people."

"Right. I think as long as that Mexico experiment is closed down, we've done enough."

At that point Joel and Nathan came through the front door dripping wet from their tubing adventure. "Mom, it was so cool. We went over these big rocks, kind of like a waterfall, and I only turned over once. And that time I got back up really easy."

"He learns fast," Joel said, rubbing Nathan's shoulders with a towel. "Next week we're going to try from farther up the creek where there are more rapids. You should come."

"Thanks Joel," Sharon said.

As I noticed the warm look that passed between them, I thought the resilience of human beings is our saving grace. Like the creek, life has its rocky spots and sometimes we turn over. But usually we're up again and back for more challenges in no time.

42

Monday morning I drove over to Shady Terrace. I hadn't been there for a week, more time than I usually let go by between visits. In the main lobby area, most of the office doors were closed. It was quiet on the Alzheimer's unit, too. The staff I saw were working quietly, the residents were calm.

I found Gramma in her room looking at a book of paintings by Henri Matisse. She turned the pages quickly until she came to a picture of a fishbowl on a pink porch table, with plants and flowers in the background. Four bright orange goldfish swam in the small water-filled bowl.

"Whose fish?" she asked, looking up at me.

"I don't know, Gramma. Matisse painted those fish a long time ago."

"Where do they live?"

"In France, I guess. That's where Matisse lived." Not that she'd make any sense of that, but sometimes I can't come up with good answers to her questions.

"Who feeds them?"

"Whoever lives there with them."

"I don't like fish." She looked slightly annoyed.

"That's okay, Gramma, you don't have to like them." I reached toward the book to turn the page, but she pulled it away from me.

"James will take care of it later," she said.

I sat on her bed and watched her turn the pages, stopping at one or another for a longer look. She didn't say anything more about the pictures. I wondered whether she had any thoughts at all about the art she looked at. Probably not, but it helped me to think she might.

After about half an hour, I went out to the nurses' station. Tanya was there charting. Surprisingly, she looked up and smiled at me.

"Martha's doing much better," she said. "She's been sleeping better at night and not wandering as much."

"Is she still on the Ambien?" I asked.

"No. Dr. Dubose—the new Medical Director—took her off the Ambien. Didn't anyone call you?"

"I haven't been around much. But I don't recall any voice mail messages from Shady Terrace."

"I'll make sure Dr. Dubose calls you. You'll like him. He wants us to deal more directly with behaviors, without so many meds. We've been trying herbal tea with Martha in the evening like you suggested, and it does soothe her. And we've been keeping her more active during the days, so she'll sleep better at night."

Amazing! Just when I least expected it, good news hit me in the face! I thanked Tanya for the information, gave Gramma a joyful kiss, and headed back to my office. It wasn't easy to focus on clients, but I had to do it. All my Nancy Drewing had begun to affect my livelihood.

I wondered what would become of Waycroft's complaint against me, now that he was dead. I couldn't see how it could go forward without a living complainant, so I called the Department of Regulatory Agencies to find out. Like any bureaucracy, they were unwilling to make a definite commitment, but I had the distinct impression I wouldn't need to be worrying about it anymore. I called Bruce, my funder, to give him the good news.

I'd been worrying all day about getting together with Pablo that evening to talk. I didn't want to have an ugly argument, but I wasn't ready to admit I'd made foolish mistakes, either. I knew I had taken risks, but how else would we have gotten to the bottom of this messy situation? And, Tyler had been insistent that I "ride the wave." But of course I couldn't talk to Pablo about Tyler.

I decided I would at least try to stack the odds a bit in my favor by choosing a location that would set a festive, possibly romantic mood. So I called Pablo and made a couple of suggestions. We agreed to meet for dinner at Terrace Maya, a funky Mexican restaurant on North Broadway. It's fairly convenient for Pablo coming from Longmont, and it has a huge outdoor covered patio, where we'd likely be able to talk without being overheard.

I took time to change into a pale green cotton sundress with spaghetti straps. It's one of my favorites because the color matches my eyes. I hadn't been out to Terrace Maya all summer, but its kitschy cantina look hadn't changed a bit. Strings of plastic beer signs for Corona, Cerveza and Bud Light decorated the fence surrounding the patio. The awning that covered the patio was hung with strings of twinkly lights, luminous colored balls and stars. Looking out to the south between the top of the fence and the bottom of the awning, you get an excellent long view of the city nestled into the foothills.

A few people sat on barstools at a tiki bar with a wood-shingled roof on the southern edge of the patio, but otherwise it was sparse. North Boulder doesn't have the cache of the Pearl Street Mall, where people tend to hang out on summer evenings. This place gets its main crowds on weekends for the live salsa music.

Pablo showed up just after I got there. He wore a soft blue shirt that set off his blue-black hair, and he had that adorable just-out-of-the-shower look. We took a round glass-covered table near a fountain whose water bubbled cheerfully between two kissing ceramic birds, and ordered a pitcher of margaritas, and chile rellenos smothered with the restaurant's famous green chili. I took a couple of big swigs from my margarita glass to fortify myself before I began.

"Pablo, this has been such a long week, I can hardly remember back to the beginning of it. And it's hard to remember what I've told you, and what I haven't at this point. So tell me what you want to know."

"There's a lot I want to know, Cleo. The last time we talked was on Thursday when you wanted me to arrest Erik Vaughn for kidnapping Sharon and Nathan on a camping trip, and then changed your mind and said they were okay. The next thing I knew I heard that you, Sharon and Elisa almost got yourselves killed at Donald Waycroft's lab on Saturday. And now Waycroft is dead, Elisa's in the hospital, and as far as I can tell Erik Vaughn has disappeared leaving his herb growers with no way to get their money."

"Right. It has been a tough week. Where do you want me to start?"

"Let's start with Erik. How much did his brother tell you about his background?"

"He told me Erik has basically been ripping people off his whole life, he's been married at least three times, and the people close to him have suffered a lot. Do you want the gory details?"

Pablo wanted to hear it all, so I went through the whole story Harry had told me, as much as I could remember it. He refilled my margarita glass a couple of times, and we ordered another pitcher when the waitress brought our food.

"I'm surprised he told you all of that, Cleo. He didn't want to say much when I talked to him. Maybe it's because I'm a cop."

"Or maybe it's because I went to Minneapolis and talked to him in person."

"Just one more part of your tough week? How come you didn't tell me before this?"

I chuckled at his surprise, and gave him the details of my trip, taking a few pauses to savor the spicy green chili. Pablo ate, listened, occasionally looked surprised, but refrained from making any critical comments. After I finished explaining, he asked, "So, did you ask Erik about any of this?"

"Some. I promised Harry I wouldn't tell Erik what he'd told me, so I couldn't ask about most of it. But then Erik told me the police had been investigating him, and he was closing his businesses and leaving town. Was that your doing?"

"I set a few things in motion. We were hoping to surprise him, get some proof he'd scammed people, and arrest him before he got away. But he's a pro—saw what was coming and left without a trace. No more Vaughn Holistic Healing website. The phone at Natural

Herbal Remedies is disconnected. His brother Harry doesn't know where he is."

"I'll admit you were right about him all along. It's even worse than you know. Sharon's husband Adam had invested in Erik's business. She'll never see that money again."

"So I guess you think Erik pushed Adam off that trail. Good luck trying to catch him and prove he did it. I'd say Sharon should accept the ruling of accidental death and move on. Especially now that she's lost her father—although it may not be such a loss from what I hear. Tell me about him."

I went through the Donald story—leaving out the part about Adam—and told him how Elisa had caused the car crash. "I guess he didn't know Elisa very well, or he wouldn't have picked her as his hostage," I said. "She never lets anyone push her around."

"I doubt if he'd been any better off with you, Cleo. You've been going after people pretty hard lately. Now that you almost got yourself killed are you ready to hang up your detective career?"

"I never said I was a detective. I just did what I had to do in the situation. It wasn't easy, but I'd do it again if I needed to."

"I wish you'd rethink that, Cleo. If you keep taking chances like you have been, you may be spending all your time with that Tyler character in the spirit world or wherever."

I let the Tyler slur go by. We'd had that discussion before, and I didn't see it going anywhere new. The waitress came to clear our table, asked if we wanted coffee. I looked at Pablo. He looked at me. "We're good," I said. "Just bring the check."

Back at my house, our conflicts melted sweetly away, like ice cream in the sun. We didn't talk any more about Erik or Donald or Adam or Sharon. We made love slowly, then dozed in each other's arms.

Around ten o'clock, Pablo's snoring woke me up. He was out cold. I got up to get a glass of water. In the shadows of the kitchen, I saw Tyler, perched on a countertop. He was quiet, just watching me—which was actually a bit unnerving as I had on almost nothing.

"Tyler! Why are you here? Can't you see I'm not dressed?"

"Cleo, stay cool. I don't see your body, I see your soul."

"That's strange. I see your body."

"You see what you want to see, Cleo."

"Are you saying I'm making you up?"

"Whatever works for you."

"That doesn't work for me. Are you real or not?" I heard my voice rising. All I needed was for Pablo to wake up and find me arguing with a ghost.

"Okay, whatever, Tyler. I'm going back to bed."

"You did it, Cleo. You rode the wave."

Acknowledgements

Cleo's Contact Project was partially inspired by Raymond Moody, M.D.'s *Reunions* (Villard Books, 1993), in which he reports on experiences of people who have contacted apparitions of the dead.

Many friends and family read drafts of this book and provided support and valuable feedback. I appreciate the time and enthusiasm they brought to this project.

I am especially grateful for the extensive editing done by Laurel Umile, Laurie Castleberry, and Sally Barlow-Perez; and by Vicki, Carol, Thora and Joann from my Sisters in Crime critique group. Their comments, suggestions and edits made this a much better book.

There is no way I can ever sufficiently acknowledge the contributions of my husband, Allan Press, and my daughter, Laurel Osterkamp. They believed in my writing long before I did, and kept after me until I wrote this book. They read and edited draft after draft and helped me resolve sticky plot points. Their love and support kept me going for the years that it took me to finish this novel.

Finally, my father, who died too many years ago, got me started reading mysteries and piqued my interest in the possibility of making contact with dead loved ones. I regret that I've been unable to tell him about this book.

For information about Lynn Osterkamp's other books,
visit our website at:

pmibooks.com